The Author

The author is a ... elsh hospital. He foolishly boasted that during thirty years of working life he had only taken ten days sick leave. A week later he fell off the garage roof, badly fracturing his pelvis and spent many months either in traction or with a walking frame. In an unsuccessful attempt to entertain him and to cure his bad temper, kind friends fed him a diet of thrillers. He grumbled that the plots were unexciting, none of them were humorous and he could write more readable books himself. On a wet November afternoon he decided to do so and this is the result.

LIFELINE

LIFELINE

by

GERALD RATCLIFFE

CENTRAL PUBLISHING LIMITED
West Yorkshire

© Copyright 2001
GERALD RATCLIFFE
The right of Gerald Ratcliffe to be identified as author of this work has been asserted by him in accordance with copyright, Designs and Patents Act 1988

All rights reserved. No reproduction,
copy or transmission of this publication may be made
without written permission.
No paragraph of this publication may be reproduced,
copied or transmitted
save with the written permission or in accordance
with the provisions of the Copyright Act 1956 (as amended).
Any person who does any unauthorised act
in relation to this publication may be liable
to criminal prosecution and civil
claims for damage.

All characters in this publication are fictitious and any resemblance
to real persons, living, or dead, is purely coincidental.

Paperback ISBN 1 903970 22 9

Published
by

Central Publishing Limited
Royd Street Offices
Milnsbridge
Huddersfield
West Yorkshire
HD3 4QY

www.centralpublishing.co.uk

Lifeline

Chapter 1

Anyone running a terrorist - or freedom-fighting organisation, the title depends on your viewpoint, needs money. Certainly there is no requirement to pay VAT, National Insurance contributions or income tax but there are still many expenses.

The meeting of the IRA Council was chaired by Fintan Lalley with his usual brisk efficiency. His predecessor had allowed free-range discussion so that the meetings were long and sometimes confrontational. An additional problem was that discussing operational matters meant that the whole Army Council knew their details. There had never been any suspicion that a member of the Council had ever been turned by British Intelligence, but a more realistic worry was that members might confide the details to lower ranking friends when drunk, or merely when wishing to impress them of how they were at the centre of decision making. Fintan had given offence when he pointed this out to the Council but after a little shouting, they each realised that whilst personally never indiscreet in drink this might not apply to their colleagues. The Council now dealt in general principles only.

It was now thirty minutes into the meeting, which was

held in a remote farm in County Kerry. Enemy surveillance was unlikely in the Republic whereas in the Six Counties, there was a risk of being stopped by a routine patrol or followed as a known IRA man. The matters considered so far were important. The first was whether to step up activities in mainland Britain. The decision was yes and to do so in smaller towns where security was less tight. This would result in a need for increased policing and a further economic burden on the British Government.

The next problem was the drug epidemic in young people in Belfast and Derry. Much of this was the responsibility of the usual lowlifes found in any community but during the last year, the trade had become increasingly infiltrated by extremist Loyalist organisations. Their aim was both fund-raising and a determination to increase drug use in Republican areas in an attempt to destroy their social and family structures. A cocaine or heroin addict could always be persuaded to grass to his supplier in exchange for drugs. This technique was proving a useful source of low-level intelligence for the police and Loyalist groups. The Council agreed that any pusher entering a Republican area should be executed with no warning and the body left with a card around the neck to explain the reason for execution.

The final decision was straightforward. Fintan explained that there had been a large recent shipment of arms and semtex from Libya to the UK. A sympathiser with no criminal record had bought a small farm in Wales. A barn next to the farmhouse had been excavated to give a cellar with a concealed door. It contained the armoury and £250,000 in £20 notes to fund the needs of Active Service Units. This necessary expenditure meant that funds were running low. It was agreed that a fund raising appeal should be instituted. This was IRA humour for a bank raid. Only three people in the room would know where this would happen and who would do it. These would be the

Chairman, the Armourer and the Intelligence Chief.

After the meeting, the three men sat at the table with a bottle of Power's whiskey. "So, only two problems," said the Chairman, "where and who," and he looked at the Intelligence Officer. This was the man who knew everyone in the Organisation, their talents, their secrets and things they did not even realise about themselves. "The North is too risky and the South is pissing in our own bathtub, so that means the mainland. Wales is out because we want no one sniffing around our armoury. London is a bit tight after the last bomb, so Birmingham needs another turn and has plenty of motorway exits for getting out. We can leave the details to the boys doing the job. I think you know the pair I mean." The other two nodded because the choice was so obvious.

Seamus and Blondie made ideal members of an Active Service Unit. They had Army experience and understood weapons, detonators and explosives. Neither had unusual distinguishing features except for Seamus' cauliflower ear and Blondie's hair, but both these features could be hidden by hats. Their most valuable asset was that they did not have Irish accents. An Irish voice gave rise to instant suspicion of the most innocent activity. In a recent letter to 'The Independent,' an Irish priest working in a London parish had complained that on three recent occasions, when indulging in such activities as buying a railway ticket or a suitcase, he had caught the person serving him making a note of his description in case he was a terrorist and there was subsequently a bomb explosion in the area. The Intelligence Chief knew that they were both highly effective, loyal and secretive. Their only disadvantage was their habit of shooting anyone who got in their way, especially policemen. He knew that the recent mysterious gunning down of two motorway patrolmen was a result of a routine stop because of a non-functioning rear light. One of the cops asked Blondie to open the car boot which contained an Armalite rifle. Seamus shot both men and then coolly sat their bodies in the front seat of their own patrol car supported by the seat belts. The car lights were left on and passing motorists assumed they were watching the traffic and cautiously slowed down as they passed the patrol car.

The cover used by Seamus was that of a self employed television repairman. His only employee was Blondie and the business made a small operating profit. They used assumed names and had bought National Insurance numbers from a small-time criminal who they promptly strangled. All taxes were paid and if the pair were away on a project, the business answerphone informed customers they were out on a job and would get back if they left their name and number. The notorious unreliability of the self employed British tradesman meant that if the call was not returned for a few days, then the customer was not surprised.

Seamus was feeling disgruntled. He had headed their two-man unit for five years. During this time he had carried out four carefully planned operations, all of which had been successful. It was a constant strain to avoid capture with a necessity to be suspicious of everyone and a need to avoid drink, making friends or becoming involved with women. The income from the TV business was small and inadequately supplemented by the Organisation. Seamus believed in the cause, but felt that the risks he ran and the contribution he had made were not appreciated. Another worry was that no one ever retired from an Active Service Unit and he saw no end to the present way of living. No matter how careful a man was it was inevitable that, sooner or later, he would be caught and imprisoned for life in a high security jail where the only way out was horizontally by committing suicide. He sensed that Blondie was having similar thoughts, although he had never been very coherent in expressing ideas even simpler than this. The time had come to change direction but that would mean acquiring money and a safe hiding place. His life had never lacked excitement and he would be lost without the challenge of his bombing activities and the opportunity to injure the hated Brits.

If these were to be carried on he would need the continued presence of Blondie because all terrorist activities need at least two people.

Four days later, a hand-addressed envelope with no stamp was posted through the letterbox of the TV shop. The instructions were simple and unsigned - 'A large television, £250, spares in usual place'. Decoded, television was bank; £250 meant £250,000 was needed and the usual place was the Welsh farm where armaments and expense money were held.

Jason Williams was the manager of a large branch of the Central Bank on the outskirts of Birmingham. He had the usual problems of a forty-five year old English businessman, that is those at work, and those at home.

The work problems were alarming. As bank profits increased, their rise was paralleled by more redundancies in the name of increased efficiency. This was a euphemism for more loot for the shareholders. During the preceding week, Jason had to tell two counter clerks that they were redundant. One was a single mother with two teenage children who had never taken a day in sick leave during the ten years of her employment and her prospects of getting another job were remote. The other was a lonely depressed bachelor who lived with a domineering mother. The other bank staff covered up his inefficiencies because they felt sorry for him. He had taken the news of his dismissal in stunned silence and Jason had spent a sleepless weekend worrying that the man might commit suicide. During the same week, Head Office instructed Jason to get rid of the chief clerk, Mrs Simpson. She would be replaced by a more junior grade with an annual saving of £5000. The manager had worked with her since his appointment and he had a high regard for her abilities.

In the early months of his new job her advice had frequently rescued him from disaster. Jason had spoken to a colleague in another bank and fortunately his enthusiastic recommendation meant that she would have another post to go to. Nevertheless she felt hurt and rejected by the bank to which she had always given loyal service. Even his own job was insecure. In modern banking, fifty-year-old managers are rare and the only older men are directors. In promotion terms, movement is either up or out and Jason had not been promoted for five years. The role of the branch manager was rapidly diminishing. The wealthy clients were assigned to a separate division called Personal Banking, whether to grant loans relied on a computerised checklist of questions. Managers could overrule the computer's decision in borderline cases but rarely did so because should the loan default, it was clear who was at fault. The main function of the manager seemed to receive admonishment and exhortation to further efforts from a remote Regional Office. The business in his own branch had suffered during the recession but, fortuitously, had been rescued by the construction of a large shopping mall in the area. Unfortunately its tenants were more financially sophisticated and demanding and recently some had transferred their accounts to other banks. Jason was worried that this would reflect to his disadvantage with his superiors.

The home problems were of a different type. Jason had married for love at the age of twenty five. The woman seemed loyal and affectionate with a determination to have a large number of children. After a year, it became obvious that she was promiscuous, alcoholic and sterile, following a bout of gonorrhoea acquired from a Turkish wind surf instructor during a holiday. Jason did his best but the marriage was doomed from the start and ended in divorce. Over the next ten years he had become lonely and had realised that life and the chances of having children were passing him by. Dr Johnson once commented that second marriages were a triumph of hope over experience and for Jason, this turned out to be the case. He found that women of forty were either divorced for excellent reasons or unmarried for excellent reasons and he then made the common error of marrying a woman fifteen years his junior. Delia was extremely pretty but empty headed, with a whim of iron and expensive tastes. After five years of marriage they had three-year-old twins who were highly trained insomniacs. Delia was bored, permanently exhausted and unable to work because of the children. She resented the fact that many of her childless contemporaries led exciting lives with foreign holidays and much dining out. Jason never seemed to want to look after the children when he came home and always seemed preoccupied and worried about his boring work. The marriage was coping but there were many tensions and Jason accepted that many of the problems were his fault. He could see that if he lost his job and income, the marriage would not survive and was terrified at the prospect of losing the twins who were a delight when not being insomniacs.

This Monday morning his timetable had become very pressurised. On the Friday before at 3 p.m. his deputy had inserted an appointment into Jason's appointment book for 11 a.m. the next Monday and this meant that two other appointments had to be cancelled at short notice. The assistant manager had taken a telephone call from a Mr Anthony Trelawney who said that he represented Nokura Electronics and wished to speak to the manager. This rang an immediate alarm bell because Nokura Electronics had featured in the National financial press during the preceding week. They were seeking a British site for a new factory that would employ 2000 workers in skilled and semi-skilled jobs. The location had not been determined and although Birmingham had been mentioned as a possible site, the journalists felt that it was at the bottom of the list. The assistant manager explained that Jason was out of the office at a meeting. In fact, he was buying lunch for a solicitor who was an excellent customer of the bank and whom Jason suspected of being grossly dishonest. When asked the nature of his business, Trelawney stated that it was highly confidential and he would only discuss it with the manager. He was leaving the area at midday on Monday and required an appointment with the manager for 11 a.m. Banks respond rapidly to bullying and an appointment was arranged.

Jason mused that if Nokura moved to Birmingham and used the Central Bank, then this would represent an enormous personal coup for him. He felt he needed something to cheer him up, as Delia had looked particularly depressed and frosty when they parted that morning and words had been exchanged.

The farm was a mile outside Fishguard. A sunken track led directly from the main road to the farmhouse so that visitors could enter and leave without being seen by neighbouring farmers. Seamus had met the farmer previously and remembered him as a gloomy widower with a permanent sniffle. The man had farmed in Kent for thirty years after emigrating from Donegal. His only son had returned to work in Omagh in the Six Counties and had become involved with the IRA. At that time, the Organisation had acquired the technique of triggering bombs using radio signals of a particular frequency which could be varied for each detonation. This meant that bombs could be laid beneath bridges or road culverts and detonated by an observer up to two miles away who had a view of the road. The Army and police had experienced serious losses and one was of an entire six-man patrol. They had resorted to using expensive and scarce helicopters to supply outlying bases. A brilliant countermeasure was the use of a device which produced radio waves in the range of frequency used by the IRA. A series of impulses were emitted with a considerable range playing up and down the frequency range. This process was known as playing the piano. The farmer's son was arming a bomb in the quiet of his house when one of the radio operators struck the lucky frequency. The son, his wife and their three small children died in the blast. The farmer attended the funeral which was accompanied by full IRA military honours. He indicated to one of the men wearing dark spectacles who fired revolver shots over the grave that he was available if they ever wanted a safe house in mainland Britain. This information was passed back to the Army Intelligence Commander who never forgot anything.

Seamus always made the man uneasy because he was uncommunicative and exuded an aura of violence. "I have orders to give you what you want," the farmer said.

"Two revolvers, one silenced and thirty rounds for each, two thousand pounds in cash, and do you have any semtex?"

"Two hundred kilos because we've just had a supply in of semtex and rifles."

"Just one kilogram and the detonators will do me," replied Seamus. "This is a small job."

"There's a weight of hay to move," said the farmer in his usual depressed manner, "and I'm getting no younger so you'll need to help." Seamus went out to the barn with the farmer and moved twenty bales of hay from one end of the barn to the other. The farmer pulled back a sliding door in the floor to reveal a ladder and he went down it into the cellar. Without saying a word, he threw up a plastic bag of bank notes to Seamus and climbed back up the ladder carrying two more plastic bags; one containing guns and the other semtex and the detonators. "It's not going to close itself," said the miserable man and nodded at the door which Seamus rolled shut and then replaced the hay bales. The farmer offered nothing to eat or drink and did not reply at Seamus' parting invitation to have a nice day.

"We need to talk about our futures," Seamus told Blondie. Blondie was startled as he was just thinking the same thing, but hesitated to discuss it in case any questioning of their present situation might provoke a violent reaction from Seamus. Blondie was unique as the only mercenary employed by the IRA. When Seamus had offered the Organisation a package deal of the pair of them or neither, Seamus' talents were in such demand that the package was accepted and the IRA Intelligence man conducting the negotiations knew that Seamus would never work with anyone he did not trust absolutely.

The problem for Blondie was that the work was dangerous and the pay less than he had earned in the Army. Like Seamus, he had begun to realise the difficulties of resigning and knew that if he did manage to get out, his position did not carry a pension.

"We have done a lot for the Organisation" Seamus told him, "but if we carry on much longer like this, we'll be caught. The more successful we are then the harder they look for us and there is always the worry that someone like that miserable farmer will shop us for the money. The problem is that I have job satisfaction and would like to continue but only doing the cheeky jobs that appeal to me and get up the Brits' noses and I need to carry on with you because I cannot trust anyone else."

"I've been thinking about it myself," admitted Blondie, "but we could never hide and would have no money or access to armaments."

"All these problems are solvable once we decide to opt out," his friend said. "Now here's what we do."

At ten minutes before 11 o'clock the man presented to the reception desk at the bank. He wore an expensive pin stripe suit with a shirt that shouted designer. The day was hot and he wore one of the Panama hats which had become fashionable during the recent heat wave. "Trelawney, appointment with Mr Williams at 11 a.m.," he announced.

The receptionist invited him to sit down. She had been told he was important and telephoned Jason to say that his next appointment had arrived. Jason told her to bring him up to his office and she shepherded him through the security door. She made small talk on the way and he seemed a typical polite businessman.

"Trelawney," the man said to Jason. He was invited to sit down and refused an offer of coffee from the pot on the manager's desk. "How can I help you?" asked Jason. "I understand that you are acting for Nokura Electronics."

"Perhaps the quickest way to proceed would be to start by showing you my authorisation." The man sat on the chair on the other side of Jason's desk and placed his Panama hat next to the coffee cup. The manager noted an odd deformity of his right ear. Trelawney opened a black leather briefcase and pulled out a large handgun which he pointed at Jason. "This," and he pointed at a swelling at the base of the barrel, "is a silencer. If you have an alarm button and press it then you are dead. If you do exactly what I say, then the only losers are the bank's insurers. Now, telephone your wife."

Jason hesitated. "Telephone her immediately or you both die and maybe the twins as well". He dialled his home number. A male voice answered with a number. "Who is it?" Jason enquired. "A friend of Mr Trelawney who is sitting opposite her and the kids. If you do what you are told she goes free and if not, she dies."

Jason was stunned at the rapidity at which his usual boring day had degenerated into a nightmare beyond his control. "Put the telephone down," said Trelawney, "what I want you to do is quite simple."

Mrs Simpson immediately went up to the manager's office when he sent for her. She felt that recently Jason had begun to look older and more strained and when she went into the office she thought that he looked even worse than usual. She concluded that his wife was giving him a bad time. "Mr Trelawney," Jason told her, " is acting for

Nokura Electronics and has given me a banker's draft for £250,000. He needs cash, can we manage it?"

Mrs Simpson was an effective cashier who always had the answers at her fingertips. "We can do it because it is Friday afternoon and the shopping mall tenants are paying in their takings. How would you like it made up Mr Trelawney?" She turned to the man whose hands were folded on his lap beneath a Panama hat. "As much as possible in twenties and the rest in tens, if you would be so kind."

The cashier was worried at this unusual request. Strictly speaking the procedure was correct, but she had not met it during a long banking career. She confided her anxieties to her friend and deputy head cashier. "Mr Williams is too boring to be dishonest unless the tartlet put him up to it," said her friend waspishly. The tartlet was the bank nickname for Mrs Delia Williams who was perceived by the bank staff as a greedy young shrew. "Besides, there is no way you can check it unless you telephone Head Office. Knowing Mr Williams, everything will be above board. At present you have a month's notice and an excellent reference for the new job. If you make a silly complaint, you will not be back on Monday and that will be the end of the reference."

Mrs Simpson considered. If Mr Williams was up to something odd then she could not be blamed. He was bound to be caught and serve him right for sacking her; after all she had done for his career. If he got away with some sort of swindle, good luck to him and she would have no sympathy if the bank lost money. She suppressed her anxieties.

The next half-hour seemed to stretch into infinity for Jason. He had previously given firm instructions that his important meeting should not be interrupted by messages or telephone calls. Any attempts at conversation with Trelawney were answered by a command to shut up and the man seemed to have nerves of steel. Jason knew that the Panama hat on his lap concealed the revolver which was pointing at his chest. He tried to keep his mind off the situation by memorising the man's description. He was about five feet ten inches with the cauliflower ear, but apart from this feature he seemed a standard English businessman.

Mrs Simpson returned with the money. The £20 notes were in bundles of 100, each fastened with an elastic band and there were 125 of them. There were too many to fit into Trelawney's briefcase, but the ever-efficient Mrs Simpson had experienced this problem in the past. "We have a suitcase in my office which we keep just in case. A new one will cost £20 and if you want to give me that for a replacement, you can have it to carry the money" she said with a smile.

"You have a most impressive staff," Trelawney congratulated Jason. "I shall mention it to your Head Office when I discuss our future transactions with them." Mrs Simpson was delighted because she knew that Jason needed all the credit he could get with Head Office. "Thank you, that will be all," the manager said, dismissing Mrs Simpson.

"You will never get away from here," said Jason. A few people have seen you in the bank in addition to myself and you must have a record."

"Let me worry about that," Trelawney told him. "Just telephone the receptionist and tell her I am coming down to the security door and will be carrying a suitcase so that she will not be surprised." Jason did as he was told and Trelawney stood up. "Thank you for being so co-operative and sensible," he said, and there was a faint phut from the silencer as the shot hit the manager in the chest. Jason had no sense of pain, but just a feeling of sorrow that he had quarrelled with Delia that morning and his body slumped to the floor.

The man carried the suitcase downstairs and patiently waited while the receptionist unlocked the door to let him out. "Do you need a taxi, sir?" she enquired. "Thank you for asking but I have a driver and car," he told her.

Delia waited in the car outside the bank in a state of terror. Blondie had said little to her but she realised that he was a man operating under different rules to the rest of the normal population.

Seamus hefted the heavy suitcase into the car boot. "Drive nice and carefully to Selwyn water, my man," he told Blondie. "You and the kids can go free after that if you behave," he told Delia. "Have you harmed Jason?" she asked anxiously. "Not a hair on his head," lied Seamus. As they pulled into the parking lot Seamus shot Delia in the back of the head from the rear seat with the silenced revolver. The twins were sitting alongside Seamus and screamed in fear. Blondie thought for a moment that he would shoot the kids as well. "Mummy is asleep," he told them, "now go and see if you can find the teddy bears in the wood." The twins seemed anxious to escape and ran off into the trees. Blondie transferred the suitcase into their own car which he had left in the clearing next to Delia's.

At 9 p.m. that evening the farmer received a telephone call telling him that the lambs would be ready at 10 o'clock tomorrow. This was code to expect a visit from an Active Service Unit at 10 o'clock that night. An hour later he heard a car pull up into the farm courtyard. Seamus and Blondie emerged carrying the plastic bags which he had given them a few days before. "Just returning the goodies, but only half the money," Seamus told him. The farmer knew that Active Service Units were meticulous about returning unused expenses money. The slightest suggestion that they had misused it would result in interrogation, trial and a rapid execution if their dishonesty were confirmed. The farmer made no enquiries about what the two men had been doing and knew that if he did, he would get no answer and would be reported to the Intelligence Officer for asking.

"If you think I'm moving that lot by myself then you're wrong," moaned the farmer and with a show of reluctance the two men agreed to help and the sliding door was again revealed. "You go down on the ladder and we can hand the bags down one at a time," offered Seamus. The farmer rested on the ladder with his head at the level of the floor and Seamus handed him the bag containing the detonators and semtex. As he did so, Blondie shot the farmer in the back of the head with the silenced gun and the blood and brains sprayed onto the ladder and cellar floor as the body fell. The men climbed down into the cellar avoiding the bloodier patches on the ladder rungs. On the walls were racks of rifles and handguns and a large tube which they recognised as an anti-tank bazooka. In one corner was an old suitcase. Seamus opened it and Blondie could see large piles of banknotes. They helped themselves to four Armalite rifles and ammunition and they put these in the car boot with the money. At the back of the cellar were ten bags each weighing about 20 kg. They recognised the white substance inside as semtex and with a lot of effort, transported the bags to the car where they distributed them between the boot and the floorwell of the rear seats. They covered the material in the boot and rear of the car with some old horse blankets and returned to the cellar.

Seamus took about 1 kg from a bag of semtex and set the detonator for four hours.

"We could be over the English border in two and a half hours," complained Blondie. "If we set the charge for four hours, someone might come along and find him."

Seamus was patient. "He is such a miserable sod that I doubt if he has any friends, but just in case, we can put some of the hay back. The extra hour or so is just in case we get a puncture down the road and get stuck next to an explosion."

They carefully washed their hands in the kitchen sink and drove carefully west along the M4 to London.

All his life people had drummed it into Blondie that he was stupid. In fact he was not, he was dyslexic at a time when that condition was not recognised. The child whom his peers assess as backward has a hard time and in Blondie's instance, the situation was made worse because his single mother abandoned him and he was raised in an orphanage. When he became sixteen he was magnetically drawn to join the British Army. He thought it would give him an adventurous life and would substitute for the family which he had never had. His travel was limited to the bleak Catterick camp in Yorkshire, and a dreary barracks in the North German plain. His linguistic talents were poor in English and non-existent in German and the Army was a lonely place where bullying was even worse than the orphanage; his life was one of misery.

Two months after he had been transferred from Yorkshire to Germany, he was having a particularly bad time in the hut assigned to his platoon. One of the corporals was a shaven-headed muscular thug who enjoyed power over the younger, weaker members of the platoon. One evening the corporal, Jones, was sitting holding court in the platoon surrounded by three of his lackeys.

"Boot polishing time Blondie," the corporal said and held out a large dung covered boot on one of his smelly feet. Blondie's heart sank. For the last three weeks every Friday night, he had been forced to polish the corporal's boots. The first time he was asked to do so he refused. The corporal seized a large section of Blondie's flesh between his neck and shoulder until he screamed in pain. There was nothing he could do except obey. He got out the corporal's boot cleaning kit and set to work. The bully sat and gave his opinion on the Welsh - "ignorant gits," and was holding forth on the Irish - "even more ignorant gits," while Blondie polished away ignored. The door opened and a thickset man with a cauliflower ear came in.

"Evening all," he said, "been assigned to this platoon,"

and dumped his kit bag on the nearest bunk which happened to belong to the corporal. With all the crisp command of the English language within his vocabulary, Jones said, "Take your fucking kit off my bunk or I'll sort you out," assuming that the command would be instantly obeyed, "and Blondie, that's not a polish it's an apology, now lick it clean before you start again." Blondie considered what to do. If he licked Jones' boots he would be licking them once a week for the rest of his service, but he knew that if he refused he would be set on until he did it.

The new man said quietly, "Hi, Blondie," although they had never met previously. "I have a better idea, the corporal can lick your boots." The insult combined with the realisation that the new man had not removed his kit from the bunk, slowly penetrated to the Neanderthal brain of Jones. He sensed a challenge and had dealt with these many times before. In a troop of apes he would clearly have emerged as the dominant male.

With a terrifying shout of rage, he got up off the chair and hurled a kick at Blondie's ribs in passing, causing him to fall to the floor in agony. With bullet head at waist level he charged in intending to butt the new man in the belly and then kick him when he fell to the floor. The stranger stepped back a pace so that the corporal's roundhouse swings did not connect and then brought his knee up sharply into the corporal's nose. Jones raised his face and his nose had a distinct new tilt to the right and poured blood. Enraged, he swung a further right hand which would have decapitated the recipient if it had landed. This time the new man moved inside the punch which whistled past the back of his neck and let loose a left hook into Jones' stomach. Jones bent forward in reflex fashion and the left hook was followed by a right hook which put the corporal unconscious onto his back. The platoon was silent at a demolition of such clinical effectiveness which had brought their tormentor down. The new man stepped above Jones and quite coolly stamped once on each hand with his boot - there was a crunch of bone on each occasion and the agony caused the corporal to sit up. He put his weight on his right hand to help this process and screamed in agony when the broken bones grated together.

"Now, where were we?" said the new man. "Very rude of me really but I didn't introduce myself. Name is Reilly and I am only going to tell you two things about me. I am Irish and the corporal had something to tell us about that didn't you? Now tell us that all Irishmen are princes amongst people." The corporal could barely speak and gave a groan. Reilly's boot pinned his broken right hand to the floor. He pressed gently and the man screamed. "Say it!" said Reilly. "All Irishmen are princes," he groaned. "Now it's your turn Blondie. Sit in the chair," and Blonde did as he was told. "Now, lick his boots clean, especially that lump of mud on the right heel," and he pressed further on the trapped hand. The corporal licked. Blondie was frightened and knew he would pay for the night when the corporal caught up with him.

"There was one other fact about me I promised to tell you. One was that I'm Irish, even if I have an English accent because I went to school there; the second fact is that I was the middleweight champion of the French Foreign Legion for five years. Now corporal this has been an interesting conversation. If you touch Blondie, or even give him a nasty look, I'll give you a proper sorting next time. In the morning say that you had gone out for a walk in the town and got jumped by some lurking Highlanders. Everyone will believe you because they are all psychopaths and the Germans call them the King's Own Scottish Murderers."

The barracks room was silent, save for the groans from Jones who had been deserted by his cronies.

Over the next few months, Blondie attached himself to Reilly. Reilly was clearly a very experienced competent soldier who said that he had often been offered promotion but had always declined, so it was no longer proffered. He never spoke of his own background and never enquired about that of Blondie. The rest of the Platoon left them alone and Reilly's reputation became well known in the Unit after Jones had appeared the next morning. The Officers knew that the origin of Jones' injury was not in the town because the guard had not admitted any injured man and Jones' injuries were, to say the least, noticeable. They disliked the man who had a reputation as a bully and made no formal enquiries about the source of his injuries which were attributed, like most disorder in the Army of the Rhine, to the Gordon Highlanders.

Blondie always felt embarrassed that he owed a favour to Reilly which it was not possible to repay. He would never accept cigarettes or beer from Blondie except in a strict rotation. Three months after the fight with the corporal, the Unit was taking part in a night exercise. An unidentified enemy called Redforce (an inspired code name by Intelligence to simulate the Russians) had invaded the German plain. Redforce was stationed East of the Rhine and had penetrated to the riverbank. The defending Unit (it was a Conservative British Government at the time so Intelligence deemed it Blueforce) sent a reconnaissance in strength over the river to capture members of Redforce for interrogation and to report on the disposition and strength of the enemy troops. The night was very dark and getting in the boats was accompanied by much whispered swearing as weapons banged into heads and crotches and Army boots were carelessly put down on hands. Blondie and Reilly were in the same boat when a fat subaltern stepped into it as its commander. His foot carrying 120 kg of fat went straight through the thin rubber boat bottom. He leaned right and with a shouted obscenity, fell into the river up-turning the boat. Blondie was amused. Although wearing boots, his weapon was free and with the safety on, and as the boat turned over he threw it to the bank remembering a sergeant once in Catterick who had frequently informed them that the squad was easier to replace than rifles. He heard a bubbling gurgle on his right and realised that Reilly's head was under water. He dived down into the rapidly flowing current and emerged swimming backward with Reilly's head above water. "Just lie still," he said amused at finding a situation where he was telling his hero what to do. He swam into the bank where helpful hands pulled them ashore. "Thanks," said Reilly laconically, "I never learned to swim after my father threw me into the sea to teach me and I nearly drowned. I owe you one."

The matter was never mentioned between them again, but Blondie felt it was now a partnership rather than a dependent relationship and he felt easier knowing this.

Their mutual relationship was that Reilly was a protector whose reputation was such that nobody fooled with either of them. Reilly was secretive and never spoke of his earlier military experience, his background or his family. Blondie was quite happy to tell anyone about the difficult life he had had before joining the Army.

After seven years of service, Blondie assumed that both of them would continue in the Army until reaching maximum pensionable service of twenty two years. Shortly before signing on again they were sitting over a beer in a pub in England. "Ever thought about going independent?" asked Reilly.

"You mean soldier of fortune, security guards, that sort of thing?"

"Not really, what are your feelings about politics in Ireland?

"None. No interest. Nothing to do with me unless I get posted there when I'll kill any bastard I'm told to."

"Yes and get paid the usual rate till you get shot in the back. Look, I'm in touch with the IRA. I was born in Belfast and lived there till I was six. My father was a carpenter and not well off but he saved his money and bought a little motorcar. Two weeks later he took my mother out one evening for a meal and left me with a baby-sitter. A local resident said that the car was stopped at a roadblock by the police and there was an argument. It was a Catholic area and the police hated to see a Catholic with a car because it meant they were prosperous. They claimed the car did not stop when ordered to do so and they emptied their automatic rifles into the back of it. Both my parents were killed instantly. The witness who said there had been an argument was a Protestant and she got a visit from some paramilitary heavies so that she changed her evidence at the Inquest and said that the car had not stopped when the RUC ordered it to. I was sent to live in England with my mother's sister, but I am determined to pay the English back. The way to get the best military training seemed to be to join the French Foreign Legion and then I finished my military education in the British Army. Before joining the Legion I went back to Belfast and contacted the IRA to tell them of my plans. They were surprised at first but checked out my story about my parents and that I was who I said I was because in Belfast I stayed with my mother's other sister who would vouch for me. Now I'm a good man on explosives and a better soldier than most in the British Army. I know how the Army works from the inside, in fact that is why I joined. Now I've graduated and I want to go back and work for the IRA. I've told them I have another British soldier who would not stand out in mainland Britain in an Active Service Unit. If you want to come with me you can, and you'll get paid double. If you're not interested, no harm done. I trust you not to talk."

Blondie sat and pondered. He owed Britain and its Army nothing, for both had treated him badly. Reilly was the only friend he ever had who had always treated his opinion with respect and the thought of the Army without Reilly and of the inevitable revenge of corporal Jones, finally persuaded him. "All right, I'm with you and will be resigning from this lot," he said.

Superintendent Herrington was effectively in command of the Midlands Regional Crime Squad. Although he was theoretically responsible to a higher chain of command, these more senior offices spent their time strutting in heavily decorated uniforms at conferences, Rotary lunches and Masonic events, whilst the Superintendent looked after the shop and covered their backs. His advancement had not resulted from a formidable intelligence but from tenacity, low cunning and an ability to spot and promote promising juniors. A week before, he had given instructions to a young Inspector in the department and the meeting he now chaired was to consider this man's report.

"Right, Wilson," said the Superintendent, "the Birmingham bank job - we are stuck completely. Quarter of a million nicked, the manager and his wife needlessly killed. No clues, no fingerprints, nothing from the informants. I want your analysis."

The Inspector was regarded with suspicion by everyone in the Crime Squad except the Superintendent. He had a degree in history, which provoked scornful laughter when he told his colleagues, and was a teetotaller - something unique in the CID.

He began slowly. "The features of this crime are so odd that they could be helpful. Bank robbers come in two kinds. The single-handed incompetent who goes in with a gun, often a dummy, and asks for the contents of the cashier's drawer. They usually get picked up from the pictures on the security cameras and sometimes they are so stupid that they try to rob their own bank or get over-excited and shoot their dicks off. The other sort is the professionals. They work in a group of at least four or five; one of whom is always a driver. They often have inside information, carry real guns and will use them only if pushed. At least two or three of the group will have previous form and we usually get useful descriptions from the bank staff and customers, even when they use stocking masks. The usual informers often get to hear about it or spot that one of them is suddenly in funds.

These two characters stand out as quite different because there are only two of them. The next oddity is why they unnecessarily killed the two people. They must have known that this would immediately ratchet up the heat of the pursuit so why do it? The only reason I can think of is that they did not want anyone to have their description. We know nothing of the man who held the wife because nobody ever saw him. The other man is aged about forty, of medium height. He wore a good suit, was white and had a standard non-regional accent - about as useless a description as possible for us. However, the bank receptionist said that he wore a Panama hat, both entering and leaving the bank. The only living person to see him without the hat was the chief cashier. I have spoken to her again. She recalls that he was sitting sideways on to her and she does not recall any distinguishing features. Few men now wear hats. This man wanted to be inconspicuous, so he must have had a reason for wearing a hat. The cashier only saw the left side of his face. I wonder if he had a scar or deformity on the right side of his head or upper face on the side she never saw. He might have used the hat to hide it.

The final strange feature is the silencer on the gun. The gun must have had a silencer because the assistant manager in the next room could hear the buzz of a conversation but never heard a shot. Silencers are extremely difficult to come by in the criminal world. They make a gun bulky and inaccurate. Forensic tell us that he was killed by a single shot in the heart from three metres".

"Now Sir," the Inspector said to his boss, "let's see where we are. One of these men is an intelligent professional who is middle class and possibly has a very distinctive feature or scar on the right side of his head. He is a marksman, so must be ex Army or a member of a pistol shooting club. The other man is a mystery but his friend must have great trust in him to turn up with the manager's wife outside the bank in the car. Had he not, number one would almost certainly have been caught carrying a suitcase with a good description from the bank staff. I'll stop for a moment before making a jump, but any comments so far?"

There was silence. "You've made a lot of jumps so far," a sergeant said sarcastically, "so you might as well keep jumping."

"Carry on, it's very interesting, but not really very concrete" said the Superintendent who was impressed with the way in which the story had been built from minimal evidence.

"Something clicked when I was running through this lot in bed at 3 o'clock this morning," the Inspector said, and paused. He had the attention of his audience. "Do you remember that the bank robbery took second place in the newspaper headlines the next day?" The audience looked blank. "The main headline was an explosion on a farm near Fishguard. They found the farmer's body shot in the head in a cellar packed with guns and an anti-tank missile. The farmer had a son who was killed in the IRA and the local police concluded that they had stumbled on an IRA armoury.

"I wonder if our friends in the bank were fund raising for the IRA and got their guns from the Fishguard dump. They might have quarrelled with the farmer when they returned the guns or might have executed him if they suspected he was an informer. I would suggest, Sir, that we run this idea past Special Branch in case they recognise this pair from other operations. It might be worth tactfully asking them if the farmer, the banker and the wife were killed by bullets from the same gun."

Five days later the Regional Crime Squad met again and on this occasion were addressed by a quiet policeman not wearing uniform. "Gentlemen, and lady," he said in deference to the single statutory female cop, "congratulations for some good thinking." The Superintendent smiled modestly. "We have had four terrorist incidents in Britain recently, for which the IRA has not acknowledged responsibility. In all but one there have been reports of two men in the vicinity never seen doing anything suspicious and without any particular description, except that they always wear baseball hats. One witness heard the younger one buying train tickets and thought he had a faint South London accent. The next straw in the wind was an informant in Northern Ireland who heard a buzz that the IRA had recruited two ex British Army men for operations on the mainland. We have looked through all British Army records for the last five years, looking for a pair who served in the same unit, left at about the same and had pistol training. We ended up with two hundred possible pairs. The next thing was to see if any of these two hundred pairs had subsequently vanished without trace. There was only one such couple. Since leaving the Army, they have never claimed any Social Security benefits, nor paid Income Tax or National Insurance. They are not known to any bank, and they must have false identities. One is Seamus Reilly. Irish parents, educated in England and left University suddenly in the middle of a degree course and joined the French Foreign Legion for five years. After that he entered the British Army and they must have been delighted to acquire a pre-trained soldier. He left the Army five years later and left with an honourable discharge. His mate was Carl Carrington who answers to the nickname of Blondie. He is rather thick, but slavishly devoted to his friend. Both were excellent marksmen. We got the Provost's department to talk to the corporal in their platoon. He didn't want to say anything and was clearly terrified of Seamus who seems to have beaten him up. The Provost had to threaten him with flogging and stopping his rum - or is that the Navy, but the upshot was that the corporal said both were outstanding marksmen and Seamus never talked about himself. We've alerted all points of entry to Britain and their Army photographs have been sent to every police station in Britain. Here's a set for yourself and remember, they are five years old". The pictures showed a blonde man in his thirties and an older man with dark hair. The picture of the older man clearly showed a right cauliflower ear.

"These are dead men," said the man from Special Branch. "They will inevitably be spotted by a policeman somewhere in Britain, but what is even more interesting is that we have had two separate reports from informers that two IRA men were responsible for blowing up the armoury in Fishguard. The buzz is that they escaped with a lot of money and semtex. The IRA has offered £50,000 to anyone who finds them so if we don't get them, the IRA will. I will be surprised if they are not dead or in jail within a month."

He remained surprised.

Chapter 2

The British public perceives barristers as wealthy, useless parasites who feed on the misery of others. Whilst this is certainly true, the life of a barrister can have a downside. Many aspirants fail to make a living and fall off the career ladder. The successful become Queen's (or King's) Council and no doubt in ten years time, they will be dubbed Royal person's Council. In order to take silk it is essential to have achieved a good income as a junior and it helps not to be female, black or an overt homosexual. The income of a successful QC would be expected to be at the level of £200,000 to £1 million annually. A disadvantage is that no self-employed person likes to turn work away and there is a tendency to take on too many briefs so that much of the work has to be done at night or weekends. Success in a case relies on persuading a judge or jury that your interpretation of the facts and the law is preferable to that of the other side. A failure to do this is done in public and in front of members of a profession addicted to gossip and backbiting. The combination of having too much money and too much stress inevitably produces problems and barristers have a high incidence of failed marriages, alcoholism and a fondness for the more bizarre outer reaches of the expression of human sexuality.

Roderick Atkins had been a very successful QC. He had a keen mind and a pleasant manner and clients, solicitors and judges liked him. He had established a considerable reputation at the Criminal Bar. His name was recognised by the general public for his remarkable success in prosecuting the Welham Street gang.

In this case four IRA activists were charged with planting a bomb in a rented house next door to the Welham Street Police Station in London. This was a high security building used for housing those detained for questioning in terrorist and major drug cases. The explosion had killed ten policemen and twelve civilians in surrounding houses and business premises. Immediately before the trial there had been considerable publicity following the release by the Court of Appeal of two groups of men sentenced to ten and fifteen years each respectively for conspiracy to cause explosions in Sheffield as part of an IRA campaign. Their solicitors used new forensic techniques to show that their confessions had been confabulated. One of the junior policemen involved at the time had been overcome by his conscience when he was dying with cancer. He made a dying declaration that the statements attributed to the men were dictated to him by his Chief Inspector. The same Chief Inspector had supervised the case against the second group of defendants and both had always protested their innocence. These revelations had resulted in much public suspicion about the conduct of police enquiries in alleged IRA cases.

The evidence in the Welham Street affair initially seemed damming. A fingerprint of one of the Defendants was found on a teacup in the remains of the house next to the police station. Special Branch would give evidence that the Defendants had been witnessed meeting with known IRA activists in two pubs in Kilburn in North London. An informer claimed that towards the end of a heavy drinking session, one of the men charged had stated that "the pigs' wives would be wearing black next week." The men were employed by different small building firms in London but shared a flat. Their descriptions matched those of four men who had been seen entering the Welham Street house during the week preceding the explosion. Their alibi was that on the night of the incident they were all at home watching the television. Their alibi was confirmed by the mistress of one of the men who claimed that she had been with them throughout the evening. A combination of bribes and threats by the police was unable to shake her story. When the police searched the flat, they found a Webley revolver in the attic.

From a prosecution viewpoint, the case went disastrously. The judge knew although the jury could not, that all four defendants had previous convictions connected with storing or transporting explosives for the IRA. The informant was shifty and evasive and admitted to a string of minor offences involving petty theft and dishonesty. He admitted that, apart from Social Security payments, his only income was from acting as an informer for Special Branch who paid him for low-level intelligence which he collected from his fellow Irishmen in pubs and illegal bars in Kilburn. At the end of his evidence, the judge sighed eloquently and the jury looked unimpressed.

The evidence of the fingerprint on the cup seemed extremely damaging to the Defence barrister who tackled it head on. He accepted the evidence of the forensic scientist that the fingerprint on the cup was indeed that of one of the Defendant's and the next witness was the young policeman who had found the teacup and put it into the evidence bag. He had previously appeared as a witness in a Magistrates' Court but had never done so in a Crown Court. The aura of such a Court is frightening. The bewigged judge sits high above the witness and matters are conducted in a formalised ritual fashion. The policeman took the oath and licked his lips nervously conveying a totally false impression to the judge that he had something to hide. Charles Rance was defending and before opening, used his standard ploy of sipping a glass of water and shuffling his notes whilst the witness stewed gently. In police canteen culture barristers are credited with superhuman intelligence and an ability to gaze into the souls of witnesses and then to expose them as either fools or scoundrels, or preferably both. The policeman had spent an agonising hour in the waiting room nervously rehearsing the answer to the questions he anticipated from the barrister. He consoled himself that his evidence was simple and non-contentious. The first question completely upset him because it was unexpected.

"Constable Williams, are you aware of the Billingham case which recently came before the Court of Appeal?"

"Vaguely," stuttered the policeman who seemed to remember that it was something about unreliable police evidence in court. Oh God! What did the barrister know that he did not?

"I will refresh your memory on that case. The defendant was found guilty of murder and the conviction rested on finding his fingerprints on a glass found at the scene of the crime. Subsequently, another man confessed to the murder and gave details about it which could only have been known to someone present when it was committed. The second man had no connection with the person convicted and it was clear that there had been a gross miscarriage of justice. Following an independent police investigation, a police sergeant involved in the original case was convicted of falsifying evidence. He had offered the prisoner a glass of water in his cell at the police station and then subsequently 'found' the glass with its attached fingerprints at the murder site."

Rance stopped and there was a silence. He found this was often a useful manoeuvre because, although he had not asked a question, witnesses often panicked during a silence and blurted out something helpful.

Constable Williams' mind was in turmoil. He was clearly being accused of faking evidence. He remembered that the sergeant in the Billingham case got eight years, and the newspapers described with great relish how he would have to be protected in the area of the jail reserved for paedophiles and grasses, although in practice the other prisoners always seemed to get to them eventually with razors or knives. He had a flashback of an American film in which an innocent but convicted cop had been gang-raped in the prison laundry. He managed to survive by becoming a sex-slave to a very perverted and enormously fat gang leader who made him dress up in a skirt and a blonde wig. The silence persisted.

"I did not plant any evidence in this case," the young man said in horror.

"Why are you denying something of which I have not accused you ...yet. You said 'in this case!' Does that mean that you have planted evidence in other cases?"

Shit! How could he have known about that, thought the now hysterical witness?

"It was only a marijuana cigarette," he blurted.

Rance utilised another eloquent silence. "I am sure that the jury will give due weight to that remark. Now, let us consider another matter."

Williams prayed. The last time he had done that was ten years previously during extra time at the Cup-Tie when Chelsea was drawing two-all. His requests had not been answered and he had been instantly converted to atheism.

"I would like you to examine Document 33 in the bundle before you."

The constable's sweaty tremulous hands found it difficult to reach the relevant document but eventually he got there.

"This is the police station log of the relevant period when the defendants were detained, is it not?"

"Yes," said Williams, wondering what it had to do with him.

"About half way down the page, you will see the entry 'prisoners given a cup of tea'. I will take you through a series of similar entries on approximately four occasions every day over the prolonged, indeed unnecessarily prolonged, period of detention of the defendants. Are you with me so far?"

"Yes," croaked Williams, his throat dry with terror. Perhaps they might put him in a jail near home where at least his mother could bring him food and cigarettes.

"Now, let us turn to the police station manning roll and this is Document 63 in the bundle." Both sets of lawyers and the judge thumbed through the documents. "I draw your attention to the record for Sunday, June the first. That was the day of the explosion at Welham Street, was it not?"

"I can't remember," panicked Williams, who by now was incapable of adding single digit numbers if there were more than two of them.

"You cannot remember," thundered Rance. "Your memory seems very selective." Rance firmly believed that the policeman was basically honest but his fishing trip had caught a whale and he was experiencing the sort of emotional high which made a barrister's life enjoyable. "You may accept my assurance that the entry was for the relevant day." He looked meaningfully at the jury who, for their part, gazed at the whimpering policeman who showed all the body language of a detected liar.

"This roll shows, does it not, that you returned to the police station from the scene of the Welham Street explosion at three p.m. and that you returned to Welham Street at 6 p.m?" The policeman agreed. "Now why did you return to Welham Street?"

The constable was relieved to receive a straightforward question to which the answer might deflect criticism from himself to someone else. "The sergeant sent me because they needed more men to control the press and the crowds."

"So, you returned because your superior sent you?" Rance said slowly and deliberately and turned to the jury. This was a useful technique for suggesting that some innocent activity had an important sinister motive which such an intelligent jury would certainly perceive. "Let us return to Document 33. Now you see that entry half way down the second page timed at four p.m. Would you read it to the court."

With a sinking feeling, Williams read out 'Prisoners given a cup of tea.'

Rance dropped his voice. This is a useful technique in acting when delivering an important line. The judge and jury leaned forward to miss nothing.

"I put it to you, Constable Williams, that you are a dishonest policeman who has admitted to this court that you have previously planted evidence in other cases and that in this case, you took tea to the Defendant, O'Malley, and then returned to Welham Street where you planted the cup in the rubble, where it was subsequently found."

"No, no!" protested the policeman.

"That will be all Constable."

The finding of a revolver in their flat seemed fairly hard evidence for the criminality of the accused. However, they had only occupied the premises for six months and protested that they knew nothing of the weapon which could have been left by any of the previous tenants or even their visitors. At this stage, the prospects of a conviction seemed remote. Atkins had done his best in damage limitation, but his instincts told him that the sympathies of the jurors were not with the prosecution.

The final witness for the Defence was Anne Robinson, who was the mistress of one of the accused. Rance took her through her alibi evidence. She was a good witness who was quite clear that the men had been watching television with her throughout the whole of the relevant evening. She remembered the date because they had all laughed at the poor acting in one of the situation comedies.

Atkins rose to question her. Robinson was a petite, attractive woman in her mid thirties. She wore a rather severe black dress with short sleeves revealing attractive freckled pale skin which contrasted with her long jet-black hair. Atkins felt it unlikely that he could shake the witness and any attempt to harass such an attractive woman would antagonise the jury. He saw no real weakness in her evidence so far, and there seemed little point in re-covering the ground already set out by the Defence.

"Were you born in England?" he asked.

"Yes, in Sheffield."

"Do you have any sympathy with the IRA case?"

"None at all."

Something was bothering Atkins about the witness who stood demurely in the warm sunlight shining through the windows of the court. It was something odd about her appearance. It suddenly registered. The sun revealed a faint down of ginger hair on her bare forearms. Ginger hair on her arms and freckles - but the hair on her head was black. Of course, a wig!

"Would you mind taking off your wig?" said Atkins and Rance leapt to his feet.

"Your honour, I really must protest. My learned friend is attempting to humiliate the witness."

"Mr Atkins," intervened the judge. " I am minded to agree with Mr Rance and will not allow your request unless you can justify it."

Atkins swallowed hard. If he was wrong the case was lost and he would receive a severe judicial rebuke.

"Your Honour, I have reason to believe that the witness is using a wig to disguise her true identity from the court." There was a gasp and Rance again leapt up to speak. The judge raised his hand to silence any intervention.

"This is a very serious allegation Mr Atkins, but I will allow your request. Please remove your wig, madam."

The woman slowly removed her hairpiece to reveal

short cut ginger hair.

"Do you still maintain that your name is Anne Robinson?"

"I do."

"I put it to you that we previously met in Nottingham Crown Court approximately ten years ago when I was Junior Counsel for the prosecution in the trial of three IRA men who were subsequently convicted for possessing arms. You were charged with harbouring them but you were acquitted. At this distance of time, I cannot remember the name under which you were charged but it was not Robinson. The records of that name and your fingerprints can easily be checked."

The woman said nothing.

"Was it you?"

"Yes."

"The prosecution rests its case. Your Lordship may wish to order the witness to be detained in custody on a charge of perjury or conspiracy to pervert the course of justice."

The Welham Street trial took place during August when hard news items for the media were scarce. They realised that Atkins' astuteness had resulted in the conviction of a gang of dangerous terrorists. His clerk doubled the brief fees but there was an avalanche of requests for his services. He foresaw an enormous income but with even less time for his family and his hobbies of old cars and painting in watercolours. He arranged for some senior colleagues and his Head of Chambers to drop hints that he wished to become a judge and within six months was invited to do this by the Lord Chancellor.

The life of a County Court judge, or indeed any judge in the Crown or High Courts, is very different to that of a barrister. The salary is much less but the life style is easy and predictable. The working day is from 10 to 12 a.m. with a two-hour lunch and an afternoon session from 2 to 4 p.m. There is a certain amount of paperwork outside these hours but no necessity to work at weekends with long vacations and a guaranteed pension. Randolph Atkins did not remain a County Court judge for long and was soon appointed to the Crown Court on Circuit.

The life style of a Crown Court judge is bizarre and flattering to its possessor. He (and very rarely she) is housed in very luxurious "lodgings", often a stately home with resident servants provided. The judge is transported to and from court in a chauffeured limousine with a police escort. As he passes through the foyer of the court an usher commands all present to stand whilst he passes. Within the court his word is law and he is treated with great sycophancy by barristers. If he takes a dislike to a barrister or to the manner in which he conducts the case, then the barrister's life can be made extremely difficult. Being a judge is a good life.

Roderick's present case on trial was rather boring. A solicitor was charged with forging documents in connection with obtaining house mortgages, in conspiracy with a dishonest estate agent. Considerable sums of money were involved. The case was complex and hinged on the interpretation of endless piles of documents which both Prosecution and Defence Counsel dissected in enormous detail. Gentle hints that they should get a move on fell on deaf ears and he suspected that Defence Counsel regarded the case as a major contributor to his pension plan. It was certainly a contrast with the preceding trial of Dermot O'Connor. He was a convicted INLA hit man serving a life sentence for killing a soldier in a siege shoot out in Dartford. Last year someone had smuggled a firearm into the prison and O'Connor shot a warder during an unsuccessful attempt to escape. He was given a second life sentence which seemed to pre-suppose having two lives but that is the way the law works. It was a source of humour to his judicial colleagues that both as a barrister and a judge, Atkins specialised in cases involving Irish terrorists. In fact it was sheer coincidence.

The police car which escorted the judge always arrived at the court at precisely 4 p.m. By the time the great man had shuffled a few papers and had a cup of tea, he never emerged from the court before 4.30, but it was axiomatic that judges must never be kept waiting and the two elderly policeman, one with cartilage problems and the other with sciatica, were always happy to sit in their warm police car and set the world to rights while they waited. On this Tuesday afternoon, they had a leisurely cup of tea in the police station canteen and sauntered out to their car which was parked in a reserved bay outside. As they fastened their seat belts, both rear doors opened simultaneously. They turned round sharply and saw two men pointing guns at them from the back seat. The policeman with the sciatica registered that the bulk of the guns meant that they were fitted with silencers. "Now boys, no heroics," said a man of about forty who was wearing a flat cap. "Just drive away and park in the forecourt of that empty sweet factory about four hundred yards down the road." The policeman did as he was told. "Now, back up the car so that it is about three feet from that wall." They were next ordered to remove their hats and jackets and pass them back to the rear seat passengers.

"Now, one at a time, you first," he told the driver. "Get out and go to the back of the car. My friend will wait for you outside the car and will have a gun under the raincoat on his arm. If you run or give the alarm, your friend gets it as well."

The driver did as he was instructed. The second man raised the boot lid and ordered the driver to get into the boot and lie down on its floor. The second policeman went through the same sequence.

"Now just lie there quietly and we are going for a ride," said the man with the cap. Immediately before he closed the boot, he quickly raised his gun and there was a double soft report as he fired a single shot into the head of each policeman. The men were wearing black shoes and trousers and when they donned the caps and jackets of their victims they appeared to be credible policemen. They parked in front of the court at 4 p.m. on the dot in the place where their previous observations had shown that the police car normally awaited the judge.

At 4.35 p.m. the judge appeared at the main door of the court and received a smart salute from the policeman on the door. He got into the large Daimler awaiting him and the chauffeur flashed his headlamps at the police car in front to signal the procession to start. It headed in the direction of the Lodgings, which modest title masked an Elizabethan manor house situated ten miles outside the town. Traffic lights along the route were manned by policemen who stopped traffic in the opposite direction if the judge's procession met a red light. All saluted smartly in the approved manner but only one subsequently remembered that the policemen in the escort car were not the usual faces, although he was unable to describe them further.

About two miles before their destination, the police car accelerated away from the limousine and then pulled into a lay-by behind a black Ford Granada. The officers stepped from the car and walked into the middle of the road indicating that the Daimler should pull into the lay-by. The Chauffeur assumed that this action was a result of a message they received since one of them was talking into his radio set. One of the policemen walked up to the chauffeur who wound down his windows. The man pulled a gun from beneath his jacket and shot the chauffeur in the neck and he fell sideways onto the seat with a groan. The other man opened the rear door, pointed a gun at Atkins and said "Out." Atkins obeyed and his eyes hunted round but the road was deserted. "Now get into the Ford or I will kill you," he was told and the man calmly closed the door of the limousine. They drove off with the judge.

The videotape was posted through the letterbox at the

home of the London correspondent of the CNN Television network, together with a hand-written note. The note said, 'This is from the Irish Freedom Fighters who have lifted judge Atkins. Play the tape, copy it but do not give it to the British police or they will confiscate it. Take the tape with you on the next plane to New York and arrange for the copy to be delivered to the police after your plane has taken off.' The correspondent played and copied the tape and knew that he was sitting on the hottest new story he had ever met. He realised that the kidnapping of the judge had not been publicised because it would have been the subject of a D notice which forbade any mention of its occurrence. D notices had no effect in America.

The video and the news of the kidnapping appeared world-wide on CNN Television News and the British security forces withdrew the D notice because the matter was no longer containable to those with a need to know about it.

The video showed only the head and shoulders of the judge taken against a white wall with no other means of identifying the venue. The judge looked exhausted and emotional. The frame did not show his hands which were tied to the arms of a chair, or his fingers which had been battered with a hammer.

"I have been captured by Irish Freedom Fighters," the judge said woodenly. "They have treated me well and I wish to admit that throughout my career, I have helped to persecute those who have fought for Irish freedom. I wish to apologise for my actions. My captors have asked me to say that I will be released in exchange for the freedom of Dermot O'Connor. I want to tell my family that I love them." The tape stopped abruptly at this point.

The Government was in an impossible dilemma. There was no way they could release a convicted double murderer and no Government could survive such a humiliation. The kidnappers were evidently professionals and the judge's prospects of survival seemed remote. The

Prime Minister summoned a meeting of the COBRA Committee at number 10 Downing Street. This group was chaired by the PM and contained the Directors of MI5 and MI6, the Home Secretary and representatives from the Armed Forces. It called in experts from any discipline where advice was needed.

The Prime Minister briefly stated that the kidnappers' proposal was unacceptable and the judge would almost certainly be executed. The judge was widely admired by the media and the public and the PM knew that his death would be a political embarrassment for the Government.

"Gentlemen," he concluded cynically. "We lose whatever happens. Our only hope is that we can find where they are keeping him. I want the SAS on standby and if we find them, they go in hard and take no prisoners. If we rescue the judge we will have shown superb coolness and judgement. If he gets killed in the rescue, we can probably talk our way out of it by saying that, in our judgement, they were going to kill him anyway and it seemed worth a try and at least our brave lads killed two terrorists. In the meantime, we stall and tell the press that we are considering the practical implications of swapping O'Connor for the judge."

The next evening there was an anonymous telephone tip off to Vine Street police station in Central London. The informant claimed to be a disenchanted member of the Irish Freedom Fighters who despaired at its continued level of violence and the kidnapping of an innocent man. The message was that the judge was being held at a rented house in a named street in Folkestone. The caller refused to repeat the message or to be detained in any way on the call. The local police were contacted. They telephoned the next door neighbour in the street where the house was situated. He confirmed that two men had moved in a month before but he had never spoken to them. The man was told that his wife and himself should get into their car and go immediately to Folkestone police station without contacting anyone else about the conversation. The neighbour demurred at the inconvenience but was told that it was a matter of life and death which would be explained when he arrived. Meanwhile, the SAS men and their toys were despatched from Hereford in a helicopter.

When the neighbour reached the police station he was rushed into an office filled with large tense men. He was unable to give them any further useful information. When it was explained that his next door neighbours were probably the abductors of the judge, the man and wife were terrified. They gave their house keys to the police.

Soon after six SAS soldiers sidled into the house using the owners' keys and the house next door was surrounded quietly by armed police and soldiers. Using microphones applied to the intervening walls, the SAS men were unable to detect the judge's voice but from one of the upstairs rooms, heard two men discussing when to kill someone and whether to move afterwards to the farm or the chalet, where they could hide until the pursuit had quietened down.

The situation was evidently critical and the decision was made to go in. A simultaneous assault was made by two teams, each of three men, through the front and rear windows. These were smashed in and percussion grenades were hurled into the two downstairs rooms. At the same time, smoke grenades were fired into the upper rooms at the front and back from concealed grenade launchers. The assault teams in their black combat clothes found nothing on the ground floor. Two men ran up the stairs covered by their colleagues; their action tripped a pressure pad beneath the stair carpet and detonated a one-kilogram charge of Semtex. All eight SAS men were killed and a number of police and soldiers sustained severe blast injuries. In the wreckage of the house was found the body of Roderick Atkins with his throat cut and his fingers battered. A tape recording was also retrieved and surprisingly, still played a discussion between two men about when they should kill the hostage and where they should hide after they had done so.

Chapter 3

My name is Eamon James Gallagher. I was born and brought up in Drumundra in Galway, Ireland. It is regarded as one of the most boring small towns in Ireland. This is a title for which there is much competition, yet for a child it was a marvellous place to grow up, with a harbour and large sandy beach.

I was fortunate too in my parents. In Ireland, and I believe even in England, no child had a mother who was less than saintly and mine is saintlier than most. My mammy had three children, which resulted in much local sympathy for her infertility. To her we were all paragons. My elder sister, Mora, was indistinguishable in her virtues from the Blessed Virgin Mary; save that she was more pious. My mother anticipated that my elder brother and myself would either become Pope or (on a gloomy day) a cardinal, or become famous cardiac surgeons. It is a sadness in my life that I never fulfilled these extravagant dreams for her. She had a quality of cheerful optimism and patience and firmly believed that God's major concern was to smooth life's path for her children, which was all they deserved. I felt sorry for God when he failed in these tasks because Ma was fierce to those who did not share her viewpoint on the kids.

My father was treated as child number four, with the difference that he needed formal instructions to do the more complex tasks in life, such as sweeping up the leaves on the front path. This always struck me as odd because outside the house, he was a tough competent foreman for a local firm of builders. At work he had a rough tongue and to my horror, I once heard him swearing and using words which I would not have expected him to know. At home he was quietly spoken, never argued with my mother and was gentle with the children. He had a failing which revealed itself once a year with great predictability. On Christmas Eve his work would stop at midday and he would go to the pub with his workteam. Every year he promised my mother not to do this but inevitably agreed to have just one quick one. He would return home at 7 p.m. very drunk and contrite to receive a tongue-lashing and would then fall asleep. With considerable brutality my mother would then wake him and drag him from bed to go to midnight Mass and the poor man must have suffered greatly but dare not refuse.

The Church formed a central part of family life. It is customary to portray the church as an oppressive, stultifying institution but to us it was as central in our lives as eating dinner or going to school. Sunday Mass would not be missed except for some fairly formidable illness.

Desmond, my elder brother, was five years older than myself, and Mora, my sister, two years older than he was. Mora was bright, and outside small town Ireland, would have attended university. I regarded her as the source of all wisdom while Desmond had infinite knowledge about football and history. When I was twelve years old, my life suddenly changed for the worse. Desmond left home to work as a plasterer in Belfast and Mora emigrated to train as a nurse at the Royal Free Hospital in London. I missed them formidably while my mother was bereft. Neither my brother or sister was an enthusiastic or even competent correspondent and my mother would look out of the front window every morning for the postman while her imagination envisaged scenarios of her children being seduced, run over or paganised.

In school I lacked enthusiasm for anything save football and at the age of sixteen, left to work as a labourer in the same firm as my father. I was six feet tall and the hard physical work made me put on muscle. My life consisted of work, church, playing football on Saturday and drinking with my contemporaries on a Friday night. I knew nothing different and was quite content. It was good to have money and to be independent of my parents.

The football team went on tour every Spring, and when I was seventeen I went with them to Bristol where we played against a local team and then went over the Severn Bridge into Wales for two fixtures at Newport in Gwent. It was the first time that I had left Ireland and I enjoyed the different atmosphere and the beery hospitality of the Welshmen. A shy, Catholic boy like myself did not meet any Welsh women, but one of our opponents claimed they made the best wives in the world, being pious in Chapel, economical in the marketplace and tigers in bed.

The last match of the tour was on a Sunday at a small mining village in a valley north of Newport. The village was a dismal strip of houses running along the valley floor and we lost by three goals to two on a pitch which had a definite tilt to the left. The locals claimed that they bred a successful race of footballers that had one leg longer than the other. By this time I was missing home and my family.

My mother insisted that I telephone home every night when I was subjected to a relentless inquisition on my activities. She meant well but still thought of me as being aged eight. The conversation followed the usual lines:

"Did you go to Mass today Eamon?"

"Yes mammy, and I did a biggy on the toilet this morning," I said sarcastically, but sarcasm was wasted on my mother.

In spite of the score and the depressing surroundings, our opponents were very hospitable and kind. Soccer players in the Welsh valleys are a persecuted minority because rugby football is much more popular and the soccer players show a lot of solidarity amongst themselves. A Welsh male voice choir entertained us in the Miners' Hall and halfway through the programme the compere suddenly announced a surprise departure from the planned programme. "Eamon Gallagher, the talented centre forward of our respected opponents, has his birthday today." There were cheers and the choir sang, *"Happy Birthday To You,"* whilst I blushed with embarrassment.

"Now Eamon," the man said, "at enormous expense and by means of some very complex arrangements, we have two very special guests. Ladies and gentlemen I would ask you to welcome two people to our village. They are Eamon's brother from Dublin and his sister from London." To my amazement, they stepped onto the stage from behind curtains at its side. Desmond grabbed the microphone. "Eamon," he said, "you are a member of the worst football team in Ireland and we were ashamed when we watched the team this afternoon." The Welsh cheered in approval and the Irishmen looked glum. "Fortunately, you were playing the worst team in Wales and you were unlucky to lose." There was an appreciative roar from the Irishmen and the locals laughed at their own discomfort. "Now let me give you some goods news. Your sister Mora has been given an award as the best student nurse of the year." Both teams and supporters cheered loudly and a pretty personable young girl went down well with both groups. I was my usual emotional self and rather overwhelmed at seeing my brother and sister and the general atmosphere of friendliness.

"How did you know I was here?" I asked them.

"Mammy kept us informed," said Mora, "and there was no way you were having a birthday on your own, so I telephoned your captain, Liam O'Connor, and told him we were both coming this afternoon."

It was marvellous to talk to them both again. Mora clearly loved her job and Desmond was his usual quiet reserved self except that when the Welsh choir finally croaked to a halt, he got up on the stage and thanked them. He told them that Ireland had an entirely different tradition of song. His country had never been oppressed by the Welsh, but for 800 years it had been dominated by the English and their songs reflected this. He intended to get revenge for three hours of Welsh choral music and defeat on the football field by giving them two Irish songs. In his lovely tenor voice he gave them *"The Wild Colonial Boy"* and *"The Cliffs of Dunoon"*.

The audience were spellbound and demanded more. By 2.30 a.m. Desmond was getting hoarse and I felt proud of my brother and sister and congratulated myself on my good fortune in having such a marvellous family.

I knew something was wrong when I came home from work on a Thursday evening in November. A Garda car was parked outside the house and the doors were all open in the neighbours' houses. No member of the family had ever been involved in any criminal activity and I was alarmed that my mother would be shamed by the neighbourhood gossip at seeing the police visiting the house. When I went in my mother was sitting in a chair with a white tear-stained face, while my Da who was a big powerful man, seemed smaller and older. "He's dead," said my father.

"Who's dead?" I said, thinking that our old tomcat had been run over after a lifetime of close misses.

"Desmond," my father replied, and my world fell in.

"He was shot by the Paras," said the Garda man, "while in the process of robbing a Post Office in Fermanagh. It was an IRA job and someone informed so they were set up and the bastards shot him. The Paras are bitter men who have lost soldiers to the IRA and that sort of work is a real treat for them."

I had no inkling that Desmond had any interest or involvement in the Nationalist cause. Later I was hurt that he had never confided in me until I realised that if I knew nothing, then I could never be accused of betraying him if anything went wrong. Desmond had always had an interest in the history of Ireland and its music. His dreamy romantic personality had led him into Nationalism whose only effective avenue of political expression was through the IRA.

I had never had strong political leanings but felt a bitter hatred towards the soldier who had murdered my brother.

"How are we to tell Mora?" asked my father. "It will destroy her."

My mother dissolved into further tears. "Get the girl home," she said. "She should not be in England all alone at this time."

Da said that he would telephone her, but it was clear to me that he was incapable of holding a telephone conversation with my sister without breaking down and distressing her even more than the news he had to tell her. I told him that I would speak to Mora, but when I telephoned her flat it was answered by a man. When I asked to speak to my sister, he told me that she was not there. I explained that it was about an important family matter.

"You can't speak to her because she has been arrested," said the man. "My name is DI Willis of Special Branch and your sister is at Paddington Green Police Station."

"For God's sake, why?" I asked him.

"Because her brother is an IRA murderer and we have evidence that she was involved."

"What evidence?" I asked him.

"I regret but I cannot divulge that," he said in that curious wooden voice only used by the police.

"I will need to see her," I told Willis.

"You cannot," he told me, "because she is held under the Prevention of Terrorism Act so that you have no right to see her and she has no right to legal representation for seven days." I got the impression that the policeman was enjoying himself at my distress.

"How can I find out what is going on?" I said, desperately trying not to scream at his arrogant insensitive voice.

"You can't," was the answer, "but if you telephone Paddington Green nick every morning, we can tell you whether she is to be released, charged or held to further help our enquiries." I shall never know how I managed to deliver this news to my parents.

"I can believe how Desmond got involved with the IRA," said my father, "but Mora, never. The poor girl must be in a terrible state knowing about her brother and then to be locked away and interrogated by the police, and her totally innocent."

That night the house was full of our neighbours who tried to comfort my parents. The neighbours were incoherent, but their presence helped my mother although my poor father clearly wished that they would go away so that he could sit down and think it all out. Father Neil, the Parish Priest, arrived half an hour later, since bad news travels fast, and he sensibly just said that his prayers and the support of the Parish were with us and that Desmond was a devout boy whom God would welcome because his sins were small and he was driven by high ideals even if they were wrong.

About ten o'clock, I opened the door to a knock and saw three men with a pair of cameramen behind them.

"Are you the brother?" said one with a Russian hat and a fat face. "I am," I said, and a camera flashed in the dark front garden. "How do you feel about it?" said fatty and I realised that he was a reporter. All night I had been bottling up my feelings in order to protect my parents. I had been awash with sadness, anger and pity, mixed with anxiety about Mora. "How do you think I feel - amused?" I asked him, and kicked him in the crotch. He collapsed in agony and after a few minutes, threatened to get the Garda and have me charged with assault.

"Never," said a voice behind him. I recognised the figure of Maggie Corcoran, a tough gossip from a house on the other side of the street. "There are three neighbours here and we all saw you strike the poor wee boy who was only defending himself. Now bugger off the lot of you before we get our men on you! In fact, we don't need the men we would sort you out ourselves." They were a formidable and frightening group. The reporters ran to their cars and roared off, no doubt to report an exclusive interview in their columns.

James Miles was a dinosaur. Like a dinosaur, he was large and ugly but it is worth remembering that dinosaurs survived on earth for millions of years, indeed much longer than man has existed, so they must have had something going for them. He was the last of a breed of senior MI5 officers and on this Monday morning, was even more cynical and gloomy than usual. He had entered the Service from the Army which he had joined as a private soldier and had risen by his abilities to the rank of major. He had not performed any outstanding acts of bravery, but it must be admitted that these were rare in the ranks of the Catering Corps. His promotion had resulted because everything he did was competently and neatly done. He credited his seniors with his good ideas and did so in front of their superiors. He entered MI5 at a fairly low level, but those qualities which had resulted in advancement in the military, proved equally useful in the Service. He rose steadily in rank and survived the purges which followed economies or betrayals and which had removed many young high flyers who would have been expected to outstrip him.

His particular expertise was in Northern Ireland affairs and he had an encyclopaedic memory for names, faces and events. Unfortunately his personality defects were becoming an increasing problem, especially since the death of his wife five years before. He publicly announced his intention of getting through to retirement in two years time without ever learning how to use a computer. Over the door of his office he had put up a wooden plaque painted with the motto 'Service with Pride.' People found this odd but harmless, until a fresh faced Oxford graduate pointed out that it was the motto over the gate of Nelson Mandela's jail at Robben Island. Cynicism was just about acceptable but his unforgivable crime was to laugh at the traditions and personalities of his seniors and the Controller (North of Ireland) found this increasingly exasperating. A final insult was when a memo arrived on James' desk to which he clipped a note reading 'show to the Fat Controller'. Unfortunately the records clerk did just that but forgot to remove the note. The Controller was sensitive about his obesity which resulted from gin-lubricated lunches with Permanent Secretaries and politicians at gentlemen's clubs around Whitehall. James had once described him as a legend in his lunchtime and this, too, had been relayed back to his boss.

People often wondered how James had survived. The reason was that once every year or two the dinosaur would produce some startling flash of intuition or knowledge. The most recent was six months before when a sergeant and corporal in an Army recruiting office in Balham had been shot. Subsequently the IRA had claimed responsibility using a recognised code word. A security camera in the office had captured an unidentifiable masked gunman carrying out the assassination. At the edge of the film he could be seen escaping into an E-type Jaguar car which was stolen and was subsequently found burnt out in a wood in Surrey with no forensic clues. The public bayed for blood, and at one of the regular meetings between Home Office, MI5 and Special Branch, the police inferred that they had no idea how to advance their investigation.

James Miles sat quietly whilst increasingly desperate lines of investigation were suggested. As the meeting tailed to an inconclusive close, the Fat Controller said sarcastically, "Nothing helpful to add, James?"

"Just enjoying listening to people talking crap," he replied politely in the way which so endeared him to all arms of Government. "Take a look at a man called Donny Flavin. He retired from active service twelve years ago but before that he had two convictions for stealing E-types." There was a strange silence and one of the Special Branch underlings hurried out, after his superior had whispered in his ear. After five minutes he returned and announced that there were no records in the computer for Donny Flavin. "Yes sonny," said James, "that's because you used the computer. The computer records started ten years ago and the convictions were twenty years ago, before you or computers were envisaged. He used to live in Castle Street in Derry and if he's not there, one of the retired men will tell you where he moved."

The next day it was confirmed that Flavin had been located. His paper shop said that his daily paper had been stopped during the week of the shooting because he said that he was having a holiday in Spain. He was put under surveillance and picked up when he met a well-known IRA activist and previously convicted gunman. They were so astonished to be arrested that when charged with the Balham shooting, Donny blurted out that he could not have been involved because he had not driven an E-type for twenty years and would have forgotten how to do so.

The police had not released the fact that the camera showed an E-type to be the car involved and both were convicted of murder.

On this particular Monday, Miles was worried because a summons had arrived for an interview with the Fat Controller (Northern Ireland). James realised that he had done nothing recently to deserve congratulations and that even if he had, the Controller was unlikely to bestow them. Recently an increasing coldness in the Controller's manner towards him and the increasing use of the phrase 'value for money' by politicians, which inevitably preceded a pruning of civil servants, had led him to believe that his time in the Service was going to be short. He began to realise that he had ambivalent feelings about being forced into retirement. He would no longer need to humour the ambitious fools who were his superiors, but enjoyed the company of the younger recruits who seemed to treat him as a wise old owl in which they could confide.

"Come in James," said the Controller in friendly fashion - a well-known danger sign to the older members of the department. "Well, things seem quiet at the moment in your area, all the known players sitting quietly at home and I'm beginning to think that at last we've got them on the run. Don't you agree?"

"No," said James and the Controller sighed theatrically.

"When the buggers go quiet that's when we have to worry."

"James," said the Controller, "it's time that we had a little chat. Life in the Department is becoming faster and more stressful. You're not a young man and you've given loyal service. Our masters have insisted on economies and putting it all together, in your own interests, it would be better if you retired although we should greatly miss you. There is no hurry and if you formally gave me three months' notice, we could come to a gentleman's agreement that you need not come to work after the end of this week.

I insisted to the Permanent Secretary that your years of loyal service should be recognised and he will make a strong recommendation for a CBE." The mixture of bullying and bribery was impressive and James felt a sense of defeat. "Fair enough Controller," he said. "I'll tidy up the loose ends!"

I never realised how many practical details need to be sorted out when someone in the family dies. The police in Belfast sent us an impersonal notice that there would be an inquest in ten days' time and after this we would need to make arrangements for the funeral and for the transport of Desmond's body.

My family felt that the whole world assumed that Desmond was a committed IRA terrorist and that his family must have known of his involvement with the movement. My personal feeling was that I could never become involved with this sort of terrorist movement but that I understood why Desmond had done so.

The following day a battered old Ford Cortina stopped outside the house and two men got out. They did not look like reporters. One was a muscular, blonde man in his early forties who stood outside the car carefully looking up and down the street. The other, slightly older man had greying hair and he walked up to the door and rang the bell. When I opened the door it struck me that he might have once been a boxer because he had a cauliflower ear on the right side with startling blue eyes. "We've not met," he said, "but my name is Reilly and I am a friend of Desmond's from Belfast." I noticed that he had an English accent. I asked him to come in, thinking he would be a friend from Desmond's work, in spite of the accent.

"Desmond was a marvellous lad and the Brits murdered him in cold blood. Only five people knew of the Post Office raid which was to raise money for the Organisation. One was me and three of the others I would trust with my life. The car driver in the raid was the fifth and we found he had major debts to a bookie. We lifted him that night for interrogation and he was very helpful after a little persuasion. We put him into an incinerator at one of the Belfast hospitals and that should discourage anyone else thinking of informing. His friends have been told what happened to him and word will soon get about."

I had never previously met anyone who admitted belonging to the IRA. Initially he had seemed a normal man, but his bitterness against the British and the laconic description of torturing and killing a man horrified me. I knew that Desmond would have had nothing to do with this sort of violence.

"It's not for you to know the details," said Reilly, "but Desmond will be avenged, so watch the television tomorrow night. I'd like to check the funeral arrangements with your Da because Desmond would have wanted a Nationalist funeral as a soldier who died in action."

"You'll not see my father," I told him, "he's had more than enough sorrow so keep away from the funeral, the IRA have done enough harm to my family already and we want nothing to do with you. Do you know that my sister, Mora, has been arrested by the Special Branch in London and we don't know what is happening to her?"

"I know nothing of that," said Reilly. "I can understand your feelings even if I don't agree with them, but if you change your mind about the funeral or you want any help from the Organisation, just put a chalk cross on the front gate of the garden and we'll be in touch." He went back to the car and after another good, hard look around the street, the blonde man got into the driver's seat and they drove off.

That next night there was news of a mortar attack on the SAS Barracks in Hereford, when two soldiers had been killed and three wounded. A telephone message to the Samaritans a few minutes after the attack gave an IRA code and claimed responsibility, saying that the attack was a revenge for the death of Desmond Gallagher and the score was now 2:1. Once again, that night, the press was at the door. I told them that the Paras had murdered my brother, but that his family had no wish for more deaths, even of Paras, and that judgement was best left to God and not the IRA. I was ashamed then to mention Mora's arrest to them because it had not been reported in the newspapers.

The following week was a nightmare. We went to the inquest and had to run the gauntlet of the press including the fat man who glared at me as I went in. My mother was greatly hurt at a crowd of Orangemen outside the court who yelled, "One less murdering Fenian bastard," as we went in. It was as though someone had struck her and for a moment I thought my father was going to hit them but he maintained his dignity and just walked on. A policeman gave evidence that Desmond and another man had got out of a car outside the Post Office. The police had warning of the raid from an informant and had asked for military support. Through a loudspeaker, the policeman said that he had warned the two men that they were surrounded and should raise their hands in the air. He claimed that Desmond had made a move to take something from his jacket which the police and military had assumed to be a gun. The Paras, who were the military support unit, then opened fire. Desmond fell dead and the other man was wounded in the arm but managed to escape in the car which was driven by a third man. The policeman was rather evasive when asked how two men had escaped from a police and Army cordon, but when our solicitor pressed him he admitted that the driver of the getaway car was an informer and it would have been impossible to shoot the wounded man in the car without the inevitable risk of killing the informer. "And he might have been useful to us in the future," he added rather callously.

When our solicitor asked that the informer be required to give evidence, the policeman stated that Intelligence reports suggested that he had been executed by his own Organisation but that no body had been found. A pathologist reported that ten bullets from high velocity rifles were present in Desmond's body and it was very clear to any unbiased observer that the Paras intended to kill him as soon as he emerged from the car.

Every day we telephoned Paddington Green Police Station. When we identified ourselves the person answering often made an audible aside to someone else in the room using phrases like 'It's the Mick's family,' or 'It's the IRA girl's relatives'. For the first four days they merely said that Mora was being questioned and refused any other information. On the evening of the fourth day, we were watching the television news which said that a female suspected IRA terrorist would be attending a court hearing when it was anticipated that the police would ask for an extension of the period when she could be held for questioning. At the end of the programme, the commentator announced that the suspect was Mora Gallagher from Drumundra in Galway. My parents gasped because the news of Mora's arrest would be known to everyone in the town and many would equate the arrest with guilt.

Desmond's funeral was attended by most of the population of the town. They were the sort of people who found it excruciatingly difficult to talk to bereaved parents, but they wanted to show their support to the family in their grief. Father Neil was in a difficult position when speaking of Desmond's life and manner of death. He tactfully talked about his gentle manner, his love of sport and that over hundreds of years, many thousands of Irishmen had died with a perception of a justified war. He stated frankly that it was a perception which he did not share and whilst he felt that Ireland should be united, that violence was not the route to achieve it. Young people often felt more passionate about politics than their elders and it was sad that their idealistic beliefs could be channelled into violence by older, less scrupulous men.

Ten days after the arrest, we received a telephone call from the British police that Mora was to be released without charge the next day. That afternoon I flew to Heathrow. I went to Mora's flat, paid the outstanding rent and gave notice to her landlord who seemed glad that she was leaving in view of her supposed link to the IRA. I packed her few belongings and stayed overnight in the flat. It was cold and lonely and I was depressed and foolishly drank about half a bottle of Bushmills which did nothing for my head the next morning.

At Paddington Green I told the desk sergeant that I had come for my sister. "We couldn't prove anything with her," he said, clearly believing her guilty of some ill-defined act of terrorism.

"Will I use that for a reference?" I asked him, but the sarcasm was wasted.

I was horrified when Mora emerged from a door in the wall which was opened with a double lock. She was pale and had lost a lot of weight and had a tense frightened air.

"Get me out of here please, Eamon," said my sister and as we went out of the door the desk sergeant jeered, "See you again soon, love."

We took a taxi to a pub off Kensington High Street which the cabby recommended. It was a quiet place where you would go for a chat. She said very little in the taxi and just chewed on her lower lip in the way she had always done since childhood when she was worried or upset.

I ordered a stiff brandy for my sister and a pint of beer for myself. When I returned to the table the tears were streaming down her cheeks. "You're the first person I could talk to about Desmond since he died. Poor, poor Desmond. I did love him." We talked about Desmond for half an hour because she needed to and then I said to her, "And yourself, why did the police arrest you?"

"Presumably, on general principles, if my brother was a Nationalist and I was Irish, then I was guilty too." The tears started running down her face again and she had difficulty in speaking. I was never any good at coping with women when they cry and it was even more difficult when it was my sister, so I went to the bar and ordered more drinks while she collected herself.

"They told me they had reliable information that I was active in the IRA and wouldn't listen when I told them that I was not political. I had nothing to eat or drink for the first twenty-four hours and had to use a pot for the toilet, sometimes with policemen looking through the window in the cell door. I felt hungry, dirty, cold and frightened," she said. "On the second day they interrogated me for twelve hours without stopping. One stood behind me and screamed questions in my ear - did I know so and so? Where was the semtex kept? Who were my contacts? In the night, I think it was often midnight but I had no watch, they did the same thing for two hours and this went on all the time for the past ten days. I feel exhausted and the awful thing is that they still feel I am a terrorist who cannot be cracked. I can never go back to a job in England and it has left me feeling completely humiliated and frightened."

"They told me that they knew I was involved with Desmond and unless I gave them some useful information, they would charge me with a terrorist offence. They could keep me for as long as they wanted without charging me and it would be easy to put one of my fingerprints at the site of the Sheffield bomb or find semtex in my flat."

That night, we took a flight back to Ireland and were met by my parents who were shaken by the change in Mora. The next morning we left her to have a lie in to catch up on her sleep. At eleven o'clock my mother took her up a cup of tea but ran back downstairs with a frightened look on her face. "She's not there!" she said, "and the bed has not been slept in." I got the car out and drove down to the Garda Station with a sense of alarm and reported her as missing. The Garda on duty was the same man who had come to tell us the bad news about

Desmond. He looked embarrassed and said, "sit down, son, I'll just get the Inspector," and he vanished into the rear of the Police Station. An older policeman emerged and beckoned me into a rear office. I felt that he had something to tell me but that he was uncertain where to begin.

"I may have some bad news for you. We had a report earlier today of a body of a young woman in the Park Lake. She has not been identified but the report about your sister is worrying. Would you be prepared to identify the body?"

I felt that my world was collapsing and I was living in a nightmare. The policeman was a kind man and so emotional that he could barely speak. "Sit down, have a cup of tea and we can get it over after that," he said.

All I wanted to do was to know whether my sister was alive or dead. I insisted that we go straight to the hospital mortuary which was just down the road. The mortuary was a brightly lit bare room containing two metal gurneys each with a body covered by a stained white sheet. "All you need to do is to see her face," said the policeman. He lifted the sheet and I saw the cold grey face of my sister. I knew that she had killed herself because she felt that she had brought shame to the family and that the lives of myself and my parents would be marked forever.

That night I put a chalk cross on the front garden gate.

James Miles hated the Millbank Headquarters of MI5. It was an undistinguished building, decorated inside in the usual civil service colours and furniture. Most rooms contained a standard issue picture of the Queen seated on a horse (the Queen was the one at the top of the picture). In James' office at the usual site of the Queen's picture, was one of Mickey Mouse and this produced gratifying irritation in any senior colleague who visited his lair. Such visits seemed to be becoming rarer and he gained the impression that he must have developed the MI5 equivalent of underarm odour.

For his farewell party he sensed that his senior colleagues were straining to make an effort to be pleasant, no doubt buoyed up by the knowledge that he would have to hand in his security pass on the way out of the building that evening, so that they would never need to see him again. Before the 5 p.m. start of the official event, he had a small private get together with some of his junior and secretarial staff whom he had known for many years. The private party was well lubricated and he had been kissed by more women in the last hour than during the preceding twenty years. The men just shook his hand and said, "Thanks for everything" in that serious English tone which indicates terminal emotion.

At 5 o'clock they all transferred to the official party. The Fat Controller (Northern Ireland) looked even shiftier than usual and told James quietly that, "There was a little problem with the CBE old boy - bloody politicians! I'm afraid it's to be an OBE." This was delivered in a tone of voice suggesting that the news was of a type which could give a well-balanced man a complete breakdown. It had been James' intention when initially told of the CBE that he would decline it to the great embarrassment of his proposers. The news of his impending demotion only caused him to smile which puzzled the Controller (Northern Ireland).

The Controller blew into the microphone to test it and then authoritatively tapped a glass with a teaspoon to obtain silence. The effect was made more impressive when the glass shattered and the Controller instinctively shouted, "shit!" directly into the microphone. It certainly gained attention and gave satisfaction to some of the audience.

The Controller launched into a predictable series of clichés - 'long and valued service, much missed, long and enjoyable retirement'. This culminated in the presentation of a cheque from the Service of the standard amount of £26. This represented £1 for each year of service. The sum was not £27 because the final year of service was only in its tenth month and the finance department regulations were that the sum should be rounded down. The Controller, on behalf of himself and the senior management, then presented James with a mock leather travel bag.

James' long serving secretary, Hilary, then announced that she wished to say a few words on behalf of the administrative staff and secretaries. She had always secretly been in love with James, a fact known to everyone in the building except James. She made a pretty speech about his kindness to the young and to the secretaries and how the Service would be boring without him. The Controller (Northern Ireland) nodded thankfully at the latter. She presented him with a small leather container about five cms in diameter. He was intrigued as to what it was and opened it with some curiosity. The case contained the keys for an open MG sports car and Hilary told him that he could pick it up at the agents in Croydon the next day because she doubted if he would be fit to drive home tonight. James recalled a conversation two years before at a Christmas party which had been accompanied by too much wine. Hilary asked him what he would buy if he won the National Lottery. James replied that he had always wanted an open sports car. The conversation had ended there, but his reply had evidently been noted. He knew that the cost of such a vehicle was about £18,000 and there was no way in which a group of secretaries and trainee operatives would raise such a sum of money. Hilary told the audience that she had invited contributions from colleagues whom James had trained over the last twenty-seven years, many of whom had risen to positions of considerable eminence within the Civil Service and in industry.

James had an impression of his own personality, not shared by many, of being a tough, unemotional, objective man. He was ashamed to find his eyes full of tears when the time came to reply. "I am terribly touched by your extraordinary gift," he began, "and it will be useful to transport my travel bag." At this the Controller shuffled uncomfortably. "The Controller," continued James, "has spoken with his characteristic kindness and generosity and he is a man who inspires loyalty and affection in his staff." The Controller smiled appreciatively and the audience smirked.

"One of the sad things about leaving Millbank is that I shall never discover the identity of the man with the BULLSHIT rubber stamp who so often disfigures our notice board." It was well known to everyone, including the Controller, that the identity of this Scarlet Pimpernel was James. Vital notices put up on the board such as 'Emergency taxi fares will only be reimbursed if pre-authorised by a Senior Officer (above Grade 8)' would lose their commanding and threatening tone if BULLSHIT was stamped beneath the signature. It seemed to particularly enrage the senior members of the Department and some of the sharpest intellects in Britain had unsuccessfully attempted to nail the culprit over many years. Recently they decided to utilise modern technology and placed a mini fish-eye lens in a light fitting above the notice board. The lens was connected to a recording camera via a fibre optic cable. The Director was not aware of this manoeuvre and on the first day of its installation, the camera picked up the Director groping a gorgeous pouting secretary who was bending over a photocopier. Matters were compounded because the secretary was male and these propensities of the Director were previously unknown. The experiment was abandoned after the first day and all concerned were sworn to secrecy but, like all office secrets, it leaked out. The reference to this incident drew an angry glare from the Controller and appreciative titters from the rest of the room. The formal side of the evening dragged on.

A few days after, there was a telephone call to the house which I answered. "Is that you Eamon?" said a voice with an English accent, which I immediately recognised as that of Reilly. "Be outside Heenan's Bar in twenty minutes and we'll keep an eye that you're not followed." I went down the road to the Bar and half way there the old Ford Cortina pulled up alongside me, driven by the blonde man. "Get in", he said. I did so and he said nothing, but drove for ten minutes to a picnic area in a local forest. "Just walk along that path and you'll be met," he said. I did as I was told and after two hundred metres, recognised Reilly who was standing against a tree.

"My sorrow on your sister," he said, "but if you want we can get back at the bastards."

"I will do whatever you want," I told him. "My family have been destroyed and my poor sister was not even involved."

"You will need to work in England. There is a big construction job in Hastings for a shopping complex and they want builders. Arrange to start in a month and we meet here at the same time in two weeks for your briefing. If you discuss this conversation with anyone, you will be killed." He walked off down the path and left me to walk home by myself.

Over the next fortnight I thought over my conversation with Reilly and began to regret it. It sunk in that involvement with the IRA meant an acceptance of violence and murder and however much I hated the Brits, I could never kill anyone. I began to think deeply and to develop an idea in my mind. I bought a large recent map of Great Britain and the ideas developed further.

I met Reilly at the same place and when I left my car in the car park, spotted the blonde man silently watching me and ensuring that I was alone. Reilly was now more direct. "We need you for an Active Service Unit. You have no military skills but we need someone to plant explosives. I spent ten years in Ordnance in the British Army so I can look after the semtex and the detonators and you can plant them because your face is unknown to the Security Services in Britain."

"I don't want to kill people," I told him, "not even police or Paras but I am very happy to put bombs in places where no one gets killed."

"Well we know where we stand with that," said Reilly, "it was better you told us at the start, but you're no good to us with that sort of conscience."

"Not unless I could promise a spectacular."

"What sort of spectacular?" So I told him. He said nothing for a few minutes while we walked up and down the path.

"Meet me here in two nights at the same time. I want to give it thought. It's certainly an unusual idea."

The proposal which I had made to Reilly seemed so blindingly obvious that I was astonished that no one had done it before. Some minor enquiries in the local reference library had confirmed my initial conclusions.

South and South West Wales have a population of two million people. There are two ferries to Ireland from SouthWest Wales and connections with other countries through the ports of Milford Haven, Swansea, Cardiff and Newport. Apart from these routes and rail connections, the main road access is over the old and new Severn bridges, plus two smaller bridges north of these over the River Wye. (This is shown in the figures).

When I toured South Wales with the Drumundra football team we crossed the Severn over the new Severn Bridge. It struck me that connections with South Wales would be very difficult if both Severn bridges were destroyed. When I looked at the map the other two smaller bridges over the Wye were very close to the Severn bridges and seemed vulnerable. If all were lost the effect would be catastrophic.

On the day after our last football match on the Welsh tour, my brother and sister both had to go back to work. I had a hangover and asked one of the Welshmen where I could go for a walk to get rid of it and that there seemed to be a path beneath the new Severn Bridge. He very kindly agreed to take me for a walk. We started at Chepstow and walked down to the new Severn Bridge. The whole procedure took two and a half hours and ended up with another alcoholic lunch in a pub. This, for a man who only six hours before, had given up drink for the rest of his life.

To summarise the situation, the Old Wye Bridge (Bridge 1) and the New Wye Bridge (Bridge 2) are both part of the Gloucester - Chepstow road which then can either rejoin the M4 to South Wales or continue directly west parallel to the M4 by the smaller A48. On the English side of the Severn going west, the M4 divides into the Old (Bridge 3) and New (Bridge 4) Severn crossings. The road west of these two bridges unite into the M4 again, with a spur road from Bridge 3 to Chepstow to join the roads emerging from Bridges 1 and 2 west of Chepstow.

If Bridges 3 and 4 were out, then the effect would be serious. If all four, then it would be disastrous. The uproar would be enormous, the financial cost vast and the embarrassment to the Government a joy to behold to any Nationalist and for me a repayment for the harm done to my family. It would give the IRA headlines in the International press and would at last make the British Government realise that their occupation of the Six Counties was not sustainable and they would sue for peace rather than risk any more damage to the economy of mainland Britain.

I had no doubt that the British Security Forces would have considered the possibility of an attack on one of the Severn Bridges. When bridge 4 opened they probably congratulated themselves on having a spare bridge in case anything happened to the other. They might not have considered the audacious possibility that Bridges 3 and 4 might both be attacked. Bridges 3 and 4 had surveillance cameras and these were particularly thick on Bridge 4. Ostensibly they observed traffic but it would be sensible to assume that they would monitor any suspicious activity of people

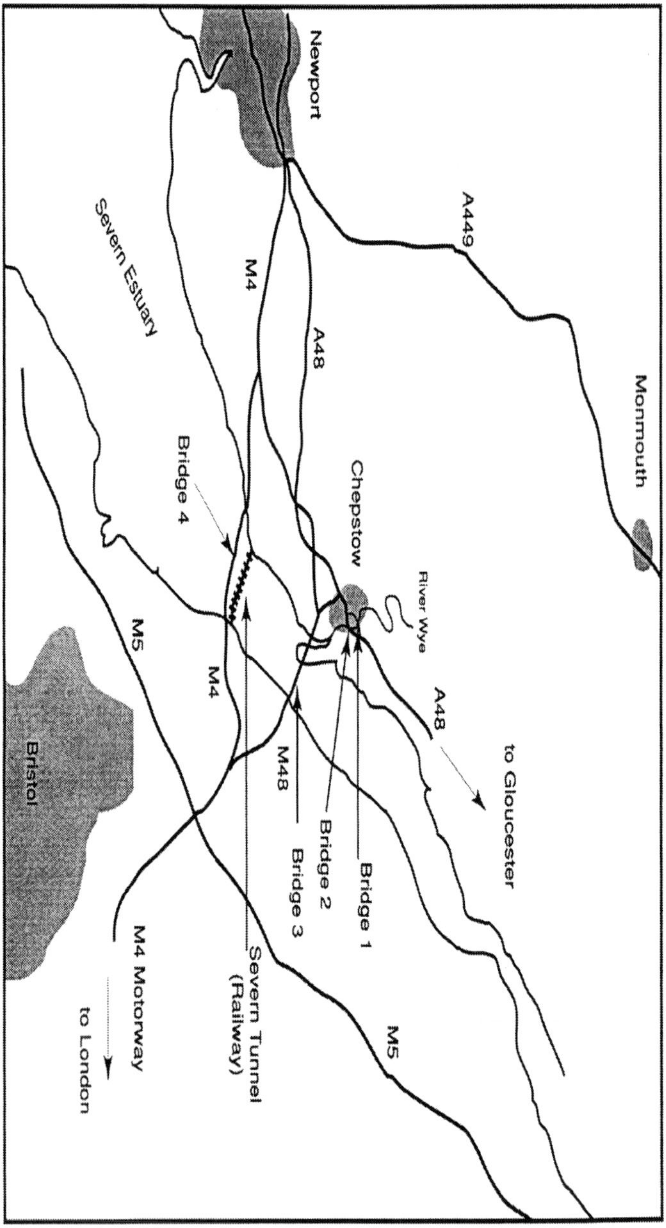
Newport
A449
Monmouth
Severn Estuary
M4
A48
Chepstow
River Wye
Bridge 4
A48
to Gloucester
M5
M4
M48
Bridge 1
Bridge 2
Bridge 3
Bristol
M4 Motorway
to London
Severn Tunnel
(Railway)
M5

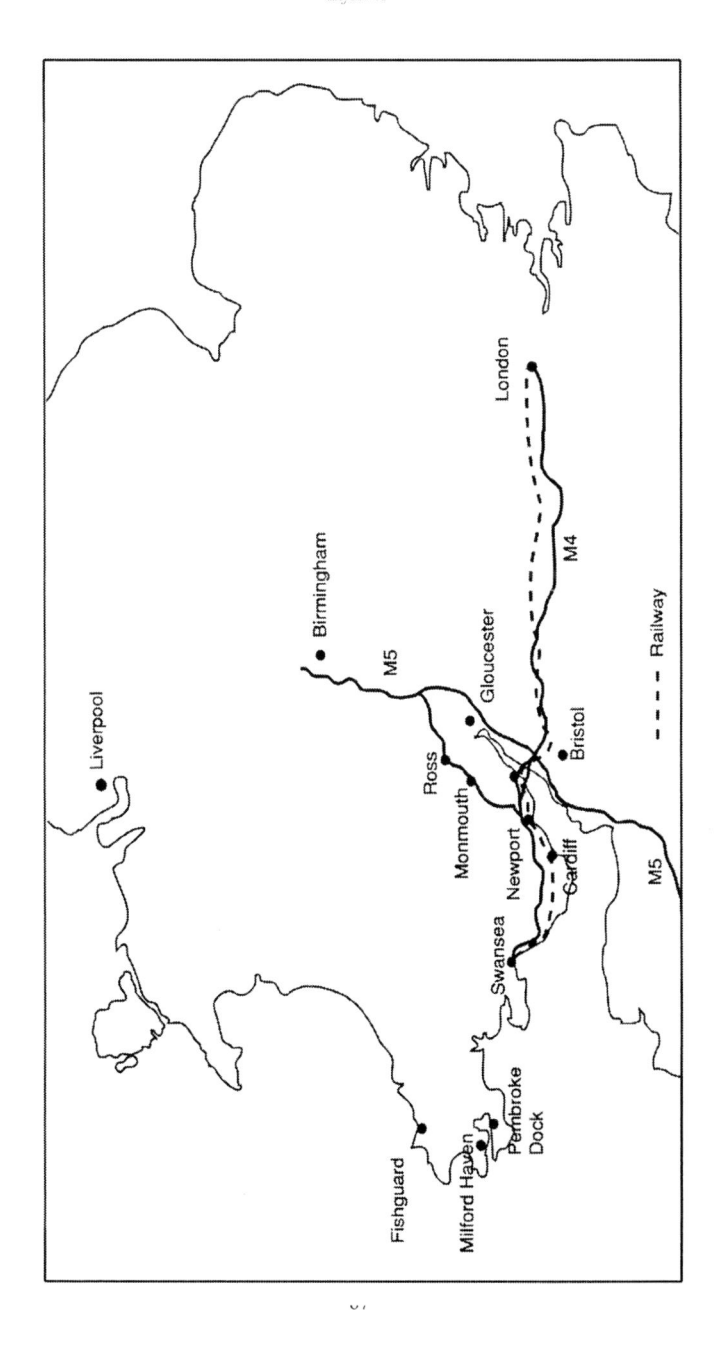

Lifeline

or traffic and the operators would be likely to report anything unusual to the police patrols. The second problem was that both Bridges 3 and 4 had police stationed at the tolls. Their main function was traffic control, but it seemed likely that they would have received special training about detecting possible attacks on the bridge structures. The third unknown to us was surveillance by combinations of plain-clothes police and any special units. I had no information about this last possibility. My walk after the football match revealed a startlingly vulnerable area beneath bridges 3 & 4 where there were no cameras or other security. There were additionally no cameras on bridges 1 & 2.

We met again as Reilly had suggested. "It will need a lot of planning," Reilly said, "but I like the idea. Go to Hastings as we arranged. You have a thick Galway accent that will stick out like a sore thumb to any Englishman, let alone a policeman, so here's what you do. You get cheap, respectable lodgings with a good English Catholic landlady. We'll do some research and find one for you. You get a job on the building site; the foreman is Irish and a sympathiser. He knows nothing of this job, but has been told that your application should be successful. If anyone asks why you have come to England, it is to get a job and you have no interest in politics. If anyone attempts to discuss the problem of the Six Counties with you, just say that both sides are mad and need their heads knocking together. Join a local football team because that will give you cover for being out a few nights a week and on Saturdays if we need you and tell the landlady that you train three nights a week. Go to church every Sunday, never get in a fight, never get drunk. Never commit any legal offence because you must never meet policemen." There was a lot more instructions and we met several times before I left for England.

The lodgings I found on his recommendation were

quiet and clean with a soft hearted landlady about sixty five years old who felt sorry for me because I was so far away from my family. The job was little different from that at home and my fellow labourers regarded me as a hard working reliable man with an enthusiasm for playing football and for following the fortunes of Manchester United.

The football club passed the evenings and Saturdays but I had no close friends and life was monotonous and lonely as I missed my parents whom I telephoned every Friday night. They were puzzled why I had gone to England and probably rationalised it by concluding that I wanted to get away from the depressed atmosphere at home.

One night at the football club, I was sitting at the bar having a beer after a training session. One of the team came in with his girlfriend who I knew, and another girl who he introduced as her sister. I had never been too good with the girls, being shy with a terrible tendency to be struck dumb and the more attractive the girl, the more dumbstruck I became. On this occasion I was very dumbstruck indeed because she was very attractive with dark hair, large hazel eyes and was rather small. It is odd how a great lump like me is so attracted to small women; perhaps they make me feel protective. After saying hello I ran up against my usual problem and my conversation died, until I remembered that she had sat in front of me at Mass on Sunday on a few occasions. What a marvellous opening gambit. To my horror I found myself saying, "I'm sure I have seen you at Mass but I've only viewed your backside before." Initially she thought I was being offensive and tried to look very dignified, but when she saw the look of horror on my face and my red blush, the whole bar roared with laughter and the ice was broken. For some reason she seemed to find my inane conversation interesting and I quite forgot that normally I was tongue-tied in the presence of women. The evening seemed to pass in a flash and for the first time in my life I realised what an overwhelming force an attraction for a woman was.

Normally I never went to the football club on two consecutive nights and the next evening it was only after I found myself sitting at the bar did I confess to myself that it was in the hope that Kate (for that was her name) might be there. After sitting alone for thirty minutes over a half-pint of shandy, Kate came in with her sister. Kate did not catch my eye but her sister did and they both came across. I suspect that her sister sensed my interest in Kate and after I bought them a drink, her sister claimed that she had an urgent need to talk to one of her girlfriends about arrangements to go to a dance on Saturday night. Whether Kate was shyer than I was it was difficult to tell, but there was an awkward silence.

"So tell me about your family," she said. The question embarrassed me. I had an urge to tell this stranger about my brother and sister, but Reilly had given me strict instructions never to mention them under any circumstances, so I told her about my parents and what lovely people they were.

"Do you have any brothers or sisters?" Kate asked. When I said I hadn't, I knew how St Peter felt when he betrayed Christ. She seemed to sense my unease and in order to change the subject, I asked her about her family. There were three sisters who were very close but fought like cats, something which seemed difficult to believe, and her parents sounded just like mine. By the end of the evening, I felt entirely at ease with her and wished we would talk forever. When we said goodnight, with uncharacteristic boldness I asked her if she would like to come for a walk along the cliffs with me the next Sunday. To my surprise she agreed and I looked forward to it. Over the next six months I forgot about the IRA and even football and realised that I had met someone with whom I wanted to spend the rest of my life and to have children with. I met her parents and got on very well with them. They seemed to think that I was the right person for Kate.

I had never met quite such a person as Kate. She was quiet but had firm beliefs about what was right and wrong. Tolerant, but her tongue would lash me if she felt I was lazy or prejudiced about something but above all, an emotional girl who would burst into tears when she watched some slushy love story on television or a film.

Chapter 4

In early June a letter arrived at my lodgings addressed to Mr E K Gallagher. My middle initial is J and Reilly had told me to keep a look out for this variation as a code between us. The letter inside was a circular from a firm selling double-glazing. They offered a 10% discount for work ordered during the next six weeks. I burnt the letter which was a coded instruction to go to one of three possible meeting places which would depend on whether the discount offered was described as 10, 15 or 20%.

The next Saturday, as instructed, I went to a pub in Wimbledon, ordered a drink and sat down at a table. A man passed me going out and although he was wearing a baseball hat, I recognised him as Blondie and he whispered, "the bus stop outside in fifteen minutes." When I went out the blonde man was standing alone at the stop. "Get on the bus and get off at the railway station and sit separately from me." I did what he said and when we got off the bus, followed him to a local park where we sat on a bench in the sun. He instantly looked around and seemed to have an obsession about being followed. "Now let's talk about the spectacular," he said.

The overall plan was simple. A separate team would survey all four bridges and assess factors such as the site of security cameras, access to the bridges and the timing of any regular police patrols. This data would then be given to the Active Service Unit through a cutout so that if either the surveillance team or the Active Service Unit were caught they could not betray each other. The Active Service team would spend at least one day familiarising itself with the ground. Blondie never revealed his name to me but we went over the outline plan and he informed me that he, Reilly and myself would go and look at the ground during the next weekend.

That weekend I told the landlady that I intended to fulfil the ambition of a lifetime and see Manchester United play at home. She gave that superior smile often affected by women at this sort of inexplicable ambition so typical of men, and she wished me an enjoyable weekend. On the Saturday morning I travelled by train to Temple Meads Station in central Bristol. In the station foyer I was met by Reilly and Blondie. Like myself, they were carrying small rucksacks and wearing anoraks and walking boots. We took a bus to one of the city suburbs where we got into a car parked in one of the side streets. So far we had not spoken, apart from saying hello and I assumed that this was because Reilly was not anxious for me to reveal my Irish accent. Once in the car, I asked him why he had not left it in the town centre and he explained that this was to avoid the surveillance cameras usually present in multi-story car parks. We crossed into Wales over Bridge 3 and two miles after crossing the bridge, parked at an open-air car park in Chepstow not having any surveillance cameras, in the lower part of the town and Blondie carefully paid for the windscreen sticker. We agreed to refer to the bridges as 1, 2, 3 and 4 to avoid confusion.

"There is no point in wasting much time on Bridge 1," said Reilly, "because there is no way that we can blow it. It would never carry much traffic in any case although it would certainly give a little help. It does give you a good view of Bridge 2 though so we can view it from there." Bridge 1 was an arched iron bridge with a plaque announcing that it had been built in 1816. Frankly, it looked it. The metal was rusty and the bridge had only one lane with traffic lights at either end. At each bank was a concrete jetty extending fifteen metres into the water with the ironwork springing from the jetties and supporting the roadway above. From the road to the jetty there was a drop of fifteen metres and it would have been impossible to get onto the jetty to place a charge without being visible from the road. After taking a long look at the bridge I told Reilly that whilst he was the professional, there did seem to be a way of blowing it. I explained this to him. "That's bloody brilliant," he said, "you're wasted as a builder!"

A footpath ran along the west bank of the Wye to Bridge 2 which we reached after about five hundred metres. The structure was about ten years old and parallel to it, and twelve metres downstream, was the rail bridge linking Gloucester to Chepstow and South Wales and Seamus had a copy of the railway timetable which showed that this was fairly lightly used. There were no surveillance cameras under the bridge. On the right side, fifty metres from the riverside path, was a pair of massive concrete supporting pillars. These sprung from open waste ground with no cover. A second set of similar supporting pillars for the road bridge were one hundred metres to the right of the path. They lay behind a slanted retaining wall which reached the ground at its far end. Between the wall and the pillars was a thick tangle of dense undergrowth which shielded the pillars. Next to the pillars on the Bridge side was an open storage facility for new Ford motor cars. The footpath fizzled out downstream from Bridge 2 and in order to reach Bridge 3, we walked up through the edge of the town and through the village of Bulwark and beyond that, to a large roundabout surrounded by a new housing estate which lay in the angle where the continuation of Bridge 3 met the River Severn Bank. Reilly explained that he would drop me at Chepstow and I would plant charges at Bridges 1 and 2 and walk to Bridge 3 to bomb that. He would go off and attack Bridge 4 and would return at a determined time to pick me up at the roundabout on the estate. "You would be rather obvious standing at a roundabout in a new housing estate," he told me, "so time the walk from here very carefully to where you can lay up between here and Bridge 3 if you finish early so that you arrive at the same time as me."

Beyond the housing estate was a field with a footpath running along the riverside of the estate. A stile led down, after three hundred metres to a tunnel running beneath the Gloucester/Chepstow to South Wales railway line and the path emerged onto a dike running alongside the river and underneath Bridge 3. As we crossed a second stile, Reilly pointed out a small wood on the riverside of the railway line and told me this was the safe place to hide if I finished early. I measured it to take nine minutes from the roundabout to this wood.

We walked along the embankment and under the bridge. Reilly showed me the two enormous pillars on the landward side of the embankment. Both were in a large field containing a herd of cows. There was a bridge over a drainage channel between the embankment and the field which was not gated so that some of the cows had come out of the field and were grazing upon the embankment. "You want these pillars," he said. They were on a mound in the field surrounded by a fence topped by razor wire with an entry gate having a padlock. The whole structure stood in the middle of the bare field and it looked horribly obvious if anyone was up to mischief with the pillars. "Now let's have a look," was his comment and he sat on the edge of the embankment and outlined the plan.

"In my haversack I have a yellow oilskin, a hard hat, some bolt cutters, a padlock and a tape measure. You can have these when we get back to the car. When you have come under the railway tunnel, go into the wood and change into the hard hat and the oilskin. Walk confidently up to the pillar and cut the lock with the bolt cutter. Put your haversack against one of the pillars and plant a charge under each on the landside where it will not be visible from the dike path and then get the hell out. On your way, replace the old lock with a new one so that the gate does not open in the wind. Change back in the wood and then nine minutes before we are due to meet, set out for me to pick you up at the roundabout."

The whole idea horrified me and I could see a whole lot of difficulties. I pointed out that I would be highly visible on a raised concrete platform in the middle of a field. He told me that there was nobody more above suspicion than someone in an oilskin and a hard hat. The only likely challenge would be from the farmer or one of his workers. If spotted, I was to start measuring the wire cage surrounding the pillars with the tape measure and noting the dimensions in a notebook. If asked what the hell I was doing, the answer should be that the pillars needed a higher security fence and that my firm was doing it. The farmer would probably ask why no permission had been obtained for access to his land. If this happened my response should be that I was a working man who did what he was instructed but that I was very happy to give him the telephone number and name of my manager and would be delighted if the farmer gave him a bollocking. The number given was that of a public telephone which would be answered by a friend of the Organisation who would identify the number as the head office of Garnet and Lacey, Civil Engineers. He would allow the farmer to say his piece and then apologise profoundly and blame his secretary who had been instructed to write to the farmer warning him of the firm's impending visit. The 'manager' would offer a Marks & Spencer voucher for £100 as a token of apology which he would personally put in the post that day.

"If they are anything like Irish farmers, he will be eating out of his hand after that," said Reilly cynically.

"Very smart," I replied, "but he will see that the lock has been cut with the bolt cutters and there may be explosives fixed to the pillar bases."

"No problem. Cover one charge with your rucksack, take your hat off if you see the farmer coming across the field and put it over the other. Tell him that some silly bugger in the firm has mislaid the lock key so they have given you a set of bolt cutters and a new lock and show him the new lock." I began to wonder what I had let myself in for and then thought of my brother and sister and resolved to continue.

"Now remember that you have to fix three bridges and I only do one, so I will have plenty of time. If you are not at the roundabout in the estate at the precise time then I will circle and return at five-minute intervals until you are." He then took me again through the timings and instructions for setting the detonators. All the explosives were to go off simultaneously at 16.00 hours, which was one hour after our rendezvous time. Reilly would telephone a contact number after we had met up from the safety of the English side of the bridges. A fifteen-minute warning would be telephoned to Chepstow Police Station telling them that all four bridges were mined. No policeman would be stupid enough to approach a primed unexploded bomb and the bomb squad could never get there in time. The warning would allow time for traffic to be stopped on all the bridges so that any damage would only be to property. Finally, Reilly told me the day of the strike.

As we walked back I said to him, "That's me sorted out, but how are you going to get at Bridge 4?"

He smiled, "I have never been caught by the British police because I always played my cards close to my chest and I have no intention of telling you now. In fact I will not even tell you whether it will be the Welsh or the

English side of the Bridge. Tell you what though, we can go back to Bristol over Bridge 4 and you can tell me how you would do it and then I'll tell you my solution when we meet for the job."

As we drove back over Bridge 4, I tried to put myself in Reilly's mind. About two kilometres before the bridge on the M4 there was a tollbooth which only collected fees for traffic passing from England into Wales. There was no corresponding toll on the other side and no charge for going from Wales to England. There were multiple surveillance cameras on the bridge and its approaches with a police car at the tollbooth, while another passed us from behind whilst we were crossing the bridge.

"Impossible," I told Reilly.

"Not easy," he said, but there's always a weak spot and you can know what it is when we next meet." He later dropped me off at Bristol Railway Station and I made my way back to London and then home.

Red Ferguson looked at the bloody mess of the Sinn Fein Councillor who was tied to the radiator with a rope. The radiator burnt anyone touching it but the rope allowed the man to keep six inches away, a distance which felt hot but not painful, that was until he flinched as he saw another punch coming when his skin would contact the hot metal. His screams were silent because of the masking tape over his mouth. Every few minutes this would be taken off and he would be re-questioned. If the answers were unhelpful the tape was replaced and the process repeated. It had been one of the less useful sessions. They wanted the names and addresses of people the Councillor knew to be active in the IRA. The man had given two names already, but these were already known to the ten members of the Red Hand Command who were present in the upstairs room of the Loyalist run pub off the Shankill Road. It was 2 p.m. but a notice on the locked pub door informed that the premises were temporarily closed for electrical work. The outsider would find it odd that electrical work was required on at least ten separate days a year, but then outsiders would be very ill advised to visit this pub. The local joke was that electrical work was likely to be performed on any stranger unrecognised by one of the drinkers standing at the bar.

Red was sure that the man had no further useful information and had got to the stage when he would grass on his granny to stop the pain.

"Anything else you want to tell us, Sean?" he enquired. It was odd how friendly the interrogator became with his victims. The man groaned. "Nothing, I'm not IRA, only Sinn Fein. They tell me nothing because there is no need for me to know. Now can you kill me clean and get it over?"

"Fair enough," said Ferguson, who nodded to one of the men standing at one side of the prisoner. He hit the man hard at the back of the head with a baseball bat and he slumped to the floor. They watched for half a minute when the burning smell made them cut the rope to release his unconscious body.

"Usual arrangement Dennis?" Ferguson said. Dennis dialled a number on the telephone in the room and said that the carpet had not been picked up for cleaning as promised. A few minutes later, a large van drew up outside the pub carrying a sign saying 'Carpets Cleaned and Supplied'. The unconscious body was then rolled in the carpet on the room floor and three of the men carried it downstairs and threw it into the van. The man would be taken to a quiet road outside Belfast and killed with a single shot in the back of the neck. His tortured body would be found and identified. Word of the killing would rapidly get around and make it less likely that volunteers would present themselves to become Sinn Fein Councillors or party workers.

The Red Hand Command was a shadowy organisation existing on the extremist fringe of the Loyalist

Paramilitary Groups. It was more violent that the others and had a reputation for conducting vigorous interrogations before invariably killing its Catholic victims. There were only ten members and all were ex military and some were, in addition, ex Royal Ulster Constabulary who had resigned in frustration because they felt the hands of the police were tied in their conflict with the IRA.

The structure of the RHC meant that all the members knew and trusted each other. Membership was entirely by invitation and this was only proffered after careful research into the person's discretion, motivation and familiarity with firearms. The small size of the Organisation made infiltration impossible and the police and security forces believed the membership to be much bigger than it actually was in view of the number of people it had killed. The retired police members of the RHC often drank and socialised with old friends who were still members of the RUC. Policemen liked talking shop and this proved a useful source of information, both about IRA/Sinn Fein activities and forthcoming actions against Loyalist groups.

Over the three years of its existence, the RHC had lifted fourteen IRA or Sinn Fein members, all of whom had been tortured and killed. This had induced a great deal of fright and anxiety in Nationalist circles, but recently the actions were beginning to become counter-productive. The IRA had bombed a Loyalist pub and killed six drinkers none of whom were in the RHC, or indeed, in any paramilitary outfit. The IRA gave a telephone message to the Belfast Telegraph that any further killings of the Catholic community would be matched by the killing of two Protestants selected at random.

The political temperature of the Province was higher than usual. The Peace Marchers marched to as little avail as usual. The fact was that Loyalist and Nationalist communities each contained a small percentage of violent, aggressive individuals. Each community was reared to regard the other as a group of sub-human fanatics not open to reason. The violence ran in families and, not surprisingly, most of these families had some member who had been killed by the other side. This gave the family a martyr figure, encouraging further violence so that the cycle continued. On either side children would be brought up and told, "These were the people who killed your Uncle Tommy in cold blood. He was a lovely, gentle man." In fact, Uncle Tommy was usually a cold-blooded murderer, but death always turned him into a saint and his manifest personality problems were forgotten.

A more immediate problem now faced Ferguson's group. It was difficult to stop killing Fenians after the threat of IRA retribution. To do so would be seen as giving in to the enemy's threats and the Organisation regarded themselves as an elite amongst the Loyalists which precluded retreat. The phrase 'No surrender' was engraved in their personalities. The immediate cause for concern was that one of their members had been picked up and killed by the IRA after interrogation confirmed by the marks on the body. The possibilities were either that he had been lifted by sheer bad luck, having been in the wrong place at the wrong time and was just an unlucky Protestant. The alternative was that he had been betrayed. Ferguson was entirely certain that there was no informer in the Group. Membership meant active participation in the killings so that responsibility was shared. A leak might have resulted from one of the Group bragging when drunk or proudly confiding to a partner that he was a member of the RHC. Six of the members drank heavily, especially after an Action and all these were potentially suspect. If someone had inadvertently leaked the name of the killed member, then the only remedy was that he would be executed.

The man lifted by the IRA was Donny Williamson and he was a hard ex-marine with impeccable Loyalist credentials. He had been one of the most expert interrogators who frequently introduced new and more effective persuasion techniques on the victims. Donny's body was missing all the fingers on one hand in addition to other forms of mistreatment. An RUC sergeant had confided to one of the RHC members over a drink that the pathologist conducting the post mortem had noticed that all the cuts were at right angles to the fingers. He had concluded that they had been caused by either a bacon slicer or a guillotine of the type used for cutting thick cardboard. Ferguson knew that no matter how tough a man was, he would talk after this treatment and knew that he would have done so himself. This meant that the names and addresses of the RHC were known to the opposition. They would be killed singly or in groups over the next ten years, and this would require that the RHC would step up their killing of Nationalists. The problem was that there were thousands of them, but only ten RHC men. It did not require much imagination to see who was going to lose that war. The only way out was to stop the spiral of violence and then start again in a different direction. He thought that both courses were feasible.

The gunmen in both Nationalist and Loyalist factions sometimes talk to each other. Each is ridden with splinter groups, informers, and men who have got out of control and common criminals who became greedy. A cleansing operation is sometimes necessary and a convenient way of doing this is to give the name to the other side with information of where they will be at a certain time and an assurance that those who normally protect them will arrange to be absent. Rarely, truces are arranged for reasons of mutual convenience or political expediency. Sometimes this is done at Christmas.

The two sides make contact through idealistic Catholic and Protestant clergy who persuaded themselves, rightly or wrongly, that they are contributing to the peace process. Red asked for a meeting with an IRA representative on Friday evening at the home of the Rev. John MacNeil, a

Presbyterian Minister. Both sides felt entirely safe attending this meeting because no matter what the level of violence, the meeting ground was treated as a neutral area.

"I speak for the RHC," said Ferguson, carefully not shaking hands with the young man on the other side of the table.

"We know of you," replied the other. "Fifty-five Albany Street," trying to intimidate Red with knowledge of his address, the threat being that they knew where to come and get him. "O'Malley, representing Belfast High Command, what do you want to discuss?"

"These killings. People are frightened on both sides and neither of us is doing much good for our image."

"You started it, so why do you want to stop?" questioned O'Malley.

"Because it's got out of hand and is doing neither of us any good. I propose a truce and guarantee we stop, if you do the same. I cannot control the other Loyalist Groups and you have your own problems with the mavericks, but the other Loyalist Organisations have not been killing over the last year so if we stop it probably all stops."

"All right," said O'Malley. "Give me twenty four hours to get word to High Command, although this was what they thought this meeting would be about and what you would offer and my instructions were to accept. Thought you might want to know that you were next on the list when you went to pick up the dole at 10 o'clock on Thursday morning."

Ferguson felt a sinking feeling because he had got into the foolish habit of going to the Social Security Office at the same time every week and his mistake had been noted.

A few members of the RHC grumbled about the truce with the IRA, largely because they did not have the intelligence to calculate that ten minus ten reached zero more quickly than 2,000 minus ten. One member was still unmoved. Mad Doug Conran never seemed concerned or frightened and was always the first to volunteer to finish off a victim with the final shot. "If we're not killing Fenians, then we're just a drinking club," he pronounced, "and all the work we have done is wasted. I hate to think of the IRA laughing because we lost our bottle." Ferguson let Conran talk himself out and recognised that his leadership was at stake.

"The problem is that you forgot your army training," he challenged. "When in a hopeless position you can either fight to the end and die or make a tactical withdrawal and fight again and perhaps win next time. What I'm telling you is that this is a tactical withdrawal."

"So when do we fight again?"

He told them.

The Duke was a liability to the Royal Family. He was not on the Civil List and was accordingly responsible for earning his own living. As a gilded youth he was the despair of his parents. Like many young men he smoked cannabis at University and, unlike most, he got caught. He was warned but not charged amidst much publicity. The newspapers pointed out that the year before, an undergraduate had been charged, fined and expelled from the University for the same offence. The only difference was that one was the son of the King and the other of a bus conductor. On leaving University, he had a variety of unsuitable lady companions, the most recent being an exotic dancer in a Soho nightclub. The satirical magazines had made the term 'exotic dancer' synonymous with prostitute. The problem for the Duke was that he was required to earn a living. Initially he managed to extract money from his father on an irregular basis. The old man would give him the money in cash and murmur, "Not a word to your mother about this; we agreed not to fund you anymore." Similarly his mother would give him money with strict admonitions that the gift was conditional on never mentioning it to his father. He fully obeyed both commands. Unfortunately the King and Queen quarrelled about their son. The exotic dancer had written an account of her love affair with the Duke for the News of the World. In truth, it had been written for her because her literary abilities were strictly limited. The reporter who actually did the writing added some fabricated details which flattered the Duke's amatory abilities and which fascinated the public. The Queen attacked the King for not being hard enough on their son and the King responded that his mother ruined the boy and had no doubt continued to give him money against his specific command. The Queen said nothing and blushed and the rarity of this combination told the King that he was correct in his assumption. Given the third degree, Her Majesty confessed that she had done so, albeit from the best motives. The King realised that they were both being exploited and confessed that he too was guilty. They made up the quarrel and even laughed at the sheer cheek of their son and both signed a letter to him pointing out that he had deceived them and that the gravy train had now come up against the buffers. Henceforth he would have to earn his own living.

The Duke was penitent, idle and without talent; save for low cunning and an instinct for self-preservation. His only attributes were his title and the Royal connections and he was determined to make the most of them. He recruited a penniless baronet of impeccable breeding who made it known that his master would be prepared to consider acting as a non-executive director of companies prepared to pay a minimum salary of £50,000 a year. No work should be involved as the Duke felt that the addition of his name to the list of directors would be an adequate return for the company. Surprisingly, there were a large number of takers even with the baronet's proviso that the annual fee was payable in advance. The baronet was on 10% commission and both thrived for two years.

Problems began when the companies began to go wrong. In one, the Holding Company in New Jersey was charged with racketeering and being a Mafia front. Witnesses at the hearing in the American courts described how the British subsidiary was used to launder money. Documentary evidence was provided to confirm this. The British press had a field day when they discovered the Duke to be a director. Questioned by a reporter, he blurted out that he knew nothing of the financial affairs of the company. The paper's editorial column pointed out that directors had a legal duty to have good knowledge of the financial affairs of a company, indeed they were responsible for them.

Troubles rarely arise singly. One of the Duke's other directorship was in a Unit Trust which had been particularly successful especially for a new Trust. It subsequently became apparent that there was a black hole in the accounts and the shares had risen because many of the investments were made in unquoted companies. This was illegal but creative accounting had disguised it. The unquoted companies turned out to be shells owned by the Mafia. At least, a newspaper pointed out sarcastically, on this occasion it was the European Mafia rather than the American.

The King was at the end of his tether. In earlier times he would have sent the lad off on a crusade. A ten-year walk to Jerusalem and back would have given him time to grow up. At a later stage in the family's history he would have been sent in command of an army to annihilate the Welsh, Irish or French with a reasonable prospect of being killed. These options were no longer available but some alternative desperate means was required.

"You need to marry a rich woman," the King said in the voice which brooked no argument.

"But…," said the Duke.

"Don't argue with me you insolent young puppy!" commanded His Majesty, "unless you can give me a positive plan." The Duke could not and was forced to agree that marriage seemed the only solution.

"No British nobility," mused the King. "Most of them are relatives and the rest are impoverished and look like horses. The Europeans are interbred and all have Hapsburg lips or haemophilia so it has to be an American. We need a dowry of twenty million pounds and she needs an income with it. No blacks, no Jews, no Catholics, no Mafia," commanded the great libertarian. "We can dig around and get a short list."

Cindy-Lou Guggenheimer had blonde hair, a happy smile and a figure to die for. She had problems in the IQ department, but most men who met her were too busy admiring her cleavage to spot it. Women uniformly hated her regarding it as unfair that anyone should possess all these physical attributes accompanied by enormous wealth. Daddykins, otherwise known as J Hamilton Guggenheimer III, was a man of obscure origin. J Hamilton Guggenheimer I had been a German immigrant who sold bratwurst in the Bronx and had left 50 dollars in his will. He changed his christian names from Johann Heinrich at Ellis Island on the way in to America. J Hamilton Guggenheimer II was a chicken farmer who left 5,000 dollars in his bank account when he died with another 5,000 in cash buried beneath the chicken run where it would be safe from the Revenue. JHG III had inherited the 10,000 dollars from his widowed father and used it to buy a small engineering business in Texas.

The business started at the onset of the Korean War and Guggenheimer rapidly switched from making tin openers to manufacturing shells for the US Army at an enormous profit. A similar line in shells of slightly different dimensions was simultaneously exported with an end-user's certificate to the Madagascan Army. The cynic might wonder why this Army with no one to shell required a million of them to do it. The reason was that a General in that Army and some politician cronies were then selling them on to North Korea and China. Such healthy businesslike activities continued over the years. He supplied both British and Argentinean Armies during the Falklands War and both sides pronounced themselves happy with the quality of the product. During the Kuwait invasion he supplied Britain, America and Iraq. Unlike some foolish competitors, he insisted on prepayment by Iraq in dollars.

His transactions were carried out through companies based in Switzerland and the Cayman Islands. Tax was duly paid on all income earned in America and he was widely regarded as a trustworthy, successful industrialist. When he passed the age of forty, he became a philanthropist, which is a career opportunity unavailable to the poor. He endowed Guggenheimer College in Cambridge, England, with a sum of fifty million pounds. The Chair of Peace Studies was one of the first in the world. It was for this piece of altruism that he was made a Knight Commander of the British Empire. As a foreigner he was not entitled to be addressed as Sir Hamilton, but his American subordinates always did so knowing that it pleased him inordinately. Hamilton had a strange admiration for procedures British, with a healthy contempt for their frivolous approach to business.

Sir Selwyn Blake-Snadely surveyed the Texas mansion of JHG III. The King had written a personal letter to the industrialist asking if the King's Private Secretary could be invited to be received by Mr Guggenheimer in order to discuss a matter of delicacy. The King would consider it a personal favour if the utmost confidentiality could be observed and the Secretary would be travelling under the pseudonym of Mr Burns. Guggenheimer was ecstatic to be addressed in such elegant Limey prose 'invited to receive,' "Marvellous!" he said. Mrs Peggy Guggenheimer (Miss Texas Rose 1953) was consulted and sworn to secrecy. What could they want? Perhaps for Guggy to be a Lord in return for endowing another College, but surely Kings didn't do money anyway. A little research showed that American citizens were not eligible for peerages.

The first impression of Sir Selwyn was that his hosts lived in a cross between the Parthenon and a wedding cake. He himself lived in a modest late Elizabethan manor house beset internally by woodworm and the deathwatch beetle and in the grounds by Dutch Elm disease and bovine spongiform encephalopathy. As he entered the gate of the Guggenheimer estate a piper dressed in a plaid unknown in Scotland paraded the grounds in the setting sun, while playing "*The Sands of Iwo Jima*". He felt at home at seeing peacocks displaying on the lawn, but was confused by the presence of two giraffes. He gritted his teeth and resolved to be tactful and appear impressed by this tasteless and ostentatious display of wealth.

"Mr Guggenheimer and surely the delightful Mrs Guggenheimer," simpered the professional courtier, "what a delightful residence. I shall feel quite claustrophobic when I return home and how hospitable was the little Scottish touch with the piper. His Majesty would so appreciate it were he here."

"Please keep talking, Sir Snadely," said Mrs Guggenheimer, "I could listen to it all day." She had quite forgotten that he should be referred to as Mr. Burns. Sir Selwyn's conversation promptly dried up.

"You go freshen up, Peggy," said Hamilton. "We boys can have some man talk in the den." He led the way into a study lined with unlikely coats of arms and a variety of stuffed animals with horned heads. "So what is the message from His Maj.?" asked JHG III in that direct approach which had netted him a fortune and whose absence had cost the British their Empire.

"A matter of delicacy, enormous delicacy and of necessity, matters are at a most preliminary, extremely preliminary stage," tacked the courtier.

"How much do you need and what's in it for me?" was the reply.

"I will be brutally frank and not beat about the bush," said Sir Selwyn. "It is in the matter of the Royal Duke, a most delightful lad but a little headstrong and wayward and needs a settling and calming influence."

"Ah, a job," said JHG III, and enlightenment dawned. "I could put him in charge of the napalm plant. Sells well and he would pick it up in no time." The courtier shuddered and foresaw the headlines. "Not quite what I meant, Mr Guggenheimer."

"What about the landmines instead?" the tycoon said tactfully. "Your kind offer is indeed appreciated, but my approach is about a very different matter - marriage." The Private Secretary winced at the indelicacy of getting to the point at such a breakneck speed.

Enlightenment dawned. "You mean the Duke and Cindy-Lou. That would make Cindy-Lou a Duchess," he said with mounting excitement. "But they have never met."

"Careful soundings have been taken Mr Guggenheimer. Your family is impeccable and your reputation as a philanthropist is considerable. Your daughter's personality is entirely suitable and she has the advantage of great beauty. Photographs have been shown to His Grace and he is most impressed. Of course a meeting would need to be arranged, and perhaps a personal invitation from yourself to the Duke to stay in your lovely residence would be appropriate if you wish to proceed."
"Perhaps you would do me the honour of an introduction to your daughter, but before that, there is a rather sensitive matter on which I need assurance."

By this time Guggenheimer was bursting with the effect the news would have upon his wife and friends. "You will, of course, be aware that a Dukedom carries enormous obligations of service to the Nation and maintenance of a certain lifestyle. His Grace's service to the Nation I can say with confidence, is second to none." He paused; hoping that Guggenheimer would appreciate the nuance. His wife always said that Hamilton had the social graces of a rhinoceros, but this was business and in business JHG III was a negotiator and would pick up the subtlest hint.

"Should my lovely daughter agree to marry the Duke, I should not of course expect her to be a burden on the Lime - British Government. It is not a situation I have previously met, but what order of settlement are were discussing?" It was proceeding better than Sir Selwyn had anticipated.

"Fifty million would seem entirely appropriate," he said.

"Fifty million dollars?" gasped Guggenheimer, torn between the magnitude of the sum and his ambition to be the father of a Duchess.

"Pounds actually," said the now emboldened Knight, "and a reasonable annual allowance. Perhaps we might discuss that later because it seems so inappropriate to talk about money in the face of young love."

The King received his Personal Secretary at Windsor.
"Well, what's the girl like?"
"Would your Majesty wish to receive the euphemisms or the facts?"
"The facts."
"Beautiful, wealthy and stupid. Ideal in fact, apart from being American. Says she's already in love with His Grace before meeting him, but probably is in love with the title. Daddy is coarse."
"What about the money?" enquired the King, in the direct manner permitted to Royalty.
"Fifty million up front and a good allowance."
"Thank God for that, let's cash in before they change their minds."

Chapter 5

Over the next two weeks I felt surprisingly calm. The decision had been made and the plan was as foolproof as possible. I was determined to change my life after the bridge action, to ask Kate to marry me and to return to Ireland to start up my own building business. Kate and I had not formally discussed marriage, but each of us spoke as though we would be spending the rest of our lives together. Before broaching the subject, I needed to clear the air about my background. I told her about the deaths of my brother and sister and apologised for not telling her before, explaining that it had been too hard for me to discuss. Her eyes filled with tears and she said that she entirely understood, which made me feel even more guilty than usual. When I asked her to marry me she kissed me and said that I already knew the answer. I telephoned my mother and for the first time told her about Kate. My mother had a firm belief that I was lonely and friendless in England and liable to be snapped up by some hard-faced English harpy. She was delighted to hear about Kate but gave me a hard time for not mentioning her before. She asked me when I would bring Kate home to meet the family and I replied that it would be in about six weeks and that we intended to get married in Ireland and live in Drumundra.

At the end of the conversation, I suddenly realised that this was probably the first really happy moment in my mother's life since Mora and Desmond had died. Now I wished that I could back out of the bridge project because anything which jeopardised my future with Kate would be foolish. There were two considerations which made me continue. One was a strange sort of idealism that it was necessary to avenge the two deaths, and the other was less worthy, that if I backed out at this advanced stage of planning it was likely that the IRA would pursue me wherever I lived and probably kill me, or certainly give me a kneecapping so that I could never work again. I dare not tell Kate of my plans being quite certain that if I did, she would issue an ultimatum that if I did not call it off she would not marry me.

In early September on a fine Saturday morning, I set off again on the train for Bristol. I told Kate and the landlady that I was going to another home fixture of Manchester United and that I would be home late on Saturday night. On this occasion, Reilly was by himself and told me that Blondie would look after giving the warnings when he received our call that the bombs had been planted.

As we drove over Bridge 3, it gave a good view of Bridge 4 about two miles downstream.

"I have been giving a lot of thought to Bridge 4," I said, "and still cannot see where it is vulnerable."

"You have to think sideways. You did not notice that after you passed the tollbooth going towards England, after about five hundred metres, a road bridge crossed the motorway. The road starts at Rogiet village and leads down to Severn Tunnel Junction which is a small railway station. Immediately before the station there is a rutted road passing over the railway on a bridge. There is no signpost at the junction but after the bridge over the railway, the road suddenly becomes of good quality and forms the road bridge over the M4. It is a public road but immediately after the motorway it ends at a Ministry of Defence firing range and presumably that is why the road is looked after. As the bridge crosses the motorway you get a good view of the tollbooth but unfortunately they get a good view of you. About ten metres to the east of the bridge is an enormous steel motorway sign warning of the toll and a hundred metres east is a security camera which is pointed to look at traffic coming from England so that it cannot view the motorway bridge behind it. You can see Bridge 4 from the motorway bridge about 1 kilometres East and there is no other entry to the motorway after it."

As I walked across the motorway bridge, all I had to do was step across the crash barrier and I could sit on the buttress of the bridge on the grass and watch the motorway traffic. As long as I did that on the east side, I was invisible from the tollbooth and I sat there for half an hour with no one disturbing me. There was no traffic over the bridge behind me and even if there was, they could not see me.

"What I intend to do is to park the car at Severn Tunnel Junction Station, stroll three hundred metres to the motorway bridge and nobody will take any notice of someone wearing a walker's outfit. I then step over the barrier and take out my sandwiches and plant the charge right next to me in the angle between the bridge and its supports. The grass is knee high and will hide it well. I will then go to the other side of the bridge and do the same. Nobody can notice that I appeared on both sides of the motorway unless they come west on the M4 twice in twenty minutes and that is physically impossible. A pair of good charges will collapse the bridge onto the motorway and will bring down the road sign as well so, with luck, a hundred metres or so of road surface will be destroyed to a considerable depth".

On the exit road from Bridge 3 to Chepstow is a lay-by and we pulled in there where Reilly gave me the charges and detonators which I put in my haversack There were six charges, two for each bridge and with the rucksack, the total weight was about twelve kgs, although it would not be necessary to carry this heavy load for long because four charges would rapidly be dropped at Bridges 1 and 2. On top of the charges I put an eight-metre coil of thin rope which I had bought a week before on a trip to London.

We reached Chepstow and Reilly dropped me off outside the castle, just before Bridge 1. He wished me good luck and reminded me that it was vital that I should be at the roundabout to be picked up at three o'clock as he had no wish to circle round the estate whilst waiting for me.

The town was fairly quiet and most of the tourism had ended as the children had returned to school. I sauntered over the footpath on to Bridge 1 and stopped about twenty metres from the castle end on the upstream side. I watched the tide flooding in and on the previous visit had noticed that this particular part of the Bridge was only overlooked by the rear windows of a house and by the blank walls of the castle. With my back to the roadway it was not too obvious what I was doing. In the lay-by I had previously attached the end of the rope to the charge for this bridge. Looking around to check there were no pedestrians or approaching vehicles, I lowered the charges and the detonators on the rope and swung them back and fore like a pendulum. After five swings, when the charges swung up into the corner between the concrete base and the start of the iron arch, I let go of the rope and the detonators and the charges landed where I wanted them with a thump. They were invisible from any aspect and the thin rope trailed into the rising tide, but nobody would relate this to a planted bomb.

Sweating somewhat, I put the haversack on my back and joined the footpath on the Welsh side of the river between Bridges 1 and 2. A few people were exercising dogs along the upper part of the path but my activities on the bridge would have been invisible to them. They thinned out nearing Bridge 2 save for an elderly woman with a poodle who was having a satisfying crap, or at least the poodle was. She avoided my eye in the manner of dog owners caught in this situation.

Once under Bridge 2, I hopped over the low wall. The undergrowth was still thick and I was unable to see the footpath from the pillars. On a Saturday morning there was nobody in the car compound behind me, but even if there was, the vegetation gave good cover and my green anorak provided further disguise. The charges and detonators stuck easily to the pillar base and just in case they were spotted, I covered them with a mixture of leaves and ferns.

As I stepped back over the wall into the waste-ground adjoining the footpath, I sensed a movement at the corner of my eye on the right side. My bowels turned to water at the sight of two policemen strolling towards me about one hundred and fifty metres away and engaged in animated conversation. They too sensed my movement and looked up towards me and I must have looked very suspicious. Inspiration struck and my right hand ostentatiously checked the zip of my trousers to give them the impression of an innocent hiker who had gone for a discrete pee before starting a walk. I gave them a cheerful wave, which they returned and began to walk, although not too rapidly, back towards the town. I waited, terrified, for a shout or footsteps behind me but felt it best not to look around. Nothing happened and I turned left to walk up the hill to Bulwark, bypassing the centre of Chepstow town.

About an hour later I reached the lane to the south side of the housing estate and went over the stile and into the wood adjoining the railway on my left. A large oak tree prevented anyone seeing me from the embankment, although it was unlikely that anyone would be on it. Once in the wood, I exchanged my anorak for the oilskin jacket and hard hat and put the anorak beneath a large stone so that the wind would not blow it away. Taking a deep breath, I set out along the embankment. The cows were gathered at the far end of the field on my right and the bridge pillars on their concrete bases appeared horribly exposed.

At close quarters, the lock on the gate in the wire cage around the pillars seemed very stout. I took out the bolt clippers which made little impression on the hardened steel of the hoop arising from the lock. The lock was low set in the door so I put the bolt clippers on the floor with the jaws around the lock and stamped hard on the clipper handles with my size ten walker's boot and heard the lock snap. The lock went into my pocket. For some strange reason, I was suddenly struck by the implausibility that a measuring job would be done on a Saturday lunchtime and that my manager would be in his office should the farmer telephone him. It was too late to start worrying about this and I had other things to do. I set the charges which were visible from the railway line, but it would be unlikely that anyone on a train would notice them or that if they did, they would appreciate their significance. I set the charges and picked up the now lightened rucksack. Before fitting the new lock on the door, I carefully wiped it to remove fingerprints with a handkerchief which had been dampened in a puddle on the way.

In a fairly intense state of terror, I walked back into the wood and changed back into the anorak putting the oilskin and hat into the rucksack. My watch showed 45 minutes before the 3 o'clock pick up. I realised that I was very hungry and sat and ate a bar of chocolate, carefully putting the wrapping paper back into my haversack because the whole area was likely to be combed for forensic evidence.

After fifteen minutes there was a low-pitched vibration indicating that a local train was approaching. It must have been travelling very fast because a few seconds later it flashed past. I realised that while I was invisible to anyone on the embankment, I was very exposed to the view of the driver or passengers on the train. All I could do was to hope that they had not seen me and if they had, would assume that I was having a quiet crap and the driver would not alert the railway police.

At nine minutes before three, I set out for the roundabout at a leisurely pace and met no one on the way. It was dead on three o'clock with no sign of Reilly's car. After standing there for twenty minutes I began to get very frightened. A few people had walked past when I had firmly stared in the other direction to avoid eye contact or any conversation. The explosives were due to go off in forty minutes. Within a short time the people who had passed me would remember seeing a young man standing at the roundabout with an agitated appearance and the police would have my description.

At 3.30 I realised there was two possible decisions. I could continue to wait for Reilly in the hope that he would turn up, although the margin for getting across the bridge before it blew was becoming increasingly narrow. If he did not arrive then I was stuck right next to an explosion with an Irish accent and no reason for being there. In addition, in my rucksack were a bolt cutter and the lock from the cage and in due course forensic would show my rucksack had carried semtex. My survival time was unlikely to exceed half an hour and the only escape route would be to walk into Chepstow and catch a bus in the unlikely event that they would still run after the explosions. If I did catch a bus, the only escape route would be back into South Wales which would become a cul de sac.

The only remote possibility for escape seemed to be to get across the bridge before it blew in half an hour. Time was extremely tight and half an hour assumed that the detonators were not fast. There was a footpath over Bridge 3 but it would take more than half an hour to cross it and I would walk into the arms of the police at the other end.

The minutes ticked away during my panic stricken deliberations. At 3.35 there was still no Reilly and the decision had to be made instantly. I scurried up a road going from the roundabout to the road from Chepstow to the approach road to Bridge 3. On the way in we had stopped at a lay-by for Reilly to give me the explosives. I remembered noticing a mirror image lay-by on the other side of the road and that there were no vehicles in it at the time to view what we were doing. It suddenly struck me that there was to be a fifteen minute warning so that, depending on the speed of the police response, the bridge might be closed any time after 3.45 using the roadside and overhead illuminated signs.

I ran along the road and saw two lorries and about three cars in the lay-by. I approached the first car and told the driver that I had been to my brother's wedding and had missed the bus back to London, so would he give me a lift. "Sorry mate," he said I'm headed for Worcester." The next car was driven by a small bald man of fifty or so who was gnawing on a tired looking sandwich and supping tea from a thermos. I told him the same story and he seemed a good sort. "Jump in lad, I'll just finish my sandwich and the tea. Would you like a cup?" I said yes, hoping that if I finished the tea it would stop him having a second cup and I gulped it down and burnt my throat while he patiently waited. I felt like screaming at him to get a move on and finally at 3.42 he drove off in leisurely fashion. We crossed the bridge and all seemed quiet.

By 4.00 p.m. we were passing Bristol on our right and a minute later there was a dull thud behind me and another minute later, a second one. Neither was loud, and my companion did not notice them. He was a talkative man and told me all about his family whilst bemoaning the habits of modern youth. He was a manager for a firm selling biscuits and shortbread and lived in East London. Once a week he travelled to different regions west of London and as far as Cardiff in order to enthuse and sometimes terrorise his salesmen. The latter seemed unlikely in such a pleasant man. He picked up my accent so I told him that I was from Cork and worked in a light engineering factory in Barnet where I lived with my wife and young child. He started asking about my six month old little boy and to my horror I found that I had no idea what capabilities they had at that age and he was most impressed that he was able to walk!

The concentration needed to confabulate this unlikely story helped to take away the horror of being caught. Just after Heathrow, he stopped at a service station where I bought him a cup of tea and a stale bun. His car had a radio, but my conversation must have been so enthralling, or more possibly such a sustained nervous babble, that he had not switched it on. In the service station everyone seemed quieter and more thoughtful than usual, but my friend did not seem to sense this. In London he dropped me off near Euston Station where I told him I would pick up the Northern Line Underground for Barnet. Once out of the car I immediately headed south and got the Underground to Waterloo.

The yellow oilskin went into the waste bin in a side street outside the Station and the hard hat was left under the seat in the train from Waterloo to Hastings. The lock and bolt cutter was flushed down the toilet at one-mile intervals after wiping them of fingerprints. It seemed unlikely that anyone finding these objects singly would link them to an explosion one hundred and fifty miles away.

I arrived at Hastings Station at 8.00 p.m. and bought a sporting edition of the local newspaper. I deliberately avoided the first page but caught the word Severn as I looked in the back for the result of the Manchester match and was able to tell the landlady that Manchester had beaten Everton 2 - 0 in a very exciting match. I did not want to read about the bombs before speaking to the landlady in case the emotion showed on my face and I wanted to establish my alibi just in case there was any future problem.

When I reached my room, the first thing was to look at the paper. On the front page was the headline 'Severn Bridge Horror'. There was a brief announcement that news had just come in that bombs had destroyed both Severn and Wye bridges with an unknown but large toll of dead and injured. In addition, there had been a simultaneous explosion on a passenger train in the Severn railway tunnel. The extent of injuries here was unknown at the time of going to press because access to the train was proving difficult. The paper said that no warning had been received before any of the explosions but it was assumed that the IRA was the likely perpetrator. All rail and road communications with South Wales had been severed including the Newport to Gloucester rail link on which Bridge 3 had fallen.

I sat down with a feeling of sick horror. No pick up for me at the rendezvous, no warning and an explosion in the Severn Tunnel, of which I had no knowledge. The tunnel explosion was presumably done by Blondie and explained why he was missing from my own action. It suddenly came to me that I had been a gullible dupe and had been used by the IRA for their own purposes whilst Reilly had consistently lied to me. Not only had I been a fool, but had got involved in murdering innocent civilians who had done me no harm.

What could I do? If I went to the police they would never believe that the plan I had been involved in did not intend to kill people. Even if they did believe me, they would rightly say that anyone causing explosions could never guarantee there would be no injuries. No doubt the bitter feelings aroused by the deaths and injuries would result in a life sentence which would mean just that and not ten years inside. I could say goodbye to marriage, children and the love of Kate. On God, Kate! What would she ever think of me if she found out?

The television news was due and I switched it on and immediately felt frightened at what it might show. The normal news was cancelled and instead, forty five minutes were devoted to the explosions. A helicopter gave aerial views of Bridges 3 and 4. On Bridge 4 the motorway bridge had crashed onto the M4 which was visibly wrecked for fifty metres. The road-signs which were ten metres high were shown blown into a field. Remnants of the cab of a heavy lorry were visible approaching the bridge with wreckage of two cars in the debris of the explosion. On Bridge 3 there was one hundred metre gap on the west side of the bridge and the stumps of the supporting pillars looked like drawn teeth. The camera lingered on the deformed corpses of about thirty cows who had wandered close to the bridge pillars. The buckled rails of the Newport Chepstow line led away from a section where the line was completely covered by the fallen bridge.

On Bridge 3 there was dramatic film of a single decker bus with its front partly over the gap in the bridge above a thirty-metre drop. The commentator said that the driver saw the explosion in front of him. Although his windscreen had shattered, he had braked hard but was unable to stop before the bus was left rocking with its front section over the edge and threatening to fall. The passengers had run forward to the only door at the front causing the bus to tilt even more alarmingly. With great presence of mind, the driver ordered all the passengers to the rear when the tilt corrected to some degree. A passenger managed to break the rear window but the remainder rapidly realised that if the back of the vehicle were lightened, the front would tip further. Some of the passengers became hysterical and had to be restrained from jumping out of the smashed rear window. Fortunately a quick-minded lorry driver behind the bus attached a towing chain and pulled the bus backwards so that the passengers could be decanted. There were also shots of Bridge 2 with large gaps both in the road bridge and surprisingly, in the adjacent Newport-Chepstow-

Gloucester rail line which was now cut at two sites. Bridge 1 had completely disappeared and the metal had been swept down river by the rapidly falling tide.

The opening sentence of the broadcast made me wish I were dead when the commentator said that casualties so far were 58 dead and 150 injured. The main carnage was on Bridge 4 on which traffic was always heavy. Two cars had virtually disintegrated and had been blown off the road into a field with six deaths. On bridge 3 a heavy goods vehicle going towards Wales had done the same thing. There were, remarkably, no deaths or injuries on Bridges 1 and 2 and an interview was shown with two emotional French teenagers who had been standing on the embankment at some distance from the explosion on Bridge 1 and who had evidently had a nasty fright.

The main toll was from the explosion on the train in the Severn Tunnel. It had occurred about two thirds of the way along, nearer the Newport end. Rescue crews had reached the train under appalling conditions and entry from the Bristol side was impossible because the derailed train had pulled down a section of tunnel wall, making access unacceptably dangerous. The Severn railway tunnel in fact consists of two parallel tunnels. In the unpredictable manner of explosions, the bomb had caused severe damage to the second tunnel, putting the pumping station out of action so that it was completely flooded and contained an abandoned goods train and the body of the driver and his mate.

Film was shown of the Royal Gwent Hospital in Newport to which casualties had been directed. There was an impressive air of efficiency about the hospital whose forecourt was jammed with ambulances. A remarkably youthful Chief Executive of the hospital explained that every year the hospital held a major disaster exercise in which some catastrophic accident was simulated occurring in the Hospital catchment area. These exercises were very realistic with volunteers covered in false blood and plastered with splints applied at the accident site for various appalling fractures. One year previously, the simulation had been of a train derailment in the Severn Tunnel. The lessons of this exercise were still fresh. All transportable existing patients had either been discharged home or shipped out to other hospitals, so that accommodation was cleared for two hundred casualties requiring admission. An unforeseen problem was that of storing the bodies of the fifty eight dead, but again, neighbouring hospitals and the local undertakers had rallied around to solve the problem. The newscaster once again repeated that no warning of the disaster had been received.

After the news broadcast, the Prime Minister was interviewed. He deplored the injuries and loss of life and the ruthlessness of the people responsible. He promised a vigorous enquiry both into how it had been allowed to happen and vowed to track down the criminals who had done it. There would be a special debate on the incident in Parliament on Monday and he would broadcast to the Nation after this.

I did not sleep that night and knew that the results of the day's action would remain on my conscience forever. I tried to persuade myself that my actions were stupid rather than vicious, but even if they had gone according to plan, there was always a considerable risk that someone might have been physically injured.

Chapter 6

The next morning I went to church feeling a complete hypocrite and met Kate.

"You look like death warmed up," she said bluntly. "What were you doing last night?"

"The team did well in Manchester," I lied, "and I got a bit carried away in a pub in Manchester afterwards. I can barely remember coming home."

She pointedly said nothing but I gained the firm impression that she had a medium term plan for stamping out this sort of behaviour and I saw a lifetime of busy Saturdays involving shopping or doing an endless list of non-footballing tasks. My guilt increased when the priest asked for prayers for those killed and injured in yesterday's disaster.

I managed to escape from my usual lunch with Kate's parents on the grounds of a tummy upset, although Kate was very tight-lipped about it in the firm conviction that the upset was a consequence of eight pints of beer. I escaped to my room with four of the heavier Sunday newspapers. An instinct for self preservation made me read every word of the account of the Manchester-Everton football match and I then plodded through their accounts of the Severn incident. The papers largely ignored the news of the rest of the world. All had aerial views of the damage with pictures of an empty M4 motorway and crowded roads where spectators had flocked to view the damage. It seemed universally agreed that only the IRA could have conducted such a massive operation and there was almost a grudging underlying admiration for the scale and surprise of the coup. In three of the newspapers, there was an expression of anger that security gaps could have allowed such an enormous operation. It was pointed out that MI5, after much political infighting, had recently taken over the lead role in dealing with IRA activities with a downgrading of responsibilities of Special Branch, Military Intelligence and the RUC. The Sunday Times stated that since the Director of MI5 had been so eager for getting the kudos of lead organisation against the IRA, then he should accept responsibility for its failure by resigning.

The police had given the newspapers a description of a man who had been acting suspiciously at the site of Bridge 2 a few hours before the explosion. A motorist had reported giving a lift from Chepstow to London to a similar individual. He was described as six feet tall, with dark hair and an Irish accent - a description which must have fitted a few thousand people living in Britain. One paper had dug further and showed blurred pictures of the two policemen to whom I had waved. The picture was captioned 'The cops who waved to an IRA murderer.' I suspect that their prospects of future promotion were minimal.

A major theme in all the papers was the effect of the incident on the economy of South Wales and of the UK. The Sunday Telegraph pointed out that approximately 2 million people lived in South and Southwest Wales. Wales manufactures 10 million tonnes of iron and steel a year which had to be exported, as did products from the electrical and mechanical engineering industries which employed twenty thousand people. Normally the Severn Tunnel took two million tonnes of goods out of Wales and these goods would have to be squeezed onto overcrowded minor roads or second class railway systems rambling up to England through mid Wales and the Borders. On Bridge 4 alone there were normally fifteen million-vehicle movement per year, and on Bridge 3 five million. Within South Wales, the explosion had locked in eight hundred thousand cars and vans and twenty thousand heavy goods vehicles.

On the political front, the Independent said that it was time to begin thinking the previously unthinkable and to ask the Irish Government to take over the governance of the Six Counties. This would remove the *raison d'etre* of the IRA at a stroke and the Irish Government could deal more firmly with the IRA that was possible for the British Administration. The editorial did not doubt that such a proposal would produce uproar in Unionist circles, but considered that in mainland UK there was no sympathy for their posturing, marching and intolerance.

On the television news that night, were reports of fifteen-mile queues on the Ross Spur and total gridlock on the road from Monmouth to Gloucester, through the Forest of Dean. Bridge 1 would require total replacement and repairs to the other three bridges could take four to six months, assuming an open cheque book. The French owners of Bridges 3 and 4 were already squabbling with the Government about who should bear the cost of repairs. The Frenchmen had a certain blackmailing ability because the Government needed the bridges open for political and economic reasons, while the Government on the other hand, knew that the owners would be missing a cash flow of ninety million pounds a year.

The tunnel was a Victorian brick structure built by Brunel. A prolonged engineering survey would be needed before work could start because of the problem of flooding from the sea. The Newport-Chepstow-Gloucester railway was a lesser problem and with twenty four hour a day working, the rubble could be cleared and the line open in two weeks. Unfortunately, it could never cope with heavy traffic and followed a circuitous route from South Wales to England.

At work the next day, I had great difficulty in concentrating so that the foreman, who normally considered me as the best of his workers, lost patience with me. My fellow builders were a cheerful, likeable bunch but I sensed an air of tension between us as a result of the Severn bombs.

That evening, the Prime Minister appeared on the television to speak to the Nation. He looked strained and haggard, but when he began to speak he gave an impressive performance. He said that although the IRA had not accepted responsibility, the explosives used were semtex and the fragments of detonator were of a type used by the IRA. He accused them of being too cowardly to accept responsibility and of taking fright at the number of innocent deaths for which they were responsible. The Severn Tunnel bomb originated in a suitcase placed in the rack at the end of a compartment. Police wished to interview a blonde man who was seen waiting for the London train at Bristol Parkway Station fifteen minutes before the explosion. It was felt likely that the perpetrator had coolly placed the bomb in the luggage rack and then left the train at Bristol Parkway. The Prime Minister had every confidence that the Security Service would catch the culprits and the Government offered a reward of half a million pounds for any information resulting in a conviction. The award would be paid without publicity and the telephone number was given for a confidential line to which reports could be made.

He admitted that the incident had revealed defects in security at the site and a disappointing performance by the

Security Service. The Direction of MI5 and the Controller (Northern Ireland) had proffered their resignations which he had accepted with regret. He expressed sympathy for the injured and relatives of the deceased and warned of economic disruption for many months to come.

The Prime Minister's manner then became more brisk and authoritative as he turned to practical arrangements. He wished to avoid inter-party disputes over management of the crisis and, following discussions, 'through the usual channels,' a Committee of thirty six members of both Houses of Parliament had been set up which contained members from all parties selected for their administrative talents. This committee would have a series of sub-committees to deal with large areas of administration, such as road transport, movement control and security. The approval of Parliament would be sought next day for sweeping emergency powers for a variety of necessary actions.

Following the Prime Minister's speech, an interview was given by the Taoiseach. He expressed his horror at the recent atrocity. He admitted that previously, many Irish politicians felt that the problems of the Six Counties had arisen because of English intransigence. This had sometimes resulted in a disinclination by the Irish authorities to share information about IRA members with the British Government. In the twenty six Counties, membership of the IRA was illegal but an unspoken arrangement existed under which a blind eye was turned to their presence if they did not carry out terrorist or criminal activities within the Republic. All this would change from today. All intelligence on the IRA would be freely shared with MI5 and known activists would be taken in for questioning and charged where proof of IRA membership could be proved or reasonably inferred.

In the newspapers the next day was an item that Martin McGrath, the Unionist MP, had issued a press release demanding the restoration of internment without trial. He called on the loyal people of Ulster to attack the popish rabble that threatened their heritage and to burn the homes of known IRA men. As a result he had been arrested and charged with incitement to murder. He had been transferred to Brixton prison for security reasons. The Director of Public Prosecutions announced that anyone from any political party who advocated violence would face similar charges.

Throughout this time it was very difficult for me to behave in a normal manner with Kate. She asked me when we were going to Ireland to meet my family. I arranged the tickets for a weekend visit in a month and then intended to leave my present job and return permanently to Ireland. I could find a temporary job in the building industry and start finding a house. Kate would then join me, we would get married and shortly after I could start up my own business.

The Emergency Powers taken by the Government had far reaching effects on life in Britain. All private vehicles were banned from the Ross Spur and the Forest of Dean link road. Any driver of a private vehicle going from Wales to England had to do so through Ludlow or Shrewsbury. To compensate, frequent bus services were provided using the Forest of Dean road. Additional air services were set up linking Cardiff airport with a range of English airports and the RAF airport at St Athans, near Cardiff was utilised as an overflow. In spite of these measures, industrial life of South Wales was being strangled and a variety of relieving legislation was drafted. Business rates were halved with temporary interest free loans for firms who were in danger of becoming insolvent and financial support for those businesses providing the improved transport facilities.

All this was expensive and there was general agreement that the resulting financial burden should be shared by the whole UK including the Six Counties. The Chancellor introduced a temporary increase in VAT from 17 .5% to 25% and a rise in all levels of Income Tax by

10%. It seemed remarkable that such draconian measures should have been relatively well received by the electorate, but there was a collective sense of shock at what had happened and an appreciation that if the Welsh economy was not propped up then the whole UK might be ruined.

The Duchess was surprisingly popular. The term the newspaper now used to describe the Duke's earlier indiscretions was that he had been a playboy who was about to become reformed because of the love of a good woman. Most females in Britain have an irrational and touching belief that bad men can be reformed by the love of a good woman, so they warmed to the Duchess. The men had already warmed to her, but for different reasons. The Archbishop of Canterbury pronounced that this was a marriage made in Heaven. This depressed the more junior clergy because all previous unions, about which he had used this phrase, ended in early divorce. It was August and the press had nothing to write about so pages of slush were churned out upon the royal romance and wedding ceremony.

"We will kill Cindy-Lou when she comes to Belfast," said Ferguson.

"You're mad!" gasped Corcoran. "Where is the advantage to us in killing the most popular woman since Cinderella. We'd be lynched by all the other Loyalists."

"Think it through," said Ferguson. "My police friends tell me that all leave is cancelled because the Duchess will be launching a ship at Harland and Wolff's yard. If she is killed in Belfast, who did it? The Loyalists will be enraged and above suspicion. It must have been the IRA. There will be a wave of outrage and sympathy for the Loyalist cause. They will produce emergency legislation to lock up the IRA and they'll take a hiding."

"Brilliant!" they all gasped. "But how do we get at her, the security will be watertight?"

"Not too difficult. Just listen and I'll tell you how."

Chapter 7

James Miles had spent the afternoon sitting gloomily in an armchair in his bungalow in Croydon. It was 4 p.m. and already getting dark. He was brooding over a difficult decision of considerable importance - whether to have fish fingers or pizza for his dinner. After summarising the various arguments, he made a command decision on pizza, on the basis that it was less work and that if he had fish fingers he would additionally need to open a packet of peas.

He had adopted the habit of having what he called a glass of wine at lunchtime. In practice this had developed into four glasses causing him to fall asleep in his chair after lunch. He would wake feeling dyspeptic and depressed at the thought of the long hours till bedtime. He missed the discipline and stimulus of work and the habits of twenty seven years.

He switched on the television which was showing an early post war romantic black and white film in which a masculine hero with a toothbrush moustache was kissing the hand of a cantilevered blonde with a beehive hairstyle.

He switched it off again and the telephone rang. Rather startled he realised that this was the first time it had done so since his retirement two months previously. "Hello, Mr Miles, Sir?" said a voice that he recognised as that of Doris, the Director's secretary. She was another of the older Millbank secretaries who were members of the James Miles' fan club of whose existence James had always been blissfully unaware. "Could you have a word with the new Director, please Mr Miles?" she said with a slight emphasis on the new. The new boss was a man of few words. "We have never met but you probably realise that the Service is in deep doodoo and I need your help, will you come and see me?"

Since his retirement James had been nursing an increased bitterness against Millbank. He felt his contribution had always been under-estimated and was now forgotten and the manner of his retirement had been dismissive. His instinct was to refuse but he realised that he was bored and lonely. The new Director had not been party to his retirement, indeed he had not worked previously at Millbank and had been brought in as a new broom. It was flattering to be asked so frankly for help by someone of such seniority in the Service. "Pleased to help," he found himself saying and made an appointment for the next morning at 10 a.m.

It seemed odd to be retracing the journey which he had made every morning for twenty seven years. As he approached the security desk at the entrance to Millbank the face of Spillane, the cynical ex navy petty officer, lit up. "Nice to see you back Mr Miles. That lot up there," - and he jerked a thumb in the direction of the lift - "couldn't run a brothel in a battleship, so go and get 'em sorted out." Spillane was notoriously blunt but unsackable because of his impeccable service record. He had a contempt for officers and the ruling classes and had saved a British frigate from destruction during a naval exercise when he was serving as a petty officer in the torpedo room of a submarine. He refused an order to fire at the frigate. The officer giving the order insisted the torpedo was a blank and Spillane knew it was not. Only then was it appreciated that the officer had a serious psychiatric illness.

It was over ten years since James had last entered the Director's office, which was referred to by the troops as the Fuehrerbunker. "Sit down Miles, do you mind if I call you James?" said the Director after introducing himself. "Last week I realised that we had no clues about this Severn business and no prospects of any. The politicians are going ape and have turned on the Service after cutting back our money for years. My survival instincts scent disaster. Two days ago I went to see Marcus Hunt." This was the Director before last who had retired fifteen years previously and whom James had assumed was dead. He had been a taciturn wise old bird with a sharp tongue but James had always got on well with him in their few dealings. "I explained our problems and asked him what he would have done." "Get James Miles on it," he said. "Awkward bugger, but best brain in Millbank and thinks sideways." "I had to explain that I had never heard of you and that you were not currently employed but that I could track you down. Your confidential personnel file makes interesting reading. There are a series of adverse reports from the previous Controller (Northern Ireland) about your attitude and your distaste for new techniques. Mixed in with this, were some pretty fulsome reports from other departments such as the Home Office and Special Branch about how effective you were when they asked for help. Reading between the lines, my impression was that the Controller disliked you. Incidentally, I shall regard it as a confidential secret, but were you the man with the BULLSHIT stamp?" James admitted that he was and the Director roared with laughter.

"Will you rejoin us? I can't offer any bribes, but you can have a promotion of two grades, a year's contract and a letter from me useable in any governmental department that they must give you every co-operation or I will personally come and cut off their pensions - or I think that is how you pronounce the word!"

"I'm in," said James beginning to be infected by the Director's staccato manner. "When do I start?"

"Now. Here's your security pass and you're in room 56 and the secretary is waiting."

James went downstairs and was delighted to see that his perceptive new Director had allocated Hilary as his secretary. "Lovely to see you Hilary," James enthused. "I feel better already," and her face went red. "Now, a nice strong cup of coffee and see that nobody interrupts me for an hour or two."

Two weeks after the bombing I was sitting in my room after work catching up on the daily paper. There was a ring on the doorbell and the landlady shouted up the stairs that there were two visitors to see me. In the hall were two men in dark clothes with ties and leather jackets whose appearance shouted police. I did my best not to look alarmed. The older taller man introduced himself as DS Carpenter and the younger as DC Manners from Hastings CID.

"I can't think of anything I've done," I said cheerfully. "What do you want?"

Carpenter explained in the usual ponderous police phraseology that he was making routine police enquiries in connection with the Severn bombings and unfortunately it had proved necessary to interview all Irish citizens resident in the UK 'to exclude them from their enquiries.' Carpenter suggested that we continued the conversation in my room and I led them upstairs with a sinking feeling.

"Now, Mr Gallagher, perhaps we could start with a few details." As Carpenter spoke, Manners got out his notebook and recorded my name, date and place of birth and the name of my employer. "On the sixteenth of September, the Saturday, where were you?" I told him that I had gone to Manchester and he immediately became interested that I had not been at home.

"How did you travel there?"

"By train."

"How did you pay for the ticket?"

"By Visa card."

"Could you give me the number of the Visa card?"

I handed the card to Carpenter who asked Manners to note the number. I had taken the precaution of buying a return ticket to Manchester on that Saturday and I knew that he would check whether the Visa account had been debited by that amount.

"Odd," said Carpenter, "that you went to see them play on that day. Had you ever done so before?"

"I did about six months ago, and bought the ticket with my Visa card." Again I knew that this would be checked.

"What time train did you catch?" I had memorised this.

"And how did you get from the train to the ground?"

"By bus, a number 23." I knew again that this would be confirmed.

"Can you remember who travelled opposite you in the train?"

There was clearly no way this could be checked so I went into great detail about a Chinese couple in their thirties and how the man had pecked at a lap top computer throughout the journey, while the woman had read a paper and then fallen asleep between Crewe and Manchester. I almost convinced myself that I had been on the train. They seemed satisfied by my replies and apologised that they were required to interview a large number of entirely respectable Irish citizens and were worried that this might result in resentment. I assured them that everyone understood they had a job to do and wanted those responsible arrested and locked up. On the way out, Carpenter asked me if I knew any other Irish people in the town. I told them there was a rather formidable Irishman who attended my local church who people regarded with some suspicion and who seemed very interested in other people's affairs.

Manners tugged out his notebook again and asked for his name. "Superintendent Bill Lacey," I told him. I thought Manners would explode as he tried not to laugh and after looking surprised for a moment, Carpenter roared with laughter. The Superintendent was a rather pompous pillar of the Parish with no sense of humour and an ability to put his foot in it. The story was still told that on arrival in the town as a young constable, he had issued a parking ticket to a vehicle parked on yellow lines. The vehicle belonged to a notoriously short-tempered Bishop who had parked outside a church which he was visiting to discipline a troublesome curate. The wrath of the clergy, Bishop and the policeman's superiors descended on his unsuspecting head. He was told to memorise the car number plates of the Bishop, Mayor and all the senior police staff and given a month of duty involving traffic direction and the issue of dog licenses. Even his thick-skinned personality realised that enthusiasm sometimes needed to be tempered.

The Northern Ireland office, the RUC and MI5 all advised the Duchess that a visit to Ulster would be an unacceptable risk since she would be a target for the IRA. All her life Daddykins had spoilt her and she was very stubborn. Since becoming a Duchess she was even more difficult to control and her new husband was becoming anxious at the thought of a lifetime of dealing with such a powerful personality. When she announced her intention to ignore the advice from the Security Services, he was not disappointed. He felt that the woman described by her father as a 'delicate Texas flower' was in fact a real little goer and he was desperate for a rest for a few days.

The launching of the super-ferry *'Sir Ian Paisley'* was a major event in the life of the province and security was intense. The decision of the Duchess to come had produced a surge of loyalty in the Orangemen. When she met the local worthies, they were all searched first and she was surrounded by a ring of bodyguards. The route of her car to the shipyard was unannounced and circuitous to minimise the risk of ambush.

The Duchess made a pretty speech about the warm welcome she had received and hurled the customary bottle of champagne from the platform at the ship. It smashed with a satisfying noise and the large ship gently started to run down the slipway as the Duchess and bystanders clapped. The platform upon which she stood was above a large crowd of carefully vetted and searched Loyalists. Sniper's rifles have a range of a mile and a shot from half a mile away from the window of a terraced house presented no difficulty for an Army-trained marksman. The Duchess slumped forward over the railings and fell onto the empty slipway behind the still descending ship. She was dead when she hit the ground.

In the late afternoon James arranged a meeting between senior representatives from the Home office, Special branch and his own department with himself as Chairman. The other two departments had said that it was impossible to attend at such short notice but had been told that the Director would use his privilege of direct access to the Prime Minister if they did not voluntarily attend and there was a hasty re-scheduling of diaries.

"It was kind of you all to come," said James, tongue in cheek. "Now first, were all known IRA players in place at the time of the Severn bomb?"

Special Branch indicated that they were, apart from members of two Active Service Units. One was known to be working in Germany and was being tailed by SAS units. The probable intention was an attack on a British Army barracks. The other had been picked up in the routine sweep of Irishmen in the UK. They were to be charged with another incident

"Put on the pressure," said James. "Any IRA, Sinn Fein or sympathisers, get them picked up and charged with spitting on the pavement, parking offences or anything else you can dream up. Anything else useful in the checking of Irish citizens in Britain?" asked James.

"Nothing except digging out the Active Service Unit," was the reply.

"Right, check all alibis again and cross check with the Irish police for IRA connections, especially any family links to the IRA. The Severn bombs must have been done by at least three or more, probably four people. One must have been an explosive expert with access to semtex and detonators, but planting the bombs could have been done by Virgins with no UK records so all the more reason for taking the Micks to bits. Can we just home in on the expert or experts? We've assumed that the job was done by the IRA because nobody else would have the motivation or ordinance. The IRA denies it but they would anyway, because the number killed was embarrassing. The Stickies (The official IRA) are mostly dead or pensioners and when last heard of the INLA were too busy fighting each other to have time for us. If it is anyone Irish, then it would have to be either someone from way back who decided to stage a comeback, or a new boy with Army explosives' training, either British Army or somewhere else."

James Miles sat and pondered and the silence around the table summarised the lack of ideas.

"There were a pair fifteen years ago, names of Reilly and Blondie," he said, after a long pause. "Real nasties. Ordinary IRA but robbed a bank for funds for the Organisation, then pissed off with half a million pounds. There was a buzz from an informer that they nicked two hundred kilos of semtex from the IRA armoury on the way out. They were never heard of again and we assumed they were caught and executed by the IRA and good riddance. It might be worth checking out their details. They predated the computer, so go back to the old manual records. Reilly was sharp and ex SAS and I seem to remember he had a cauliflower ear from boxing. Blondie was thick and survived because he did what Reilly told him to do. He had short blonde hair."

The meeting broke up at 6 p.m. and everyone seemed jaded, except James who was on top of the world and feeling useful again.

The newspapers continued to run the reverberations of the bombs. The Financial Times pointed out that after the two large steelworks in South Wales, the largest industry was the Korean firm Lucky Gold Star and there was heavy Japanese investment with firms such as Panasonic. It reported that the Korean and Japanese Ambassadors had asked to be received by the Prime Minister. At the meeting they forcibly pointed out that their countries' investors in Britain were losing money and that unless communications with South Wales were rapidly restored and firm guarantees given of watertight security in the future, then there would be no further investment by their countries, either in Wales or in the rest of the UK. On television there were, several times a week, interviews with small businessmen and executives from larger companies all agonising about the financial pressures on their businesses resulting from the bombs.

As time went on I began to feel more secure about not getting caught, but knew that for the rest of my life I could never relax about it. Unless there was some forensic evidence which I had left behind, the only danger was if Reilly or Blondie were picked up and then informed on me. They did not strike me as the informing type and there would be no advantage to them if they did so given the nature of the offence.

The images of the police and security forces were badly hit and they gave considerable publicity to some IRA activists who were arrested as a result of the intensive trawl conducted in the search for us. I suspected that this success might have resulted from information given by the Irish Government.

An unfortunate consequence of the bombs was a wave of anti-Irish sentiment in mainland Britain. There were frequent reports of Irish people being beaten up in the East End of London. A gang of fascist skinheads achieved notoriety by hunting for Irishmen at pub closing time. They made the mistake of extending this operation to Kilburn and one of the skinheads was stabbed during a fight with a collection of Irish labourers. An interesting development was the suggestion that the war with the IRA was unwinnable without the most unacceptable limitations on personal freedoms. Like it or not, was the perception, a small ruthless organisation could bring a modern state to its knees if it concentrated on wrecking the economy. In addition, there had to be an expensive menu of packed jails and increased number of police and military.

David Davies was Mayor of Cwmgwrch. He was known locally as either Dai Twice or Dai Do My Best, because this was what he always promised to do for the supplicant even if the case was hopeless. Local Government politics in Wales are ruthlessly conducted and David was more ruthless than most. He had fought his way up as a Councillor by rigid adherence to the party line and only jumped on bandwagons if they were likely to yield publicity and promised success.

His Worship, as he insisted on being addressed, even when in public by his wife, had made the occasional mistake in pursuing his political career. As a very junior councillor he once attended a Council meeting at which it was proposed that a boating lake should be excavated in a local park. Following a recent steep rise in Council Tax, the elected members were flushed with enthusiasm for spending other people's money. They unanimously agreed to put a fountain in the lake. The Chairman of Social Services proposed the erection of a central island linked to the shore by Chinese-style bridges. His brother owned a local building firm and the councillors in the same Masonic Lodge nodded through the amendment, secure in the knowledge that the brother would get the contract. The Chairwoman of Parks proposed that swans should be purchased and, having recently returned from a fact finding trip to Venice, that a gondola should be put on the lake. The young Councillor Davies saw an opportunity for sycophancy. "A marvellous idea, Chairman, and I propose we buy two gondolas and then we can breed from them."

His most recent triumph had been the adoption of his proposal that all Council business should be conducted in Welsh. Ninety five per cent of the population of Cwmgwrch spoke Welsh, so this presented no particular problem save for Colonel Smythe-Wilson who was the sole Conservative councillor and who represented a ward in the only wealthy part of Cwmgwrch. He spoke not a word of Welsh and was forced to sit glaring and disenfranchised whilst Council business was transacted.

Councillor Davies had entered the steelworks when he left school at the age of fifteen and after five years had become a full time union officer. He immediately called a strike which stopped all steel production in Wales and which is still spoken of as a legend in Welsh Trade Union circles. The post of councillor gave him a position of power and patronage in the community with access to generous expenses and the need for frequent free visits to twin towns in Virginia and the French Riviera. He had been a councillor for twenty years and it was now his turn to be Mayor. This post involved even more generous expense allowances with the opportunity to dine out every night and a necessity for much foreign travel in the cause of representing Cwmgwrch.

The invitation to Her Majesty's Garden Party came as a pleasant surprise and he knew that Mrs Do My Best would be gratified. "Inform the press," he pronounced to his secretary on opening the invitation with its impressive Royal Crest. "And tell Ianto Jones that he needs to get the limousine serviced and polished for the trip." Ianto was the mayor's chauffeur and came with the job. Over the next three months, David managed to introduce into each speech (and there were 106 of these) that Her Majesty had invited him to her Garden Party.

On the big day the distinguished couple set off for London in the highly polished stretched Ford Granada limousine. Ianto Jones had been given a new uniform and hat and David had conducted rehearsals with him for opening the car door and bowing to the Mayor and his wife. It was a long journey from Cwmgwrch to London via Ross. The mayoral prostate was becoming increasingly troublesome recently and shortly after Bath he rapped on the division in the car and asked Ianto to stop at the next Service Station. The chauffeur suffered from a similar problem and when they got out of the car, both men galloped off to the toilets followed at a more leisurely speed by Mrs Blodwen Davies. She needed to check that her hairdo, performed that morning by Myfanwy of Myfanwy Coiffeur Des Dames, was still intact.

They returned to the car and Ianto Jones pointed at the front tyre and whispered confidentially to the Mayor, "Ffucking fflat," (in Welsh the single f is pronounced v and the English f sound requires the spelling ff). The chauffeur gloomily reflected that his shining new uniform would be covered in dirt and oil after changing the tyre and he could imagine the contemptuous looks from the other chauffeurs at the Palace. There was nothing to do but get on with it and he jacked the car up. There was a crack as the rusty unused jackleg disintegrated and the car crashed to the floor.

A voice behind Ianto said "Want a hand, mate?" and he saw two workingmen in overalls, who were wearing baseball caps. "We've got a proper jack in the van here and you look as though you're going to a wedding."

"Going to the Queen's Garden Party in Buck House," said Ianto, "and this is His Worship the Mayor of Cwmgwrch and Mrs. Davies."

"Honoured to meet your Worship and Madam," said the older of the two men. "Tell you what, sir, you and your good lady have a nice cup of tea and your driver can wash his hands. By the time you come back we can have the wheel changed and you won't even be late!"

"What a nice man," said Mrs Davies over tea and indeed by the time they returned the punctured wheel was back in the boot. The Mayor insisted on giving them ten pounds which they reluctantly accepted and promised to drink his health with it.

The Garden Party proceeded well and Mrs Davies recognised Dr Floyd, an eminent physician from the local hospital, and flirted shamelessly with the distinguished handsome man. An hour into the event, there was a large explosion in the courtyard of the Palace. People screamed and ran in the opposite direction. The casualty list was five limousines, three chauffeurs and a visiting colonial Bishop. The press was enraged not only at the damage, but at the incompetence of security procedures which allowed a bomb to go off in Buckingham Palace.

The police later reported that the bomb was a typical IRA device from the construction of the timer and the use of semtex. It had been placed in the boot of the car of the Mayor of Cwmgwrch. The police wished to interview two men who they felt could help with their enquiries and who had changed a tyre on the car. The Mayor was unable to give an adequate description of the men who both wore baseball caps so that he could not even describe their hair colour. The police description was of two men of average height, one about forty years old and the other a little younger. The newspapers waxed sarcastic at this and pointed out that the description fitted fifty six Conservative MPs. The police reported that no organisation had claimed responsibility for the bomb, but neither had they for the Severn incident and the police were certain that both bore the hallmark of the IRA.

Eamon read the newspaper accounts of the bomb and formed a firm conclusion that his two acquaintances were responsible. A week later, Detective Sergeant Carpenter apologetically called at Eamon's house and Eamon was able to tell him that his foreman and workmates would confirm that he was at work all day on the day of the most recent explosion.

One evening I was walking home along the usual route from work when a car pulled up alongside me and Blondie emerged from the driving seat. "We need to talk, get in," said Blondie. There was no one I wished to talk to less except Reilly, but if I offended either of them they only had to make a single telephone call to the police giving them my name. I knew that my story would not stand up to prolonged expert interrogation, even if I had managed to fool the local CID. I got into the back and was told to lie face down on the floor. He drove for half an hour and pulled up. I heard doors opening and closing after us when the car drove on for a few metres and I was told to get out. The car was in a large wooden garage and Reilly was sitting on a crate at the other end.

"Nice to see you, Eamon," he said. "Didn't we do a good job?"

"You bastard!" I told him. "You left me twisting in the wind on that roundabout, there was no warning given and you said nothing about the tunnel".

"An operational necessity," he said dismissively. "Anyway, you're not really committed to the Cause."

"What the hell do you want out of me?"

"Not a lot. Just a little help with a final job and this time I promise we'll look after you and we need never meet again."

"No!" I said firmly. "The people who were killed are all on my conscience and I cannot sleep at night for thinking about them."

"You don't have much choice, do you?" said Reilly.

"The police would love to have your name and you couldn't tell them much about me. Anyway, it would be very sad if anything nasty happened to that young lady I hear you have."

I swung a punch at him without considering the consequences and caught him on the nose which started to pour blood. Blondie was standing behind me and gave me an agonising punch in the right kidney causing me to fall to the floor. I felt his heavy boot on my wrist. He looked at Reilly and said, "Will I break both of them or only the one?"

"I don't want him marked," replied Reilly, "but give him another in the back," and I screamed as his boot thudded into my other kidney.

"Now let's have some common sense," Reilly said. "First I personally guarantee that your woman will get a going over which will make what you just got seem like practice. That is unless you give us a hand with this last job. Blondie likes that sort of work, especially with girls. My problem is that our faces are probably all in the police files because we have both been in the British Army. There are only two of us in this Active Service Unit and we need a third with an unknown face. Yours fits beautifully and I'm not sure whether your girl has ever told you, but you have a very innocent manner."

My position was hopeless. If the price of not co-operating with the pair of them was a life sentence at this stage I could probably have accepted it, indeed it almost seemed a way of payment for the deaths I had caused. What I could never take was for any harm to come to Kate. "All right. What do you want me to do?"

"Nothing for the moment, the less you know, the less you can talk but we'll be in touch. Just stay in your job and lead a nice quiet life."

"I'm going back to Ireland in a week to introduce my girl to my parents and then fixed to go home permanently in a month." Reilly told me to let these arrangements stand, but to keep a week's holiday in hand starting on the fifteenth of November, because the job would be done during that week. "Then you can go back to a boring life in Ireland and forget you ever met me," he said.

The blonde man made me lie face down in the car again and dropped me off near work. He was a man of few words but told me that the last man who hit Reilly had rapidly died unpleasantly and I was lucky to be alive and no hard feelings about the kicking. He warned me never to contradict Reilly, especially when he had been drinking when he became extremely aggressive. I got the impression that Blondie was scared of him.

When I got home, I was due to meet Kate for a drink in an hour and I felt an enormous urge to tell her what had happened and to unburden myself. I felt dishonest and underhand at having withheld the truth from her, but terrified that she would reject me if she knew that I was a man responsible for murder. Her instinct would be to go straight to the police in the naive belief that they would help. If she did so I knew I would spend the rest of my life in jail and that she would be beaten or killed by Blondie. He impressed me as the type of man who would relish the thought of my hearing about it in prison. The only practical action for me seemed to be to carry on life in as normal a manner as possible and I was developing into a competent actor.

Three days later, James called a meeting of the ad hoc Security Committee. He got reports that the Irish police were overwhelmed with the British Special Branch enquiries about Irish citizens living in England and their relatives. They were grumbling hard at James, who, with all the cunning developed in a lifetime in the Civil Service, persuaded the Prime Minister to write to the Irish Taoiseach (copy to Chief Constable, Dublin) expressing his gratitude for the enormous help given by the Irish police. There was no news of Reilly or Carrington and to sum it all up, no advance on the last three days since the Committee last met.

Again, James Miles was more cheerful than seemed warranted. "Just keep plugging away and something will turn up," he said cheerfully. He turned to the Home Office man "Could you line me up for a chat with the IRA with Donovan McDonald. The usual rules, neither side leaks about the visit and we both deny it vigorously if the press hear of it. No arrests on our side and no violence on theirs."

"I can fix that via our usual contact," said the Home Office man.

McDonald and James had last met twelve years before. The IRA had captured a Captain from the Royal Green Jackets who made the mistake of going for a drink to a Fermanagh pub. It seemed probable that he had been executed. There was great public anxiety about his fate and the Army and police were combing the Six Counties for the captain, alive or dead. On the confidential line, James had received a telephone call from McDonald telling him the captain was alive, "at present," with the implication that this might be a temporary state of affairs. He then offered to discuss a deal. James had immediately gone to Ireland and met McDonald. The IRA man offered the release of the captain for the repatriation of six Republican prisoners from English jails to serve the rest of their sentences in jails in Ulster. In addition, he required the release without charge of the pregnant wife of a senior IRA man. The IRA and the RUC knew that the woman was not politically active. The British Government of the day depended on the votes of the Unionist MPs to maintain its thin Parliamentary majority. The arrest was popular in Unionist circles as a means of punishing her husband. The only evidence against her were her fingerprints on a revolver which had been found in a black plastic bag in the dustbin of her house during an otherwise unsuccessful police raid.

The woman claimed, and it seemed true, that she hated violence and disapproved of her husband's activities. She had found the weapon hidden in a wardrobe in her house and had thrown it out in the dustbin so that her husband could not use it.

James agreed the exchange. "There is a delicate little problem for me," said McDonald. "Some of our lads are hard men and if they knew we had negotiated the soldier's release, I might end up with some ventilation holes in my head." James promised discretion and the next night the IRA moved the officer to a different room in the house which they used for his prison. He noticed that his captors had forgotten to lock a small window through which he escaped. Neither the man nor his superiors ever realised that his escape had been negotiated. James pointed out to McDonald that he had problems of a similar nature because the Prime Minister at Question Time had reassured the House that HM Government would have no contact with the IRA until it disowned violence. Each side had kept the bargain and formed a grudging respect for each other.

On this occasion, James met McDonald at a large international hotel in Belfast. James had arrived at the hotel by taxi. He had a particular dislike of American hotel chains and this was a prime example.

As the taxi drew up, a tall figure stepped forward in a uniform reminiscent of an officer in the Romanoff Life Guards circa 1860 and wearing a guardsman's busby. The man opened the taxi door and cheerily anticipated a large tip for performing this onerous task. James did not take the hint and merely murmured, "Merci, mon General".

The receptionist was elegantly uniformed with her name on the uniform at the level of the left breast. Unfortunately, the print on the label was small and in order to read it, James had to lean over the counter and peer at the label from a distance of two feet. The lady clearly misinterpreted his interest and she retreated nervously but had been well trained.

"Welcome to the Lariat Inn," she cooed, "how may I help you?"

"I've booked a room for the night, name is Miles." The young woman pecked at a computer keyboard but nothing happened as she summoned a manager who did the same thing with the same result.

"Why don't you plug it in?" James proffered. The girl blushed and did so and after thirty seconds; the name of Mr Smiles appeared on the screen.

"Ah yes, Mr Smiles," the girl said.

"Miles, actually."

"Are you sure?"

James controlled himself. "Reasonably sure," he replied.

"Could I have your credit card please sir?"

"No".

She looked astonished. "But it is company policy to register the card," she said indicating that quoting company policy was an ultimate method of suppressing rebellion.

"And it is my policy never to give anyone my credit card."

"But why?" she cried in amazement.

"Look," responded James, "you want my card in case I run off without paying the bill, meaning you don't trust me. That is fair enough, but neither do I trust the hotel so you cannot have it."

"I see," she said and then clearly remembered the training course when the instructions were to treat awkward customers politely but firmly.

"In that case we cannot give you credit if you use the hotel facilities and if, for example, you use the hotel restaurant then you will need to pay cash."

"Your restaurant food is notorious and I shall be dining elsewhere."

The receptionist handed the room key to James and repeated the American hotel mantra, 'Have a nice day'.

"Thank you, but I have alternative plans," he said and strode to the lift. So far it had been a most satisfying day. An hour later there was a knock on the room door and James answered it. McDonald looked older and greyer than the last time they met, but James acknowledged that he had aged better than himself.

"We heard they eased you out," said McDonald. "I thought of having a party to celebrate. Presumably you want to deal about something and you haven't come to offer the British surrender."

"We've know each other long enough not to play fencing," said James. "I'm speaking with Home Office approval. We have been badly knocked by the Severn bombs and can't get your lads who did it. If you give us a deal of no spectaculars for five years, then I am authorised to offer you a swap. All IRA prisoners in British jails go back to Long Kesh. Indefinite life sentences will be reviewed at ten years instead of the present twenty five. In addition, we take off the present heat from you both, from the Irish Government and ourselves. If there is anything else you want in addition, we are prepared to look at it sympathetically."

McDonald sighed heavily. "Tempting James," he replied. "But you've always been straight with us. I'll do the same. The IRA did not do the Severn job, but I know who did and you can have their names for free."

"Would it be that you never caught Reilly and Carrington and they went freelance with a lot of your money and semtex?"

"That is so. Neither did we do the bomb on the cross channel ferry and the military hospital bomb in Chelsea. I have a strong suspicion that they killed Judge Atkins. Their actions have cost a lot of lives and made us very unpopular. We reckon all three attacks were by that pair of headbangers. The odd thing is that they are active every two or three years, then vanish off the face of the earth although we have certainly looked hard for them."

"I'm sorry that we can't deal," said James. "But what you say makes sense. The way we can play it is that if you hear anything about Reilly and Carrington, no matter how insubstantial, you tell me and I'll give you a contact number and code. In the meantime we will step down the hassle on your Organisation and ask the Irish Government to do the same. The Home Office says that in the present political climate it would be impossible to return your men to Long Kesh or to parole the lifers, but when the uproar has died down, we can slip those things in quietly."

Both men left the meeting and although each had made small gains, they felt it had been worthwhile.

Chapter 8

When Kate and I flew to Ireland she was in a very apprehensive state about meeting my parents in spite of all my attempts to reassure her. As soon as they met, they both kissed her and told her how marvellous I had told them she was. They evidently shared my opinion of Kate and I felt a great sense of relief with at least one problem off my worry list. We went home for tea and I found it difficult to get a word in edgeways into the conversation between Kate and my parents. My father sensed that I felt excluded. "Why don't you go down to the pub and have a chat to all your old friends," he said. "We can get to know Kate better without you interrupting all the time." This seemed rather hard as I had only opened my mouth twice since crossing the door, but it seemed a sensible idea.

I walked down the dark road to the pub and heard someone walking behind me. Something hard pressed into my still tender kidney and a voice said, "I have a gun in your back. Just carry on walking nice and easy or I'll blow a hole in your spine. I am going to come up and walk alongside you, but the gun is under the overcoat on my arm and if you run I will use it." The man was short with a blonde moustache and I had never met him before. "Now walk down to the Strand because I have someone who would like to meet you." We crossed the beach and continued on across the dunes where the footpath passed the derelict lifeboat station which he told me to enter. When I went in there were two men sitting on a windowsill. They were both in their forties and like my captor, seemed at ease and unworried. One of the men on the windowsill never spoke while I was there but the other taller man said, "Nice to see you Eamon, sit down." I did so. The second man was sitting on a coil of pieces of rope. He competently tied my hands and feet and stuffed a rather grubby handkerchief into my mouth so that I could only breathe through my nose.

"You've been causing us trouble Eamon," said the tall man. "But you were very stupid coming back home, although it saved us having to kill you in England. There are three things we could do with you and I don't know the best so perhaps you might care to advise me. I can give you to the Gardai and tell them you did the Severn job. They'll beat the shit out of you to get the names of your friends, then send you to England where you will spend the rest of your life in jail. You'll be a category 'A' prisoner and isolated because all the other prisoners hate bombers and will want to kill you. They always manage to pee into the soup and coffee. The other possibility is to kill you and my only problem is whether you die hard or easy and it's up to you. You can tell us everything and when you have told us what we want to know, you get a quick shot in the back of the head from my friend behind you. The other possibility is that you are unhelpful. Now, just to convince you what I mean by dying slow I can show you." He reached out and pinched my nostrils so that I could not breathe. After thirty seconds, panic set in and I felt I was going to die. There was a roaring in my ears and I lost consciousness. When I came round I heard the tall man say, "The dirty bugger's pissed himself," and, to my shame, realised he was right.

"Now," he said. "We can do that twenty or thirty times and we have plenty of other tricks, so what's your decision? I'll take the handkerchief out and there is no point in shouting because no one will be out on the Point on a winter's night and if you do shout, in goes the handkerchief and we start again."

He cautiously removed the handkerchief and it was an enormous relief to be able to breathe normally.

"Who the hell are you?" I asked him.

"My name is no matter, but we're the Provisional IRA."

"But I helped the IRA," I protested and he roared with laughter.

"You really are a patsy, it's unbelievable. You know the man with the cauliflower ear and the blonde man?"

"Yes Reilly and Blondie," I blabbed, trying to be helpful and terrified that the gag might be replaced.

"Our intelligence people told us that they had visited you after the death of your brother," said my interrogator. "We knew it was not a social call and shortly after, you went to England to work and then the Severn bombs were planted. You do not have to be a genius to put that lot together and spot that you were involved. Reilly is Seamus Reilly, and Blondie is Carl Carrington, as nice a pair of lunatics as you would ever want to meet. They went independent fifteen years ago and took some of our assets. They've been a pain in the arse since then. You'd better tell me what happened from the beginning."

I felt there was little point in lying. I owed nothing to Reilly and Blondie and was terrified at the thought of dying by suffocation plus whatever tortures they had in their, no doubt experienced, repertoire. I summarised how I had been recruited and our actions on the four bridges and the tunnel.

"You really are a fool," the tall man said. "But you

have badly hurt the Organisation. We used to have a fairly safe haven in the Republic but we are now hounded and we've lost good men to the Gardai and the Brits. We are unpopular with Irish people in Britain because they have been getting serious hassle and some of our sympathisers in Sinn Fein have resigned because they think we did the Severn explosions and went too far. I'm surprised that Reilly and Carrington failed to kill you just in case you gave away their description."

I then confessed that they wanted me to do another job in two weeks time but that I had no idea what it was. I told the man of Reilly's threat to Kate and myself so that I had no option but to co-operate.

"Let me think," he said, then seemed to make a decision. "Eamon, you are an honest fool who has wrecked his own life and caused major problems for us. I was going to kill you tonight, but I may be able to make you a deal so that you can get out of this mess and carry on a normal life. At the same time you can do a favour for us. I need to speak to someone about it. Go home and behave normally and speak to nobody about what has happened, especially your girlfriend. We have a reputation to maintain and if you run or tell anyone, I will kill you both. When are you going back to England?" I told him that I should be returning in three days as we both had to go back to work. "Meet me here at seven o'clock in the morning the day after tomorrow," he commanded. "I may have some good news for you."

The lights flashed on the priority line at the Millbank switchboard. This line was used for contacts by subversive organisations, themselves, or for moles within them. When the operator replied an Irish accent said, "This is Carruthers and I want to speak to James Miles about a carpet sale." The operator smiled because the image of Carruthers was that of a Victorian District Commissioner in Africa and whoever bestowed it on an Irishman had a sense of humour. She quickly checked the confidential code lists and read the instruction to put the call through to James Miles immediately wherever he was and not to trace the call.

"Hello James," said the man. "I have a lead on a man with a cauliflower ear and a blonde fella. We can probably plant someone on them, but the man was involved previously in a project that you've been interested in involving bridges. If he finds our contacts for us would he get immunity?"

"I would have to clear it with Sir Tufton," James said. "But he is so bloody desperate I'm sure he will say yes. Let's assume he will and I will come and meet you in the same place as last time at seven o'clock this evening."

After putting the receiver down he asked the switchboard to connect him to the Secretary of State for Northern Ireland. The Secretary of State was a kindly, well-intentioned man, universally known as Sir Tufton Bufton, although that was not his name. He had attracted this nickname because he was a product of Eton, Cambridge and the Guards and had a braying upper class English accent. For the IRA his voice symbolised English oppression and for everyone else, made it difficult to take seriously anything he said. The Secretary of State told James that he would approve any decision necessary to track down the Severn bombers, even if the price was for one to go free.

The rest of my stay at home passed in a haze of worry. My parents seemed to sense this and assumed that I was having second thoughts about marrying Kate. This induced panic since they felt she would be an ideal wife and I felt trapped and guilty being unable to confide my problems in anyone.

Two days later after meeting Reilly, I told my parents that I would be getting up early to go for a walk before breakfast. On the way to the lifeboat station, I spotted one of the three men I had met earlier. He was standing in the sand dunes looking at me through a pair of binoculars and making sure that I was not being followed. The other two men were in the old building together with a grey haired man wearing a quality of suit never before seen in Drumundra.

"The plot has thickened since we last met," said my earlier inquisitor. "This man," and he nodded at the man in the suit, "represents the British Government and you can call him James. The IRA and the British Government want Reilly and Carrington preferably dead or safe in a high security jail. The IRA wants the present heat taken off it by the Irish and British Governments. If we can give them Reilly and Carrington, they will take the pressure off. The British and the Irish are stuck into this war and no matter what we think, we are both deadlocked and both want a solution. The British are willing to get out of the Six Counties. They reckon that if Reilley and Carrington are jailed or killed, then the INLA can be blamed for the Severn affair and in practice, we know that they are a spent force. The British Government will announce that the IRA were not involved and have been co-operative in tracking down our friends who they perceive are mad dogs. The IRA will express sympathy for the dead, bereaved and wounded and as a gesture of goodwill, will announce a cease-fire. After an interval the British Government will state that peace talks will be held with the IRA. The Loyalists will no doubt start marching and killing people but the IRA will co-operate by not responding and will give its list of Loyalists killers to MI5 and the Government will respond vigorously to any Loyalist violence in a way in which they have not done in the past. After a further interval, the British and Irish Governments will issue a joint statement that the Six Counties will be incorporated into the Irish Free State. We think that the United Nations would jump at the chance of supervising the changes and concessions will be made by the twenty Six counties to harmonise the two legal systems on things like divorce."

I listened to this with increasing bewilderment.

"There has been no news of any of this in the papers," I told him.

"Nor will there be," said the man introduced as James. "It was all proposed at a Cabinet meeting yesterday afternoon and I was sent to put it to the IRA. We've communicated with the Taoiseach and the American President and have their full support. The crux of the problem is that there must be no violence and the only way we can underwrite that is by nailing Reilly and Blondie."

"That's fine," I said weakly. "But what about me while the problems of the rest of the world are being solved?"

"If you give us these two, we forget you ever existed," James said.

"You may, but they won't. They will know that the only person who could have informed on them was me and even if they are in jail, they can send some fellow lunatics from the INLA or someone like that so that my problem would be prolonged rather than solved."

James Miles looked rather shifty. "I hoped you would not have spotted that one, but put it this way, they are likely to be armed and it will be justifiable to shoot them. If they are not, we use the Gibraltar solution and those arresting them will form the impression that they are armed and will shoot them anyway in self-protection. We have used that solution before and no doubt will again."

"Never thought I would hear a Brit admit that," murmured Seamus.

"Off the record, remember," Miles said. "But judges and juries can behave unpredictably. Juries are very cautious about convicting nowadays after we made a few mistakes like the Birmingham Six."

It seemed that this unpleasant contract was the only escape for me without getting myself jailed or Kate and myself killed and I agreed to go along with it. James Miles wanted the time and place of the next action as soon as possible and the IRA man who said his name was McDonald gave me a telephone number which would be constantly manned so that I could report back through him.

James Miles looked pensive as he got ready to leave. "It seems a very one-sided bargain," James said. "I can get the Gardai to lift this lad and produce a sacrifice for the great British public. If I don't, all you are offering me is a remote chance that we can lay our hands on our two friends. Tufton would have my neck if I went back with a bargain like that."

"There is a little icing on the cake," McDonald said. "I keep giving you a list of things that the IRA never did, so here is another - The Duchess. The Orangemen did it to unite their troops and get the British public behind them. It was the RHC. We interviewed one of them at length, a most helpful man. There are only ten of them, strictly speaking, only nine now. We picked up a Prod at random in retaliation for them killing one of our men. He knew he was going to die and offered a deal, a list of RHC members if we let him go. He was desperate and very stupid. We had no idea he was active and he was just going to get the shot in the head. We put on a little pressure and he was resistant at first, but at the end he was singing like a canary and gave us the names and addresses of the members and told us that they did the Duchess job. They meet every Thursday at 1 o'clock in a room above Griffiths Ale House off the Shankill. If you raid it you can pick them all up and they store their guns there too."

"If we get the RHC lot we have a bargain," said James.

The telephone call from Reilly, came just as I was leaving for work. The landlady looked rather displeased at being roused so early as she shouted that there was someone on the telephone.

"It's your old friend," said the voice of Reilly. "I'll pick you up outside work at four o'clock today." He rang off before I could reply.

That day at work I was pre-occupied and forgetful and the foreman made a few coarse suggestions about my love life. It was beginning to get dark as I walked away from the site and saw Reilly's bulky figure standing in a doorway. He told me to walk around the corner and get into the front seat of the car which was parked there. He got into the driver's seat of a shabby Fiat and as I sat down a voice said, "Now Eamon, I have a gun at your back so don't do anything silly," and I realised that the blonde man was sitting in the back seat. We drove North towards London and then headed West on the M4 towards Wiltshire.

"Look I'm expected back at my lodgings tonight and I have a date. The last thing in the world I want to do is to go missing because a missing Irishman in the present climate will really stick out."

"Just shut up and let us do the worrying," said Blondie. "And if you don't, I'll give you a belt with this gun."

We drove on in silence, eventually off the motorway down narrow country lanes and finally up a long drive lined by poplar trees.

"Now out, and nothing funny or your dead," Reilly commanded and Blondie opened the door of an old farmhouse and put the light on. They told me to sit down and drew the curtains. Reilly poured himself an inch of Scotch whiskey from a bottle on the table and drunk it in two large sips and then poured himself another.

"What do you want me to do?" As I asked Reilly the question, I dreaded the reply because it was nothing I wished to be part of.

"Well Eamon, after our last little chat I'm sure you were very keen to help us. But just in case you had second thoughts or decided to grass on us, it seemed a good idea if we lifted you so you are going to stay here until the job is finished."

"Look, if I am not home tonight, my girlfriend will be round at the police station tomorrow. They'll be buzzing like flies at the thought of a missing Irishman. She'll give them a full description and the police will take a long careful look at my background. They have no other clues about the Severn job and in a few days, every policeman in Britain will be looking for me."

"That was something we thought of, Eamon," he said, and he took a pen from the pocket of his jacket. "Now address this to the young lady and Blondie here will take it to the main post office in the town so that it catches the last post."

"Sure and will I say, 'being held by IRA gunmen, so please don't worry'?"

"Now Blondie is not like myself and likes a bit of action, so don't be cheeky again or you'll get a good going over. First address the card and I've even donated a first class stamp." There was no future in disobeying him so I did as he said.

"Just write what I say. 'Dear whatever her name is. I am very sorry but I cannot go through with the wedding. I am sorry to hurt you but it is better to tell you now rather than later – Eamon.'"

I looked at Reilly in horror. "I can't do that it will destroy the poor girl."

"You can and you will!" and I felt an agonising pain in my right ear as Blondie, who was standing behind me, stubbed his cigarette on it. I screamed but did not move knowing that he still had the gun in his other hand.

"Remember what I told you," said Reilly. "You lose the girl anyway if you do not help us because we kill you. After all this is over, you can spin her a yarn about pre-wedding nerves or tell her the truth if you want to and then you can kiss and make up."

I realised that there was no choice and wrote the words which he dictated again, feeling terrible at the thought of Kate reading it probably after the postman, and anyone in her family who picked up the postcard after it came through the letter box.

"Show the gentleman to his suite Blondie," and Blondie opened a door off the kitchen into a large room which looked like an old storeroom and had a single slit-like window.

"Put your feet up for an hour," he said, "and I can go and post the card and then we can all have something to eat."

I heard a bolt slide on the kitchen side of the door. The room contained a sink, a bed and a chair. There was a shower and lavatory in a small cupboard-like extension but the window was tiny and there was no way of escape. I lay on the bed feeling frightened and utterly depressed at what I had just done but could see no other alternative.

After about an hour there was the sound of a car door banging and ten minutes later a tantalising smell of fried bacon. The door opened and Blondie shouted that I should come out and have dinner.

"It's very difficult if I have to keep pointing a gun at you so let's get the rules straight. If you try to escape I will shoot you with the intention of hurting and not killing you. The killing will come later - much later. You stay in the kitchen or your room when we are here and if we go out, we lock you in your room - understand?" I nodded, knowing that even if I did escape there was nowhere in Britain where I could run. I doubted if the IRA would believe a story that I had been kidnapped and escaped and even if they did, there was no reason why they should help me as I would just be a liability.

Reilly told me that he would give me the details of the planned project when it was necessary and that meanwhile, we would be doing rehearsals for a few days. He said that he had rented the farmhouse through an estate agent who was grateful for the letting since the property had been on the market for over a year, having been neglected by the owner who died after ten years of living as a recluse. The solicitors administering the estate wanted to sell, but were happy to settle for a three-month rental to pay some of the costs incurred in keeping the buildings in repair. Reilly had told the agent that he had owned a dress factory in Hong Kong for twenty years and was now returning to England because the Colony had reverted to Chinese rule. He had sold the business for a handsome sum and needed a base in central England so that he could look around for a suitable business to buy as an investment. The estate agent accepted the story as fact and had recently spent a holiday in Hong Kong so spent a long time talking about his impression of it. This presented no problem since Reilly told me that he had been stationed there with the British Army before he left it eight years ago. He paid the agent three months rental in advance in cash and hinted that he might purchase the farm if he liked the area and found a suitable business nearby to purchase. He told the agent that he had always wanted to keep a few horses and could he recommend anyone who would sell him a large horsebox. The agent was able to give him the names of a local truck dealer in a nearby town who was in the same Masonic Lodge.

"What the hell do you need a horsebox for?" I asked him.

"Well we're going to go in with the cavalry," said Reilly sarcastically. "You just wait and everything will become clear and no more questions." As our conversation took place, Reilly frequently refilled his glass with neat whiskey and his manner became increasingly aggressive as the drink got to him.

Surprisingly, that night I slept. They obviously did not trust me because I heard the door bolted from the outside as I got into bed.

The next morning the smell of bacon again filtered under the door and much as I like bacon, it seemed likely that the diet was to become monotonous. At breakfast the two seemed in high spirits. "Now Eamon," Reilly said. "You're a single man and used to fending for yourself. There's no point in looking sideways at the food because you are elected cook from now on. It'll give you something to do so you have no time for dirty thoughts. If you make a list of what you need, I can get it at the supermarket this morning."

After breakfast Reilly went off and left me with Blondie whose conversation was minimal. He spent the morning fiddling with the engine of a small white Mini-Cooper in the yard. I felt bored and washed up the dishes and cleaned the kitchen. After that I made the bed in my room and to fill in the time, decided to sweep the dust off the stone flagged bedroom floor.

After two hours, Reilly returned carrying shopping and newspapers. Blondie settled down with 'The Sun' and spent a long time gazing at a young lady with magnificent attributes on page three, who expressed an interest in a modelling career and claimed that she loved animals, so Blondie could have been a suitable lover. I carefully read 'The Independent' where there were articles about the Severn incident; one in the financial section discussed the fall in the Footse Index, resulting from the damage to the UK economy caused by the bombs. It stated that earlier estimates of the damage had been optimistic and in fact the British economy would actually shrink during the next year. The other column reported that two men, who were believed to be members of an IRA active service unit, would appear in a special magistrate's court at Doncaster where they would be charged with terrorist offences. They had been apprehended, stated the article, as a result of routine stopping and checking of vehicles which had been stepped up after the Severn operation.

After our lunch of fresh bread and cheese, Reilly announced that they were going out for the afternoon to transact a little business. I was bolted into the bedroom and heard the Mini-Cooper drive off with its characteristic raspy exhaust note. I had no wish to escape and nowhere to go, but wanted to know what they intended to do for the next attack.

When I swept out the room that morning I had noticed that one of the flagstones in the floor had a ring in it and a recessed edge. It looked like the entrance of the sort of cellar in which potatoes for the winter were stored in Ireland and seemed worth exploring. I raised the metal handle to the vertical position, but the slab had probably not been lifted for decades and it was impossible to shift it. One of my teachers once told me that Archimedes had said, "Give me a lever and I can move the world," and I wished I had access to an iron bar or a jemmy. Looking desperately around the room I realised that the broom was still in the bedroom because I had forgotten to put it back in the kitchen after sweeping the floor that morning. I put the handle under the metal ring and lifted hard on the other end. I am a powerful man and thought the handle was likely to snap and although it bent, the flagstone lifted a fraction and then suddenly gave way exposing a cellar underneath which was about two metres deep. There were no steps, but it was easy to lower myself into the cellar which was poorly lit by the light from my bedroom above. There were a few old potato sacks in the corner but no other exit and finding the cellar had been of no help. I sat on the stone floor of the cellar for a minute or two to get my breath back and as my vision accommodated to the dim light, I saw another source of light in the cellar ceiling. I walked towards it and found a grill in the ceiling which was partly blocked by weeds and dirt. Lifting myself back into the bedroom, I passed the bedroom chair down into the cellar. By standing on the chair I could get my shoulder under the grill and with my knees bent, I strained up and lifted the grill upwards. When I cautiously looked out I was in the farmyard and climbed out through the grill. I went through the unlocked front door into the kitchen. There were four doors leading off this, one led into my bedroom and another to a bathroom and lavatory. The other two were identical small bedrooms each containing a chest of drawers and a bed. A quick search of the drawers revealed no papers or documents but in one of the lower drawers were two well oiled revolvers with ammunition. I wiped the revolver with my handkerchief after handling them because if my fingerprints were ever found on the guns by the police, I would be even deeper in the shit than I was at present. It was clear to me that my two colleagues were men accustomed to travelling light who survived by cultivating a sense of paranoia.

In one of the bedrooms on the chest of drawers, there was a telephone. Finding it did not help me because there was no one from whom I could seek help. By the side of the telephone were a biro and The Independent newspaper which I had read the day before. On the top of the newspaper Reilly or Blondie had written HBG 9039282157941. The initials and numbers meant nothing to me but using the biro I wrote them on the sole of my left foot and then put the sock and shoe back on. It seemed possible that the letters and numbers were a code for a bank account or a safe deposit box.

There seemed no further information I could gather and I retraced my steps. After replacing the flagstone in the bedroom I used the brush to sweep dust into the recesses at its edges so that it was difficult to tell that the stone had been disturbed.

The RHC meeting was a solemn affair. The death of the Duchess had produced a profound reaction in Ulster, Britain and America. Internment without trial was introduced immediately and four hundred members of the IRA and Sinn Fein were incarcerated. The severe security restrictions in the province made life intolerable with no nightlife because every one was frightened to go out. The RHC members were in a mood resembling that of a young boy who has started a small fire in a derelict mansion and then found that the whole building was ablaze. They agreed that they had inflicted a mortal wound on the Nationalists who had lost all sympathy with reasonable people. It was decided not to meet for a month until the uproar had died down.

The noise of the splintering front door of the pub was followed by the sound of running heavy boots on the stairs. Two occupants of the room managed to withdraw loaded pistols from the cupboard where the guns were stored. The SAS threw stun grenades into the room before entering. As they came through the door, they saw two men with weapons who tried to put them down when they realised their assailants were British Army and not the IRA. The Paras shot them all in the manner in which they were trained.

Subsequent ballistic examination of the sniper's rifle found in the armaments cupboard confirmed it was the gun used to kill the Duchess.

Chapter 9

DC Maureen Smith was a plain ambitious woman who operated at the lowest level in the pecking order at Special Branch which she had joined because it sounded glamorous and would look good in her CV as she pursued her ambition to be the Commissioner of Metropolitan Police. So far her duties had largely consisted of taking in cups of tea and biscuits to meetings of senior male police officers who stopped talking when she entered the room. To be fair, they did sometimes make supportive and helpful comments such as 'not bloody rich tea biscuits again' and on one occasion, 'I hope this hair in my tea is from your head'. The latter comment caused her to flee, pursued by coarse male laughter. Apart from the tea and biscuits, her other duties seemed mundane and secretarial and consisted of faxing long lists of names and addresses of Irish residents in Britain to her opposite number in Dublin. After seven to ten days the names would be returned, usually marked 'no relevant records this person or family'. Occasionally, the name had a record of IRA political activity either personally or in the family and

Maureen would then pass the information on to more experienced and male policemen who would re-interview the person involved or re-check their alibi. At her level, she never heard whether anything useful resulted but presumably it had not because the dreary process continued and there were no reports of arrests in the newspapers.

The day after she had been embarrassed by the senior officer, she sat in the canteen drinking watery tea and indulging herself in a packet of fattening crisps. Her sergeant, Dave Fisher, came in and sat opposite her. "Sorry about that remark yesterday Maureen" he said. "It was over the top and the man is a bully." The sergeant was a kindly man and Maureen was grateful for his remark.

"So what do you think of Special Branch?"

"Well frankly, I though it would be more exciting."

"Any joy in Dublin with that list of names yet?"

"I don't know, no-one ever tells me, but we did have an interesting one in today. Young chap in Hastings, record pure as snow, he had a brother in the IRA who was killed by the Paras and the sister committed suicide a few weeks later. I'm going to put it back into the pool for someone to sort out."

"Maureen," the sergeant said. "Special Branch is a test bed for fliers and you have to make your own luck. Tell you what, just to convince you that not all men are bastards, I'll give you some advice. Dublin could not have had any information about this lad's sister so they must have got it from the local police. Why don't you telephone them, the name of the town will be in the details of the brother who was killed, and ask for some background?"

Maureen was bored and it seemed rude to ignore the advice, even though she felt it unlikely to lead anywhere. She dialled the number for the Drumundra police station and introduced herself. "Special Branch," said the desk sergeant respectfully. "I doubt if it was about yesterday's sensation here about someone caught parking on double yellow lines." Maureen explained that she was enquiring about the death of a girl called Maureen Gallagher.

"Ah, the poor child. You know more about that than we do because she killed herself after you interrogated her. God help her, and them such a lovely family."

Maureen replaced the receiver with a sense of embarrassment mixed with excitement. She entered the computer and checked out details of the arrest of Mora Gallagher. She had been picked up at random because of her relation to her brother Desmond and, reading between the lines, it was what was called in the trade a 'lucky dip', in the hope that something might turn up if she was interrogated. There was nothing against her, although it had taken ten days to find that out.

Maureen ran into Fisher's office bursting with the information. "Sarge, looking at this lot it sounds as though Eamon Gallagher had a right to be angry and if he moved to England after all this happened it would have been because he was recruited into the IRA."

"Maureen," the sergeant said. "Remember me when you enter into your kingdom. I'll pass it upstairs and tell them who spotted it."

The next piece of the jigsaw came from a retired police inspector from the Branch. He spotted a man who he thought was probably Reilly at a filling station on the M4. The man reporting this had been retired for ten years. He recognised Reilly by spotting the cauliflower ear when he took his hat off to get into a small car. He had no wish to confront Reilly who might have been armed, but he noted that the car was a Mini-Cooper and recorded the registration number. Mini-Coopers are now rare cars and since they are usually driven by lunatics who crash them at speed few have survived.

An all stations alert went out for the car, with instructions not to attempt to arrest the occupants since they were likely to be armed. The DVLC records gave the name of the last owner. He was shaken when a police loudhailer outside his house woke the man at 4 a.m. with an announcement that his house was surrounded by armed police and he should come out with his hands up. He told the police that he had sold the car the previous week to a man calling himself Frederick Jones who paid cash and yes, the man did have a cauliflower ear.

Miles arranged to re-interview Gallagher with the CID officer who had obtained the original statement during the routine check. They went to Eamon's lodgings at 7 a.m. on the general principle that surprise was a useful tool in interrogation. The landlady reported that Eamon had vanished a few days before, leaving all his possessions. She was not too worried because she described him as a steady lad who always paid the rent a month in advance. James enquired whether there was anyone who might know his whereabouts. The landlady told them that he had a fiancée. She did not have her address, but the local Catholic Church would because they were both regular attenders.

"Would you mind if we had a quick look at his room?" asked the CID man, and the landlady looked doubtful. "He's in no trouble, but we are worried he might have been injured," lied the policeman, "and it would be helpful if we had some clue where to look for him." The landlady accepted this pathetic line of reasoning and the team trooped up and checked the room but found nothing, save for a few letters from his mother and a picture of a pretty fiancée. They agreed to check on her.

James found Kate a helpful and attractive, but bewildered young woman. She had evidently been crying and told them that Eamon seemed to have got cold feet at the engagement and had sent a postcard breaking it off. When James gently asked her if this was a surprise she told them that she was unable to believe it. The postcard had been written in Eamon's very characteristic handwriting. "Only the evening before we talked about names for the children we would have," and she burst into tears.

"Do you have the postcard?" persisted James.

"No. I was so upset, I burnt it."

"And was there a postmark?"

"I was so upset I never looked."

"Was there anything unusual about the postcard?

Kate seemed surprised at his perception in asking the question. "Yes, there was something very odd. He signed himself Eamon and I never called him that. I called him Ted because he looked like a big old teddy bear," and she began to cry again.

James pondered. This was odd as was his observation that Eamon had vanished whilst wearing his working clothes of T-shirt, trainers and jeans. "Look Miss," he said, "we are not sure where Eamon is or why he has vanished. If you hear from him, day or night, here's my telephone number and just get in touch with me."

On the drive back, James began to form an impression that Eamon was a virgin terrorist who might have been used by Reilly and his assistant. They had probably kidnapped him to kill him as a potential informer, but it was always possible that they were planning another job. The Mini-Cooper was a useful lead and would be difficult to hide.

That evening I heard the car returning with the sound of another larger vehicle accompanied by much door slamming and Blondie, being exhorted to lift the other end and be careful. Half an hour later I was released to cook dinner. They seemed to be excited and Reilly drank heavily from a bottle of whiskey at the kitchen table. I was not offered any.

The next morning they took me out in the yard. The Mini-Cooper had been joined by a dark blue Vauxhall Astra and a large horsebox with a 'CAUTION HORSES' sign at the rear.

"Now we're going to practice your driving skills Eamon," Reilly said. The yard was quite large and he told me that we would be using the yard and the part of the lane leading up to it.

"We will start slow and speed it up, just like you do with that girlfriend of yours," said Blondie. I knew he was trying to provoke me to take a swing at him, but it would have done no good and he would have welcomed the opportunity to give me a hiding to show who was boss. I resisted the temptation.

He positioned the horsebox half way down the yard and told me to practice driving the Vauxhall up and down the lane so that I got accustomed to the controls and after doing this, I should park thirty metres behind the horsebox. Reilly and Blondie then opened the rear door of the box and let down the ramp from the interior to the ground, down which the horse would normally exit. Inside the horsebox was the Mini-Cooper with its rear facing out to the ramp. Blondie slowly backed the small car down the ramp and onto the ground so that it finished up two metres in front of the Vauxhall which I was driving. He then drove it back up into the box and folded up the ramp, closed the rear gate and put a padlock on it and locked it. We repeated the manoeuvre at least twenty times so that it gradually became more practised. On one occasion he stalled the Cooper resulting in a lot of bad language.

Over the next three days we repeated the procedure until it became almost a reflex and they could get the back open, the ramp down and have the car on the floor and back where we started in one and a half minutes.

It was difficult to work out what they were seeking to achieve but on the evening of the third day, Reilly got out a sheet of blank paper and a biro. "You need to know what we are up to if you are going to be of any use Eamon," he said. He drew a large square. This square is the one we attack. At each corner of the square is an exit road. Along the right hand vertical border of the square he hatched in a rectangle and said that this was the main target. Finally in the top left-hand corner he put a cross and told me that these represented traffic lights with a filter sign for traffic going to the left.

"Here is what we do. The Square has heavy surveillance with police and cameras so we have to be slick. You follow the horsebox into the square and we enter from the road on the bottom right corner, keeping thirty metres behind and making sure that no one squeezes in between us. Half way round the left side of the square, I pull up to the kerb and you stop twenty metres behind me. Nobody ever suspects a horsebox and anyone behind will assume I stopped because of trouble with the horses. I then leap out and put the ramp down just as we did in practice and the Cooper is moved down to the ground. I then replace the ramp and back door and padlock it and we both shoot off in the car, - but us first remember."

"So what is the target?" I asked.

"The Houses of Parliament," came the reply. "We are aiming for a Guy Fawkes job except we're going to succeed and not get caught! There will be two drums of semtex left in the horsebox."

I started to sweat as the simplicity of the plan sunk in. The bomb would be about one hundred and fifty metres from the Houses of Parliament, but Reilly was a munitions' expert and was presumably using a very large charge. The bomb would cause enormous damage to the other buildings around the Square, particularly Westminster Abbey, which was the symbolic centre of Anglican Christianity. At any time Parliament Square was packed with tourists and ordinary Londoners and the casualties would be in hundreds.

My face must have shown what I was feeling.

"Cheer up you miserable bastard," said Blondie. "Not many people have the opportunity to influence world events. If you're caught you will be famous and if we get away, you will never meet us again. Reilly and myself have been careful and lucky and after this, it's retirement for us. After Severn and Parliament, the Brits will give up and abandon the Six Counties because the voters will call a halt."

He then went over the get away plan which was for us to head immediately left from the top left corner of the Square down to Buckingham Palace and then to Hyde Park Corner where we would abandon the vehicles and catch an Underground train. The bomb would be set with the detonator timed to go off two minutes after we had left Parliament Square and on a preliminary run, two minutes had been enough time to get to the Hyde Park Corner roundabout. Experience in the North of Ireland was that when a bomb went off nearby people stopped their cars and got out. We would do the same and then walk slowly to the Underground. Blondie warned me to avoid any connection involving the Circle Line because this ran at a shallow level beneath Parliament Square and would either be damaged or closed on safety grounds. The acting ability to walk slowly after committing such a horrendous crime seemed likely to exceed my limited thespian talents. I began to get depressed as the other two became more elated at the prospect of the mayhem which would result from the bomb. I told them that I felt tired and wanted an early night.

Reilly's whiskey consumption continued at an impressive level. By the time I left them his speech was slurred and he occasionally muttered as though having an argument with himself.

It was impossible to get to sleep. I was trapped in a scenario with no possible exit and dreaded living with myself after being part of another massacre of innocent people. Even if I got away I could never ask Kate to marry such a monster and was glad that the decision had been made for me about the postcard calling off our marriage. Desperation concentrates the mind. Reilly had told me that they had left the IRA with half a million pounds and two hundred kilograms of semtex. The Severn bombs had used about twelve-kg so presumably if they used up the lot as a retirement bonus, the Westminster bomb would be enormous. My knowledge of explosives was slight, but my experience at the Severn Bridges told me that they would need detonators and the germ of an idea began to form.

The next day we did not do any further rehearsals. Blondie seemed to be a petrol-head and spent the morning under the bonnet of the Cooper which had been confined to the farmyard for the last three days. I thought motoring was probably the only subject we could discuss without argument. "So what did they do to this engine that made it so different to the basic Morris Minor Series A engine?" I asked him. This profound remark exhausted my motoring knowledge but it produced an extremely boring and lengthy response. He told me that the electrics on the engine were too low down so that it was easy to flood them in the wet.

"So where exactly are the electrics?" I requested with the air of a student seeking knowledge from a guru.

"Down here," he said and leaned into the nether regions of the bonnet. As his head disappeared I looked around for the source of his tools and saw an open toolbox beneath the nearside of the car and leant over to watch the master demonstrating the problem. After another ten minutes of excruciating conversation I managed to extricate myself and went back to my bedroom.

That evening Reilly went through the plan again and ensured that we were all certain of our roles. He then told me that the action was to be on the following day. In a matter of fact voice he told me, "In case you get all soft-hearted and ethical and decide to shout a warning before scooting off in your car, I will shoot you myself." I felt that my companions were so callous about other people that they were both probably mad.

We all went to our rooms at ten thirty after watching the evening news on the television. It made no mention of anything which interested the others, except that the next day there would be a debate on the manner in which the

Government had dealt with the effects of the Severn bombings.

On previous nights I had often heard footsteps outside at irregular intervals and surmised that Reilly and Blondie patrolled the surroundings of the farmhouse to check that nobody was interested in their activities. Around 1 a.m. I heard footsteps outside the narrow window of my room. Twenty minutes later, with my ear pressed to the bolted bedroom door, the farmhouse door opened and closed followed by the door of one of the bedrooms.

I had left the broom in the bedroom and quickly lifted the flagstone. This time it came up more easily. I quietly lowered the chair onto the cellar floor using it to stand on while I lifted the grill slowly so that there was no noise. It was a dark windy night with half a moon. The small toolbox was easily retrieved from beneath the car.

I reasoned that the explosives could not be kept in the horsebox because the rear had been open during the day and the interior was empty. The farmyard was surrounded by an empty open barn and two stables with half doors. I started by looking in the first stable and got into it by unlocking the lower half of the door. It contained only some ancient straw so I re-bolted the door and turned to investigate the second box. As I did so there were a gust of wind and the door of the first box flung open with a bang against the wall which would have woken a dead man.

My two friends were light sleepers and within a few seconds, in rapid succession, the lights went on in their bedrooms. Through the window I could see Blondie crossing the kitchen and checking that the bolt was still in place on my bedroom door. He then ran to the window and peered out into the yard. Although the night was dark, the light from the bedroom window completely changed the situation. I realised that in an attempt not to make a noise, the bolt on the lower half of the stable door had not been fully pushed home and the wind had flung it open. I dived into the empty stable just as the farmhouse door opened and the two men came into the yard. I realised that this only postponed discovery by a few seconds.

In desperation I looked up and rapidly jumped for the rafters in the stable roof and pulled myself up trying to quiet my panting breath. A torchlight shone round the yard as the lower half of the stable door banged open in the opposite direction with a further gust of wind. The face of Blondie appeared with a torch in his left hand and a gun in the right. He shone the torch carefully around the stable.

"Bloody wind," he said and shut and bolted the door. "Now cover me with your gun and I can check the barn and the other stable." I heard them cautiously moving about and then opening the door of the other stall. "Nothing here," said Reilly. "Will we go and check on Eamon?"

"I already did and the bolt is as tight as an Orangeman's smile - we can leave him to his beauty sleep."

My situation seemed desperate. There were no windows in the stable which relied for light on opening the top half of the door. The only possible way of getting out was through the roof. My position perched on the rafter was uncomfortable and the box of small tools was pressing uncomfortably into my hip so I took it out. The roof was a standard fairly steep V shape and clearly any attempt to remove a slate would make a noise. I waited thirty minutes for things to settle down. Using pliers I pressed hard on one of the slates in the side of the roof facing away from the farmhouse. Any hole in the roof on that side would not be visible from the courtyard or house and any noise would be partly masked. The slate gave way with a crack and using the handle of the pliers, I split the slate into two and slid the pieces out. Once one slate was out it became easier to remove others and the hole in the roof gradually enlarged and became big enough for me to slide out onto the roof. I dropped down into a field and approached the other stable by crossing through the open barn into the courtyard.

Very carefully I slipped the bolt on the stable door and on this occasion fixed it firmly open with a large stone to prevent it flapping. I entered the barn ducking under the closed top section of the door. My eyesight, by this time, was well accustomed to the dim light and there were two large unsealed sacks containing a white powder which I assumed to be semtex. It was barely possible to lift the sacks because of their weight. In a corner of the stall was a device with a clock and a control and with two switches marked M and H. Wires from the clock led to a metal case which I assumed was the detonator. The wires leading to the case were sheathed in red plastic and each wire entered it through a metal tunnel traversed by a brass screw for securing the wire in place just like a household electrical plug. With a little difficulty I could unscrew these with my fingers, so releasing the wires. I peeled the end of the plastic off the wires using the pliers so that about a centimetre of wire extended beyond the end of the sheathing. By taking one strand at a time and giving a hard pull, it was possible to snap the wire so that it came off a few centimetres up the plastic sheath and could then be pulled out with the pliers. After some trimming it was then possible to replace the ends of the plastic beneath the retaining screws so that they did not contain wire and there was no electrical connection. Finally, I carefully tidied up the cut ends of wire and plastic and re-bolted the stable door. I had considerable respect for Blondie's paranoid personality and replaced the toolbox beside the Mini-Cooper.

The journey back to my room was uneventful but I felt completely exhausted and to my horror saw that the time was 5 a.m. I fell into a deep sleep and was roused by the rattle of the bolt of the bedroom door at 7 a.m. Reilly looked in cheerfully and said I looked as though I'd had a good night's sleep. "I hardly slept at all," I told him, "with that wind and some silly bugger must have left a door unlocked, because you could hear it banging in the wind until one of you got up and shut it."

After breakfast Reilly issued me with a bucket of water, a scrubbing brush, a nail brush and a pair of gloves. He told me that my room and the kitchen would be covered with my fingerprints and I was to remove them; it being in my interest to do a good job. After that I was to do the same to the Vauxhall and the other two would do their own rooms and the other vehicles. He told me to keep the gloves on until I walked away from the car in Hyde Park Square.

The whole process took about two hours and by 10 a.m. we were ready to leave. After a quick final inspection of the premises, Reilly pronounced himself satisfied. The Mini Cooper was no longer in the yard and it and the explosives had evidently been loaded while I was still snoring after the night's exertions. An elegant authentic touch was given by pieces of straw protruding between the hinges of the lower part of the rear door of the horsebox.

"Just follow me gently to London," Reilly told me. "By the time we get there you'll probably be pissing yourself anyway, so just in case, we will stop at the Service Station on the M4."

"Could we not stop at the Services on the London side of Heathrow Airport, it would be an hour later?"

"No. It is well known that anyone who successfully smuggles drugs into the country through Heathrow always stops at the next Service Station to London and hands over the drugs for the big men to distribute. There is always an undercover police unit at that services so you will just have to hold your water until afterwards."

The maximum speed of the horsebox seemed to be about fifty five mph, but they seemed in no hurry and Reilly told me that the House of Commons did not commence sitting until 1400 hours. At the Service Station my companions were silent and my hands were shaking so much that it was almost impossible for me to hold a cup of tea. Every time we passed a police car on the way into

London, I broke into a cold sweat. At one time a police car going fast with lights flashing appeared in the rear outside lane and I went weak with terror but it merely streaked past and was on some other business.

The horsebox drew no attention as it drove through West London and the normally ruthless local drivers seemed to treat it with more consideration than a conventional vehicle. This was presumably in the belief that it contained horses which deserved more careful treatment than did human beings. We drove up along the Embankment and past the Albert Bridge. Outside the House of Commons, as I entered the Square, there was a police car parked with its wheels on the pavement and the driver was talking to two uniformed policemen standing on the pavement. They were engrossed in their conversation and did not look in our direction. Parliament Square was crowded with tourists, with a collection of about a hundred outside the Houses of Parliament led by three tourist guides.

We circled the Square and the horsebox slowed down and stopped at the kerb. I had carefully kept the thirty metres between, which distance was not large enough to allow a car to overtake me and interpose itself between us, but did leave enough space for the Mini-Cooper to back down the ramp. There is a limitation to the tolerance of London drivers and the slow speed of our convoy caused a taxi driver to hoot his horn angrily behind me. About twenty metres before the horsebox stopped, the traffic lights changed to red and I knew we had three minutes to go.

Just at that moment a motorcycle roared up inside and pulled up sharply between my front bumper and the lorry in front. On the back of the motorcyclist's leather jacket was a logo advertising a motorcycle courier service. Reilly saw what had happened in his rear view mirror and leaned out of his window and made a clockwise rotating motion with his hand letting me know that he intended to circle the Square again rather than ram the motorcyclist. I only hoped that the policemen on the other side of the Square were concentrating on their conversation rather than our antics. A horsebox is an unusual vehicle in central London and one circling twice around Parliament Square risked drawing the attention of a trained eye. As we went around again, the occupants of the police car were now busy talking to each other and the two policemen outside Parliament were watching the tourists rather than the traffic. The horsebox again stopped on the left side of the square and I pulled in twenty metres behind it.

I sat and sweated with a powerful urge to wet my trousers. The driver's door of the horsebox suddenly opened and Reilly shot out, unlocked the rear door and ran the ramp down. Blondie's head was visible through the back window of the Mini, whose engine was already revving. The car shot backwards down the ramp with a squeal of tyres at a much faster speed than we had achieved in practice. There was something odd about the appearance of the car and it registered on my panicky brain that there was a heavy wooden plank roped to the rear bumper with large nails protruding from it and pointing upwards. I realised that the Mini was going too fast as it shot backwards and collided with the front of my own vehicle. Reilly coolly put up the ramp, closed the door and snapped the padlock shut and then ran to the passenger door of Blondie's car which rapidly shot off. As it did so, Reilly leaned out of the window, smiled and blew me a kiss, which seemed an odd thing to do. I accelerated after him but there was a tortured shriek from the front of the car which stopped after half a metre stalling the engine. I notice that the car had a list to the right and that one or both tyres had been punctured. Once again they had deceived me and Reilly had even found it amusing when he blew me a kiss.

It had all happened so quickly that people on the pavement just stood transfixed and unable to work out what had happened. A middle-aged woman ran out from the pavement to my side of the vehicle. "Are you all right?" she asked.

"Yes, I'm not hurt."

"I saw the mad bugger and got the number plate of the Mini so if you want a witness, I can give my name to the police." It was difficult to understand her interpretation of the accident, but she seemed to think I was merely the victim of a piece of bad driving, although I'm sure she had never before seen an accident when a car accelerated backwards from a horsebox. Her mention of the police concentrated my mind and I caught a movement on the other side of the Square as the police car pulled out from the kerb to assess what was happening. I was desperate to get away but it all seemed hopeless. I got out of the Astra and told the woman and the bystanders that I was going to telephone the police and walked off at a brisk pace towards Victoria Street. As I turned into the street the police siren gave a whoop and the car skidded up to the horsebox. My last sight of what was happening as I looked over my shoulder was of three pedestrians simultaneously trying to give their version of events to the two policemen.

They must have been quick thinking because a few yards later there were shouts of, "Bomb alert, do not panic. Clear the Square." There were screams and a sound of running feet behind me. My first horrified reaction was that the spectators had realised my role in the affair and were pursuing me, but a few young fit people ran past me including a girl who was barefoot and presumably had abandoned her high heel shoes in order to run faster. I ran with them and after about three hundred metres, dived off into a side street leading to Green Park. All around I could hear the sirens of police cars. More than two minutes had elapsed by now and I knew that my attempt to disarm the bomb had been successful. I walked over to Hyde Park Corner Station and took the Underground to Victoria. There were a large number of police in the Station and the passengers were herded into the foyer. A police loud-hailer told us that there was an unexploded bomb in Parliament Square and that all mainline stations were closed for an indefinite period while they were searched for what the police referred to as 'explosive devices'. There was a groan from the crowd as rush hour was just starting. The Circle Line was closed and most commuters did not have alternative means of getting home. After an hour and a half it was announced that the trains would start running again. As the passengers passed the barrier to enter their train platform, they had to pass between two policemen who stopped people at random and asked them where they had been and where they were going. The young man in front of me made the mistake of telling the policemen that that was his own business. They seemed to be on a short fuse and whisked him off to a police van parked in the forecourt so I managed to get on the train without being questioned. An Irish accent would have been treated with great suspicion.

It was impossible for me to return to my lodgings and the first priority was to think of a plan. I got off the train at Boxhill and climbed up onto the hill. By this time I was mentally and physically exhausted and crawled under some bushes and fell asleep. I was only wearing thin trousers and a light anorak and woke shivering at 2 a.m. and walked around the hill in a desperate attempt to keep warm. It seemed too dangerous to go into the town until 9 a.m. when I wandered into a café looking like one of the great unwashed and unshaven and felt better after a few cups of strong tea and a bacon sandwich.

I was unable to avoid conversation when the man behind the counter commented that he had not seen me before. I told him that I worked on a nearby building site. The boss had the site key and had telephoned the shop next door giving me a message that his car had broken down and he would not arrive to let me in until 10 o'clock, so I could go and have a cup of tea in the meantime.

Spotting my accent straight away he said cautiously.

"What did you think of the bomb yesterday?"

I had no idea whether it had ultimately exploded or not, but it seemed safe to say that whoever planted it should be locked up for life, and the IRA campaign made life very difficult for honest hard-working men like myself. He prattled on and his version of the story was that the bomb had been discovered before it blew up. I suspected that the police and Army bomb disposal squad were taking credit for my action in disarming the bomb. They must have been completely baffled when they found the severed wires beneath the plastic case.

On the way to the railway station I bought a morning paper and read it on the London train. The paper praised the prompt and efficient action of the police and of the two policemen who had risked their lives by clearing the Square. There were pictures of the horsebox and my vehicle and a report that the police were seeking three men. There were good descriptions of Reilly and Blondie and, to my horror, there was a recent picture of me which they could only have got from Kate. The paper did not propose any reason why the second vehicle had punctured tyres and this obviously baffled them.

It was pointed out that explosive experts calculated that if the bomb had gone off it would have largely destroyed the Houses of Parliament and any other building within two hundred metres of the explosion.

An editorial headed, 'How long must we suffer?' expressed despair about the lack of success of security operations against the IRA and bitterly attacked the Government for its ineffectiveness.

In the train going to London I did my best to assess the situation and to think of some method of avoiding arrest. I had nothing to offer the IRA, indeed they must have been embarrassed by their failure to deliver the promised goods to James, the man from British Intelligence. The IRA had a formidable reputation for dealing with people they felt had let them down.

It was impossible for me to run in England because the IRA would catch up with me and escape abroad was not feasible without a passport. In England my photograph would be in every paper and my Galway accent was as good a disguise as a leper's bell. So much for the bright side. A search of my pockets revealed £7.50. I was wearing a T-shirt, light trousers and trainers. It was autumn and the nights were getting cold so I needed more money, more clothes and some sort of waterproof jacket in case it rained. If I had a few days when I could hide perhaps some bright idea might come to me which would solve my problems. It seemed preferable to just walking into a police station and giving myself up, although that would certainly make the day for some policeman.

So, money, clothes, somewhere to hide and a new accent, but the first priority was money. I am of a gentle and honest nature, at least that was what Kate told me and the thought of snatching handbags off ladies repelled me. My Catholic upbringing persuaded me that since my need was great and I was innocent, then I could justifiably steal money from some large wealthy organisation and if my life sorted itself out in future years, I would return it anonymously.

This line of reasoning was all very well but banks and post offices were out because of their levels of security. An idea struck me as the guard announced that the next station would be Clapham Junction. I left the train here and walked in the general direction of London. After half a mile I spotted two policemen strolling towards me and I dived into a video store until they had passed its front door. An older woman in the store glared at me which made me realise that for five minutes I had been gazing at the section entitled Adults Only.

The supermarket was a large one and at this time of the morning, was fairly busy with a mixture of pensioners and mothers with pre-school children. I filled my basket with a random mixture of groceries and walked slowly along the line of checkout tills. The last in the row was worked by a very fat woman aged about fifty. She was dealing with the groceries of a young woman who had a baby perched on the child seat of the trolley. Behind the trolley, a pair of grey haired old ladies were queuing and engaged in an animated conversation. Between the checkout and myself was an empty till-station.

It is an interesting fact that when men come to pay for goods at supermarkets, they have the money or credit card ready as the bill comes up. For women, the fact that they receive a bill seems to come as a surprise every time. When given it they forage in their bag until a purse emerges and this is then unzipped and after a leisurely search, money or credit card emerges. This young housewife was no exception. She went through the usual drill and eventually pulled out cash. The fat woman pressed a catch on the till and the top rose to reveal her cash balance. I quickly moved down the empty till lane behind her where she was unable to see me, leant across and snatched the contents from the containers for ten and twenty pound notes and ran like hell. The checkout girl was a slow thinker, the mum trapped behind her trolley and unlikely to abandon the child to pursue me. I heard confused shouts behind me but no running feet and quickly slowed to a walk across the crowded car park where I was indistinguishable from the other people in it. On the edge of the car park, I hopped over a wall onto the street and walked back to the railway station. In the gentlemen's lavatory, a quick count showed me to be richer by £320 and my first acts were to buy a warm padded anorak and a sleeping bag and to get a ticket to Waterloo.

I am uncertain why I possessed a peculiar belief that there would be some magical way out of my dilemma if only given time to think of one, but there it is - we are not entirely rational creatures, thank God. With some money and clothes, my problems were temporarily solved. Now for somewhere to stay and a new accent. A combined solution of these problems seemed unavailable. At Waterloo Station I spotted an empty cardboard box outside a junk food shop. The lid ripped off easily and in biro I printed a message in large, rather crude letters HOMELESS, DEAF AND DUMB. I could never fake an English accent and it seemed wiser to have an excuse not to speak at all. I had read in the English newspapers that beggars were a great nuisance in the Strand, so I asked directions written on a piece of paper and walked over Waterloo Bridge to get there. Most of the doorways were already occupied by beggars, so I walked up to Fleet Street and planted myself down on the pavement outside Coutts Bank with my piece of cardboard in front of me.

It was bloody cold on my tail end and the pickings were very thin. Inside the bank I could see chubby warm bank clerks with the men wearing curious cut away frock coats. Their only worries seemed to be the size of their Christmas bonuses. Occasionally a policeman passed by and I suffered agonies of anxieties whenever this happened. Fortunately for them, I just seemed to merge with the scenery. It struck me that my photograph would be in every police station in Britain and I resolved not to shave in order to make my recognition more difficult. There was no immediate need for money with the proceeds of my raid on the supermarket but I did not wish to repeat that high-risk procedure.

I entertained myself by trying to predict who would give me money. In general, the strike rate seemed to be about one in two hundred of passers by. The givers could be predicted because they looked you in the eye, whilst the rest looked at the floor or into the distance. As a group, the givers were female rather than male and usually younger but there were the odd exceptions. At five o'clock the employees began to leave the bank and one of them, a thick set young man, slipped me a fiver and said, "Good Luck" - the first person who had spoken to me since I had sat down.

The next problem was finding somewhere to sleep and I tried to remember a map of London. On a previous trip I recalled walking in Regent's Park and that it contained large clumps of trees. It seemed possible that I could hide up there. By the time I had walked to Marylebone Road I was tired, hungry and footsore and bought myself a bottle of beer and a plastic covered pack of sandwiches in a Pakistani corner shop. I pointed at the goods and my notice and the man just took my money and put the purchases in a plastic bag. It was dark by the time I reached the park and I found a small clump of trees near the East side where I sat down and had my beer and sandwiches, crawled into my sleeping bag and promptly fell asleep.

I woke up at 2 a.m. and was absolutely frozen. There was a thin skin of frost on the grass but the East wind was absolutely bitter and my teeth were chattering. I felt dirty, cold and hungry and knew that it would be too dangerous to walk about the streets to keep myself warm. It dawned on me that if I continued to stay where I was, that I might be dead by morning so I plodded around one of the inside paths in the park in a rather unsuccessful attempt to keep warm. By 6 a.m. I reckoned that a workman's cafe might be open and found one near Euston Station. After two large sweet cups of tea and a greasy cooked breakfast I began to feel human again. It struck me that I was on a very low rung of the ladder of human status because the cafe owner insisted on payment before serving me and evidently suspected a strong possibility that otherwise I might do a runner. I felt even dirtier than the night before, but consoled myself that this was part of the disguise and I had acquired a definite stubble on my chin overnight. In the lavatory of the cafe, my appearance in the cracked mirror alarmed me and I had more sympathy with the counterman's request for prepayment.

That day I returned to my station in Fleet Street but on the way I bought a few doughnuts. At about midday, a man of my own age passed me. He had a beard and led an old lurcher on a string. I recognised that he was in the same line of business as myself. The man stopped.

"How you doing mate?" he asked. I remembered to watch his lips as he spoke.

"Do you know a place to sleep tonight?" I wrote on the reverse side of my cardboard.

The man started writing on the piece of cardboard then blushed as he realised my ability to lip-read.

"I will pick you up at five o'clock," he said slowly and clearly and I nodded to show my understanding.

By 4 o'clock my total take was only a few pounds and this seemed to be a hard way to earn a living. I wandered across to a small shop and bought a few cans of cider and a pile of sandwiches and returned to my pavement.

A few minutes after five, my friend from earlier in the day arrived, introduced himself as Jason and told me to follow him. We walked for a few miles and I was completely lost but we ended up under a flyover somewhere near Paddington Station and where there was a collection of about thirty homeless people, most of them sitting around a fire. Some were cooking sausages and others drinking beer from cans. On our walk Jason had told me to collect newspapers and told me to sit on them and then to use them as a mattress at night. I took out the sandwiches and cider and indicated that we should share them, and a wall sheltered us from the keen wind as we ate. When the cans of drink emerged from my bag, there was a rustle of interest from a group of the older men. In dumb show I indicated that I would share the cider with them and they immediately joined us. It was very easy to forget that I was supposed to be deaf and necessary to teach myself not to turn around towards anyone addressing a remark to me. The technique was to closely watch the lips of the speaker's lips and every now and again, to misunderstand what they had said.

I stayed at the site for a week and although it was cold and uncomfortable, it was not unbearable. The major deprivation was the inability to have a bath or sit in a warm clean lavatory, but the consolation was that it was better than being in jail. The group of people under the flyover was interesting and consisted of definite sub-groups. My friend, Jason, was typical of one such. These were young males who were either from orphanages where they were thrown out at the age of sixteen, or from homes where a new stepfather did not want an adolescent in the love nest. Most had convictions for petty crimes, but it struck me that these crimes were from necessity rather than wickedness. Because they had no fixed address, they were not eligible for Social Security payments and no employer would take them on. Most of them possessed ugly mongrels who were their closest friends. Another large group was middle aged or elderly men whose lives had been wrecked by alcohol. One was a highly intelligent bank manager whose marriage and career had failed because of his problem. A small isolated group was clearly mentally ill and some of them conversed with imaginary voices. They were given a wide berth by the sane section because they were occasionally violent. Once was clearly paranoid and believed that the other people at the site were plotting to kill him.

The group had the advantage that the rest of the world perceived them as threatening nuisances although, in reality, they were largely harmless and rather sad. A nice cheerful group of people from the Salvation Army came round in a converted ambulance at about ten p.m. every night and gave out hot drinks and doughnuts and for some of the old men, this was probably the only food they got during the twenty four hours of the day. I resolved that if I ever got out of this mess, then the Salvation Army would become my favourite charity. One night I found tears in my eyes when a pretty young Salvationist put her arm around the shoulders of a lousy, smelly old man with a long beard and planted a smacking kiss on his stubbly cheek.

On the seventh night in my new refuge, I had just drifted off to sleep when there was shouting at the other end of the wall from my pile of newspapers. There were two torches moving about and behind them the flashing blue light of a police car. I began to sweat, knowing that my disguise would not stand close inspection and my photograph was probably in the tunic pocket of every policeman. The police were evidently looking for someone and were systematically waking people and shining their torches into the faces of each in turn. The dogs instantly recognised and disliked the law and an older cop with sergeant's stripes, warned the men that if any dog went for a policeman, he was guaranteed to be taken off and put down and his owner arrested on a charge that they would think up on the way back to the police station.

My back was to a wall which was L-shaped and the police were working their way long the horizontal limb of the L whilst I was halfway down the vertical limb. The choice seemed either to run or attempt to bluff it out. The younger policeman had a lean, rangy look and I am too muscular to be any good at running more than 200 metres. I decided to stay and brazen it out and then run if unsuccessful.

There was a sudden loud shout as one of the policemen shone his torch into the face of the paranoid man. He leapt to his feet with surprising agility for an old man and headbutted the older portly copper in the belly. The policeman made a sound like a punctured balloon and fell heavily backwards onto his well-upholstered buttocks. His companion was quick to react and leapt on the old man from one side and pinned him to the ground. He gave a loud shout as the old boy unsuccessfully tried to bite his shoulder through his heavy-duty issue overcoat. The older policeman got himself to his feet, shook his head and kicked the old man in the belly with his large boot.

"Leave him alone, you murdering bastards," shouted the enraged down and outs and to my horror I realised that

I was shouting too, but fortunately, in all the excitement nobody noticed my miraculous cure. The fat policeman looked rather abashed at this instinctive reaction. Had we been a group of thirty educated Guardian readers, he would have been sacked without a pension, but complaints of brutality from a gang of dossers were unlikely to get far. My friends also had a serious distrust of police stations and the sergeant knew he was safe.

"Right you lot, we lock up this nutter and then we come back to sort you all out." They frog-marched the mumbling old man across to their car and threw him roughly into the back. As the police car left the campsite, so did my friends with their meagre belongings and so did I.

The last few days had given me time to think but had not produced a solution. I then made two telephone calls which turned my life even more upside down.

James had formed an impression that Kate was an honest, straightforward girl who knew nothing of her fiancé's secret life and who was genuinely baffled at his disappearance. Nonetheless, it seemed important to keep her under surveillance either in case his judgement was incorrect, or should Gallagher want to get in touch with her for money or help or to give some explanation of what he had been up to.

Intensive surveillance requires at least nine people and two or three cars. One observer was needed for the front of the house, another for the back and the third and the other cars so that the subject could be followed allowing the agents and cars to change at regular intervals so that they were not spotted. Three teams of three are needed to cover the twenty-four hours. This level of observation was observed for a week and all the reports indicated nothing unusual in Kate's activities and no suspicious attempts to contact her. Her mail was stopped and read and the telephone tapped with no result. The Special Branch team reported that she went for long walks by herself and seemed thoughtful and depressed. After a week, the team of three was replaced by a single policeman parked in an old van 100 metres from the front door of the house of Kate and her parents. It was a job of unrelieved boredom and the policeman claimed that a tendency to constipation was essential to do the work properly.

John Williams was uncomfortable and suffered from three sources of discomfort. The hangover from a party the night before caused him to groan every time he moved his head or coughed. The cold pizza for lunch had been greasy and he had wolfed it down. It was combining with the hangover to give him severe heartburn. The most pressing problem was that it was getting towards the end of his eight-hour shift in the van. The milk bottle was full to the top with urine and he desperately needed another pee. Williams gloomily contemplated an alternative career doing something easier, like being a trapeze artist or mine disposal work. At that moment he heard the noisy buzz of a motorcycle engine and a motorcyclist in courier's gear pulled up outside Kate's house. He took a parcel from the parcel carrier, walked up to the door and handed it to a middle-aged woman who answered the doorbell. Williams leapt out of the van and intercepted the courier as he was walking back up the path from the front door. He flashed his warrant card; told the man he was investigating a serious crime and asked him for the names of the sender and recipients of the parcel. The man was taken aback.

"Nothing to do with me guv, I only do the deliveries." He fished a list of names and addresses out of one of a large supply of pockets in his leathers.

"Here it is - sender, Mr James Connolly, 15 Heatherside Road Brixton; recipient, Miss Kate Collins at this address."

Williams thought quickly. He could get his police station to ask Brixton police to investigate the background of the sender. However, if the parcel contained papers or a message from Gallagher, then they might be destroyed while the police wasted time chasing a sender who may have given a fictitious address. On the other hand, if he barged in on Miss Collins and asked her to view the contents of the parcel, then she would realise that she was under observation and if involved in some IRA plot, would be warned. Damn! He was stuck either way. "Write your name and address," he told the courier. "You can go now, but keep quite about this or I'll personally charge you for that noisy exhaust." Williams marched up to the door and rang the bell. The same lady answered.

"Mrs Collins," he said, "I am a police officer investigating the disappearance of Eamon Gallagher." Again he flashed his warrant and the woman looked alarmed. "I believe that you have just received a parcel."

"Yes, it's for my daughter, Kate. I just shouted up the stairs to tell her about it."

As the woman spoke, a very pretty dark haired girl came down the stairs. Williams, yet again, identified himself and asked Mrs Collins if he could speak to her daughter alone. The mother looked at her and she nodded when the mother retreated into a back room with a worried look on her face.

"I must ask you to give me that parcel Miss as part of my investigation into a serious crime," Williams told her in a very firm manner.

"The parcel is my property. I have committed no crime and you cannot remove my property without a warrant, indeed if I ask you to do so you must leave the premises immediately or you will be committing a trespass" the delicious girl told him. Oh God, bloody modern woman, but she's right.

"On the other hand, if you asked me nicely instead of talking like a robot and give me a convincing reason for you request, I might be inclined to be helpful."

"Sorry Miss. I'm desperate for a painkiller tablet for my lumbago," blurted Williams who was becoming increasingly aware of his full bladder. "It is in relation to Eamon Gallagher, we think he may be mixed up with the Welsh Bridges bomb in some way and that he might be communicating with you."

"If he did, the communication would received a very cool reception, but does it say on the parcel who it is from?" They examined the parcel but there was no record of the sender's name.

"The courier tells me that it is from a Mr James Connolly of Brixton. Do you know anyone of that name?"

"No, but it rings a bell somewhere." Kate wrinkled her nose in a puzzled manner and Williams though that made her look even more charming than ever.

"Hang on. You hinted that Eamon might be mixed up with the IRA. I don't believe that for a moment - but James Connolly. He was one of the heroes of the Irish Easter Rebellion in 1916 when the rebels took over the Dublin Post Office. He was wounded and the British executed him strapped to a chair. I don't know why I should be involved, but if the IRA are mixed up with this, do you think this might be one of these parcel bombs?"

Williams stepped back two paces and gazed in horror at the parcel which Kate was holding. "Oh my God! Put it on the chair and let's get the hell out of here," and he backed towards the door.

"No. My mother is in the back of the house and anyway, if it goes off, it would wreck my parents' house. Now I shall put it out in the middle of the road. Meanwhile, you can call for help and then start warning the neighbours. If you take the first five houses on the right, I will do the five on the left. There is very little traffic in the road at this time of the day and it is the safest place to put it." With that she calmly walked past Williams who shuddered as the bomb passed within a foot of his tortured bladder.

With the instinctive behaviour of the English male given firm instructions by a woman, Williams called the police station on his radio. He identified himself and the address and croaked that there was a suspected parcel bomb in the road outside and please send the bomb squad and as much help as possible, "And quickly please," he said superfluously and pathetically.

Most of the houses were empty at that time of day but a few neighbours were evacuated to a distance of two hundred metres.

"Look Miss," said Williams, "I must be the world's worst policeman, but if that was a parcel bomb, you saved my life because I would have opened it and probably killed the pair of us."

An approaching wail of police sirens told them that support had arrived. Kate saw a bald, fat policeman coming towards them with much silver braid on his cap and shoulders.

"Here comes the end of my career," moaned Williams. He recognised Chief Superintendent Trotter. Trotter was universally hated by his subordinates and was known as Porky Pig. This was not only because of his surname, but because he was very fat and bald with a pink round face and small eyes. When angry, and his uncertain temper was famous, he tended to make shrill screaming sounds. Trotter had a firm belief that the modern generation of young policemen were idle and dissolute and that he had a personal mission to correct this state of affairs. He was a believer in the naval maxim that the floggings would continue until morale improved.

The stately figure bore down on Kate and Williams. "This had better be good, Williams. I was addressing the Rotarians and I got pulled out in mid sentence because of this and the whole Division is in uproar. Now what the hell is going on?"

Williams was a little uncertain where to start the sorry story and opened his mouth to begin. Before he could say anything, Kate flashed a lovely smile at Porky and looked at him as though he personally represented the US Fifth Cavalry.

"Perhaps I can explain Officer. A courier delivered a parcel to my house. Before I could open it, Constable Williams came dashing in, snatched it from me and carried it into the middle of the road. He warned me to stay clear and then personally warned the people in the nearby houses. He was so brave and so calm."

"Very credible Williams," said Porky and this was probably a career first for being nice to a subordinate. "Now, lets retire a little and wait for the brave lads in the bomb squad to do their stuff."

At the end of the road two cars drew up with a screech of brakes and a group of men bundled out which included two carrying cameras. "The vultures of the press," Williams said to himself. With many years of self-promotion, Porky recognised them. "We need to brief the media," said the fat man pompously. He put on his hat to hide his billiard table head and sucked in his gut and cameras started to flash.

"Now come with me Williams, but leave the talking to me and I can tell them of you prompt action and the way in which we have worked together in this case."

At this stage, Williams realised that in the next 30 seconds he would become incontinent of urine and the press pictures would show him peeing himself in the same frame as Porky.

"Perhaps I could leave the press to someone of your experience Sir. That man in the house down the street says he may have seen something of what happened and it might be best if I got his statement whilst events are still fresh in his mind." With a brisk salute he ran down the street and as he accelerated off, received a wink from Kate. He ran up to an old man who was viewing the chaotic scene from his front door. "Could I use your toilet, please Sir?" said Williams, and the man nodded. There was a crash as 15 stone of large policeman shot up the narrow stairs and arrived just before disaster.

As he contemplated the lavatory tank, Williams

considered how during the last 15 minutes he had consecutively experienced the emotions of boredom, terror and basking in adulation. But the best emotion of all was the satisfaction of having a two-pint piss.

That evening, James Miles called in to see Kate.

"I have interviewed Constable Williams," he told her, "frankly his story did not hang together and he seemed furtive and guilty. He told me what really happened this afternoon and I reassured him that the secret would remain between the three of us. He behaved like a complete idiot but he seems a nice lad and learnt a few lessons today. Besides, the police have had a bad press recently and need a hero. One thing is very clear and that is that you have a fan for life there. Were the flowers on the hall table from him?" Kate admitted that they were.

"If I may say so, you are a very cool and generous customer," said Miles and Kate looked embarrassed. "I feel we owe you an explanation. Briefly, we think Eamon was very bitter at the death of his brother and sister. He offered to help what he thought was the IRA in a way which was not violent. Unfortunately he got mixed up with a psychotic pair of renegades and got completely out of his depth and was used by them. He was mixed up in the attempted bombing of Parliament Square, but they probably blackmailed him into that by threatening to harm yourself. Presumably they blame him for some reason for their lack of success and the parcel bomb was a punishment to Eamon for that."

"But how did they know where I lived?" Kate asked him.

"His landlady got the address from your parish priest so that she should could forward any of his mail here. A few days ago she got a telephone call from a man saying that he was Eamon's brother and could he have your address because he wanted to contact you."

"So where do we go from her?" Kate asked James.

"I will be frank. Eamon is in big trouble and faces a long jail sentence. He may be able to give useful information about the other two and I would ask you to contact me immediately if he tries to get in touch with you. Meanwhile, you will have an escort of two armed policemen round the clock."

Chapter 10

When I telephoned the number which McDonald had given me, a voice answered which I did not recognise. "McDonald told me about you but he is out at the moment. Phone again in two hours and he will be able to talk to you."

Later, as instructed by McDonald, I stood outside Hammersmith Underground Station reading the Evening Standard and doing an impression of someone waiting to meet another person. McDonald came towards me dead on time. "We'll take a little tour first just in case we have any company, so go and buy two tickets to Cockfosters." We got into a Piccadilly Line train and two stations later, just as the doors were closing, rapidly got off. Nobody else made the same manoeuvre nor did they when we repeated it three stops later, going in the opposite direction. McDonald told me that we would leave the talking until we had reached our destination. Leaving the train we took a zig zag course through some quiet streets and my companion constantly checked that we were not being followed. He suddenly turned into the small front garden of one of a row of small terraced houses. The door was well secured with two mortise locks and we went into what appeared a deserted house, going up the stairs to a comfortable flat with its own bathroom and kitchen and a large sitting/dining room with furniture which looked new and in good taste.

"You seem disaster prone," said McDonald, "and where the hell are that other pair of gangsters and why did you vanish?"

I told him the story from the beginning. "They seem to have a charmed life," he said gloomily. "And on past form, they will vanish for a few years while we pick up the pieces then they will come back and do another spectacular. As for yourself, you've had it. The British would like to catch three people but one would be a good start and you would do nicely. A dramatic trial and a life sentence would get the press off the politicians' backs. I can see the Home Secretary saying to the cameras that, in this instance, a life sentence will mean exactly what is says."

"What if I could find them?"

He sat back looking astonished. "If you did that we could wipe the slate clean with the Brits as far as you're concerned and do ourselves some good."

"When they lifted me from Hastings, I saw some initials and a number next to the telephone and wrote them down. It was HBG 903928157941. I wondered if HBG was the initials of a person and if the number could be a telephone number preceded by an international code. It only cost me a pound to find out so I dialled it. The person who answered said 'Hotel Bristol, Girne.' I put the phone down and checked the International dialling codes in the phonebox - 90392 is the access code for North Cyprus and 815 that of Kyrenia. Kyrenia is the Greek name for the city and the Turks renamed it Girne in 1974 when they invaded North Cyprus. Presumably, Reilly either knows someone at the hotel, or was making a booking, but I don't know why he chose Cyprus because I gather the British Army is still stationed there."

Donovan began to look very excited. "But it is Turkish North Cyprus and the British bases are in the Greek South of the Island. It explains where they have been hiding all these years. In North Cyprus they stamp your passport on a separate removable piece of paper because otherwise the Greeks will not let you into mainland Greece or South Cyprus. If Blondie and Reilly usually hide in North Cyprus, then there would be no stamp in their passports. Even if they were caught, the Brits have no extradition treaty with North Cyprus. They don't even recognise their Government who would be delighted not to comply with an extradition request just to pay them out for not recognising them. Normally tourists get a three-month entry stamp on their passports, but if they take the ferry to mainland Turkey, they can get another three-month stamp even if they come back the same day. As long as you pay your bills and do not attract notice from the police it is possible to stay there indefinitely."

McDonald sat and brooded, obviously dreaming up some course of action. "If we sent you to North Cyprus, you could finger them and we could then get the British to infiltrate an SAS team and grab them."

I said sarcastically. "I have nowhere to live, no money and my photograph is in every newspaper in Britain. I doubt if I could get beyond passport control at Heathrow. Even if I got to Cyprus they would know me and that would tell them they were being chased."

"I think we could sort out these little problems Eamon. You can stay here and I can give you a float of five thousand pounds in cash - we're funded well from America. We can change your appearance fairly easily if you buy a pair of horn-rimmed spectacles, grow a moustache and dye your hair blonde so that your granny would never recognise you."

"Not exactly a dead ringer of the photograph in my

Irish passport, and there is a little problem of the passport - I don't fancy going through Immigration in Cyprus or Britain with some forged job. I'd probably shit myself in terror and give everything away. Besides, how can an Irish citizen get a UK passport?"

"Easy, we can give you a new British one in a different name. All you need is a birth certificate and a photograph signed on the back by a respectable person such as a doctor. Once you've had the hair dyed and grown a moustache, you can get the photo. On the back write, 'I certify that this is a true likeness of Eamon Gallagher,' and sign it with the name of a local GP and write MB.BS after the signature. A friend of mine in Armagh has been a GP for twenty years and has never been asked by the Passport Office whether his signature was genuine."

"As for the birth certificate, we do it regularly and Reilly and Blondie would have done the same. We go to a local reference library and ask for the newspapers around the time of your own birth. We look at the death notices and find one for an infant where it either states the date of birth or gives some information so you can work it out, for example, died on the fifteenth of June aged three days. We then go to Somerset House and get a copy birth certificate by paying a few pounds. With the photo, we then have the complete tool kit to get a passport. It will take about three weeks. In the meantime, go to the travel agent tomorrow and tell them you want a holiday in North Cyprus because you had a lucky win on the horses in the Grand National - you remember that Flibbertigibbet won at 100:1 and was an Irish horse. This will explain why you pay in cash. Book it for three weeks time. Meanwhile stay here, sort out your hair and grow a moustache. The fridge is full of enough beer and food to last you out. There is a pile of videos next to the television and a shelf of thrillers in the bookcase. One of them is about the IRA and it must be the most inaccurate and rubbishy book ever written. Stay in unless you have to. In an emergency you can get me on the same number you used already. If you feel you are being watched, phone them on that number but I'll not come and rescue you at the risk of getting caught because the Organisation needs me more than you. I'll be in touch and the money will come by motorcycle courier at three o'clock tomorrow afternoon, so make sure that you are in. In the meantime, here's a hundred pounds in case we forget to put anything essential, like toilet paper, in the flat."

"There is another big difficulty. My granny certainly would not recognise me in my disguise because she is blind, but Blondie and Reilly would."

"Yes, I thought of that and there is a way around it that I was going to discuss next time we met."

"Yeah, I could wear a tutu and a magic wand and pretend to be the tooth fairy."

"No. Your girl. They know of her existence, but have never met her. If you went together you could keep in the background and she could get up close."

"Certainly not," I said firmly. "At present, she thinks that I am Jack the Ripper who she fell in love with and foolishly agreed to marry. Now he has called it off, rather brutally, and vanished. Besides, I could never let her within a hundred miles of that pair of murdering psychopaths."

"Think of it this way. At present you've lost each other anyway and if you fail to haul in our two friends you are going to be banged up for life. If you saw this girl, do you think that you could convince her with your story of what happened? If you can, you could offer her the option of helping. If she says no, you are no worse off and if she says yes, you have a girl worth marrying."

I thought for a minute while McDonald sipped a whiskey from the bar in the flat. "All right, if you can get her to meet me with no risk to herself, then I will talk to her about it."

"It's not going to be easy," said the IRA man. "The Special Branch or local CID will be keeping an eye on her, and her telephone will almost certainly be tapped. Does she go out anywhere on a regular basis?"

"She goes swimming twice a week but the days vary, but she never misses Mass at 9.30 on Sunday morning."

"I will see she gets a message with a place for a meeting. Even after what she thinks you have done, I doubt she would turn you in but you can never be sure. I'll have to be careful. By the way, now that we have democratically agreed that you are both going, book two holidays in Cyprus."

Three days after I met McDonald he telephoned me to say that he had fixed a meeting with Kate. One of his low level helpers who did straightforward tasks for the Organisation had been given a description of Kate and told that it was her habit to sit on the left side of the church in the fourth pew from the front. He went to the church, picked up a hymnbook and sat next to Kate. Immediately before the second hymn he picked up her hymnbook, apologised and then instead of returning hers, gave her back his own. When she opened the book at the number for the next hymn, she saw a note saying, 'I am a friend of Eamon's. He is innocent and wants to meet you. If you want to see him, put the book on the pew in front. If not, put if by the side of you.' She thought for a few seconds, flushed and put the book in front of her. As the service finished, the man, whilst looking straight ahead and kneeling beside her, had said, "I have put instructions in my hymn book. When I leave, pick it up then take them out and put the book at the back of the church. Just act normally."

Each morning I did a fast six-mile jog around the local park to keep fit and relieve the boredom. The only hazard was the dogs, both with their droppings and the threat of having my ankles nipped by aggressive terriers and Alsations whose owner always reassured me that they never harmed anyone. At this stage of my existence the last thing I wanted was a disabling dog bite when the police would, no doubt, appear by magic and take meticulous statements from me with my give-away accent.

On the second afternoon I went to Hayes in West London and found a rather grubby barber's shop. I told the barber that I wanted a crew cut and emerged looking like every respectable woman's nightmare, a man she would not like to meet in a dark lane after closing time. On the way back I went to another down at heel lady's hairdresser and spun them a yarn that my girlfriend wanted to go blonde but had changed her mind and that I might be able to persuade her to do it if I came home with the dye. I told the woman that I always had a weakness for blondes and being blonde herself she simpered at me.

When I got home I followed the instructions and a new strange face peered at me from the mirror an hour later.

Five days later I walked towards Earls Court tube station. About a hundred metres north of the station a man sat on the floor holding a card saying, 'No home, HIV positive, help me.' McDonald had told me that it was a coded message that Kate had been followed from her home and no tail had been spotted. If she had, the notice would have read 'Homeless, no job, no prospects.' I spotted Kate walking towards me expecting tears or a smile or improbably for her to fling her arms around me. I realised my disguise was good because she walked straight past me so I returned behind her.

"Kate, it's me!" I said and she whisked around.

"Good God, you look weird."

"Just keep walking normally," I said and we set off together arm in arm.

"Kate, I've been a fool and have lied to you, but I swear that I have never deliberately hurt anyone and I lied because I had no wish to hurt you."

She took a long hard look at me. "Eamon, I've invested a lot of emotion and hope in you. If you have let me down then I have been a fool and a poor judge of character. All that I've heard so far suggests that that is just what I have been, but tell me about it and then I can decide."

We walked back to the flat although McDonald would not have approved it. I poured myself a stiff whiskey, although Kate declined anything, and over an hour told her exactly what I had done and perhaps, more importantly, not done. Finally I told her of the IRA's plan to chase after Reilly and his sidekick.

At the end of this uncomfortable session she told me to go and cook something for us to eat and to pour her a small drink. I went into the kitchen to prepare the speciality diet with which I had so much experience during the last week - re-heated pizza. I looked through the door and saw Kate staring into space with the drink untouched. It seemed a rehearsal for when the jury would be deliberating when I appeared in court. The pizza went on a tray and looked like something produced by the rear end of a cow as I took it into the dining room and Kate gazed at it in disbelief.

"Eamon," she said, "if I did not marry you I would have the guilt on my soul of causing someone to die of malnutrition because you would if you lived on swill like that for the rest of your life." My eyes filled with tears as I realised that she believed me and was ready to go through with what needed to be done.

"I will keep you in the background with those two men and once we have sorted them out, we can get back to a normal life." Kate left an hour later leaving me a happier man.

It was after the Severn bombing that Blondie began to realise that Reilly was mad. In earlier jobs he had been cool, remote and professional, but before the attack on Parliament he had began to drink heavily and when he was in his room Blondie would often hear him talking to himself. The scale of the Severn incident had been alarming. Blondie had always had a rather relaxed attitude to civilian casualties but on that occasion they were so large and the pictures of the wounded on television so horrific that he began to feel distaste for what he had done. Reilly had told him that the train bomb was intended to go off in Cardiff station and not in the tunnel and unusually had been insistent on setting the timing of the detonator himself on the morning of the operation. Blondie realised that, for the first time, his friend had lied to him. He had never seen Reilly make a technical mistake in the past and the failure of the Parliament Square bomb to explode meant that Reilly must have made a mistake in setting up the device.

Blondie was worried because he felt everyone was after him, the IRA, the British police and no doubt Interpol and he saw no end to a life of constant running and hiding because Reilly seemed quite content to carry on forever. Blondie had a dream of a small holding in a remote part of the Scottish Highlands. If he had his share of the money from the bank robbery, it would be enough to see him through for the rest of his life. He had friends who knew how to get a National Insurance number for a modest payment and he should be able to get a job. He might even meet a nice girl and get married. The problem was that Reilly would consider such an action to be treacherous and he would prefer pursuit by the British police and the IRA to pursuit by Reilly. He felt that things were beginning to fall to pieces. What had previously been suppressed dreams, now became options which needed urgent decisions if he was not to face death by continuing to be entangled with Reilly.

The Prime Minister had been in opposition for six years before his party won the election. During his time in the wilderness his central objective had been to unite the warring wings of his own party and to concentrate their venom on the Government rather than each other. Unity is

Lifeline

not achieved by displays of temper directed at the awkward squad in one's own party. The required tactic was to massage gigantic but easily bruised egos. Now that the election was safely passed, the PM realised that, with a large majority, he could indulge in stamping on the lunatic fringe in his own party and on anyone else in the Civil Service who failed to meet targets or whose actions caused political embarrassment.

His cabinet colleagues recognised that a danger sign preceding an emotional explosion was that the Leader tended to relapse into his natural Yorkshire accent. In his youth he had made considerable efforts to replace this by standard BBC English speech.

The Severn affair had resulted in an awesome display of temper. In his public appearances he had managed to convey an aura of calm sensible reaction but within the confines of Number 10, tough ruthless Ministers had been reduced to tears and the well brought up secretaries in their twinsets and pearls had their vocabularies extended. MI5 and Special Branch had been selected as particular targets with a ruthless sacking of senior staff. The only happy people were MI6. Six is responsible for foreign security while MI5 deals with organisations threatening the security of the State. These ranged from vegetarians to Irish Terrorist Organisations both Orange and Green.

The failure of MI5 to prevent or solve the Severn incident was a cause of joy in MI6. Sir Crispin Stout, the Director of Six, seized the opportunity to send a memo to the Prime Minister pointing out the anomaly of having two separate security services whose functions sometimes overlapped. He suggested that the service provided by MI5 should be subsumed by MI6 into a single service with greater efficiency and fewer staff. The current budget for Six was £400 million a year and that for Five, £200 million. If Six took over then the work could be done with a total budget of only £500 million. The PM was sympathetic and intended to implement these reforms with

Sir Crispin (a sound man) at the head of the combined unit. It was 9 a.m. and time for coffee, two Digestive biscuits and the sacrosanct half hour when the PM was not to be disturbed while he read the morning papers for matters of political interest, starting with the Sun and working through to the heavies. Civil Servants read the papers first using coloured pencils to mark items likely to interest him. Green meant goods news, red bad and yellow neutral but politically interesting. He was irritated to see that the first paper, the Sun, had red pencil on page 1.

The scream from the Prime Minister's private office caused the Parliamentary Private Secretary to spill scalding Earl Grey tea onto his trousers and was matched by a scream from himself. The PPS ran into his master's office to view the alarming sight of the great man stamping on a newspaper and yelling that he intended to kill that bastard Crispin. The PPS usually scanned the newspapers before handing them to the PM in case there were requests for further information on any interesting news items. He had not done so today because the office was busy. By now, the Prime Minister had sat down with his head in his hands and the PPS was able to rescue the offending broadsheet.

'BRITISH BUGGER BANGED UP' yelled the headline. The PPS rapidly read the article. It did not take long because the print was large and the words all short to cater for the readership.

The PPS was aware that the Prime Minister, during a recent visit to a SEATE (South East Asia Tiger Economy) State had personally negotiated a contract with that Government to supply its armed forces with advanced naval and military equipment. The agreement was secret and highly sensitive in view of the repressive nature of the regime. It was the intention of the PM to announce the deal for £10 billion staged over five years. He would stress that the contract would result in 10,000 new jobs in manufacturing industry. It was, of course, a coincidence that these jobs were to be in marginal electoral constituencies. In order to soften the criticisms of the human rights lobby, the SEATE President would simultaneously announce the release of all political prisoners. During the preceding year, a large number of unrepentant prisoners had died in jail and this had been attributed to an epidemic of pneumonia. Those left for release were either ancient or broken. The article in The Sun made no mention of this background so security had evidently been watertight. The article reported that British Intelligence in the SEATE capital had decided that it would be a good idea to dig out dirt on members of the SEATE Government in case it might be useful in the future. They quickly struck oil in following up a rumour that the President had a fifteen-year-old mistress. He had recently given a rare interview to BBC Television stressing the laxity of morals in the Western World which he unfavourably compared with the situation in his own country. A small time criminal was given a vast bribe and obtained access to the love nest where a camera in an attic obtained film of the President performing activities not normally associated with high office. MI6 were delighted and the film was so important that Sir Crispin had watched it five times and issued a directive that further footage should be obtained. Unfortunately, in doing this, an obese British Agent had fallen through the attic roof onto the busy couple. He had been badly beaten by the presidential bodyguard who had immediately rushed into the room on hearing the commotion to the further embarrassment of the President. Under interrogation, and in the highest tradition of the Service, he had confessed everything including the fact that Sir Crispin had viewed the film.

The President announced that a British spy had been caught committing industrial espionage and had been shot whilst attempting to escape from captivity. In view of this, a large forthcoming order for security apparatus for the Police and Military would go to a French firm and not to the British. In order to further embarrass HMG the President released photographs of handcuffs, cattle prods and water cannon which British firms currently supplied to his State. He announced that there would be a further rounding up of dissidents and subversives who would not benefit from the gentle treatment previously given to this class of person.

The Prime Minister not only had no good news to announce, but would need to explain why his Government had given export licenses for repressive equipment for such a dreadful regime. The Sun pointed out that not only were MI5 useless, but so were MI6.

"Get Stout here," said the PM, with that terse economy for words which heralded problems for someone.

Sir Crispin was blissfully unaware of the recent sequence of events. The local head of station was aware that the fat agent had not reported in for three days, but two of these covered the weekend and there seemed no need for concern. It had happened before and the man had a drink problem but was an effective agent and was allowed the occasional lapse which did not seem to interfere with his routine work. The head of station had recently received a herogram from Sir Crispin following the film of the Presidential romp and was not inclined to be hard on the fat man.

Sir Crispin assumed that the urgent summons to Number 10 resulted from his recent memorandum. He thought that the old man was beginning to show the strains of office and seemed rather tense.

"So how are things at Six?" enquired the PM with that charming boyish smile which had gained him the support of the majority of British females of voting age.

"We seem to be on top of things at present Prime Minister."

"Including the President of one of our allies," the Prime Minister said to himself. "I have been giving thought to your idea of merging Six and Five and see many advantages. We would get rid of a lot of deadwood and could take it further because we would not require two headquarter buildings."

"Entirely agreed Prime Minister. I admire your thinking," toadied the Knight. "It would solve a lot of overlap problems."

"Excellent!" said the PM, "then we are agreed? Now your gang of incompetents fell through the ceiling onto a copulating President and lost us a 10 billion-pound contract. In addition, as a direct result, the Civil Liberties mob will be after my blood. Get out of here, but only after you've written your resignation. I never wish to see you again and MI5 will take over MI6. We can sell your nice new building to Tescos for a supermarket."

"But what about my pension?"

By now the Prime Minister was incandescent and spoke in pure Yorkshire. To his subsequent chagrin he subsequently recalled screaming, "Get out Stout, you'll get now't."

Sir Crispin fainted.

Chapter 11

Two weeks later we met in the Departure Lounge at Heathrow Airport. The place was heaving on a Saturday, security was tight and our baggage was x-rayed before we could present our tickets. Before going through passport control, I underwent a professional body search. Going through passport control with my new document was frightening but when the man saw an UK passport he waved me on and did not even examine it. We had booked in separately and I did not intend to travel next to Kate on the plane on the basis that if I was caught, she might still have a sporting chance of escape.

When we got to the final departure lounge after the flight was called, Kate sat at the opposite end pretending to read a book, but her eyes were darting everywhere returning about once a minute to see that I was safe. After ten minutes there was an announcement that the flight was delayed for an hour and a withered British memsahib sitting near me pronounced that she had been going regularly to North Cyprus for twenty years and delay of an hour was less than usual. Eventually we boarded. The plane was clean but the cabin staff had clearly been instructed never to use the words 'please' or 'thank you'. After four hours the plan landed at Izmir in Turkey. It then sat on the runway for an hour whilst ten or so people got off and a few Turks boarded. The aircraft then took off for Ircan in North Cyprus using a different flight number. The woman in the next seat explained that flights could not go directly to countries which Britain did not recognise diplomatically. What happened was that the British flight went to Turkey and then a separate Turkish flight took off for a country only recognised by Turkey and North Korea. The fact that our bums never left their seats was apparently diplomatically irrelevant.

We landed at Ircan and again faced the ordeal of the immigration counter. It was guarded by two soldiers with rifles who seemed about fifteen years old. On the counter was a pile of forms which we were invited to complete if our passports were not to be stamped and my virginal passport was returned to me with the stamp on a loose flimsy piece of paper.

The journey from the airport to the hotel took an hour in the bus and I was physically and mentally worn out by the time we got there, but at least we were now safe to sit together. When we arrived and booked in, I flung the window of the bedroom open and the warm breeze smelt of flowers. The next morning at breakfast Kate, who was more widely travelled than myself and felt an adventurer in visiting England, told me that the flower smells were of jasmine and honeysuckle.

My room was thirty-six and hers was thirty-eight and after unpacking I went along the dark empty corridor and gently tapped her door. She opened it carefully and then flung her arms around me and confessed that she had been terrified throughout the journey. I poured both of us large Courvoisiers from the bottle bought in the duty free at Heathrow. "We will start tomorrow," I told her, "but not with anything to worry you. I'll hire a car and we can see something of the Island so that at least we know how things work and where they are before we start."

I woke the next morning to a beautiful day in early summer. When we left England it was wet and cold. At eight o'clock it was already hot and the swimming pool below my balcony was empty. I went down to the pool, picked up a towel and did a quick twenty lengths in the clean warm water. The hotel was evidently going to be delightful even if the work we were doing was not. The Onar Village Hotel was perched on a hill three kilometres from Kyrenia. It had eighteen bedrooms (although mine was numbered thirty-six!) with small flats in the grounds. Breakfast was served on the balcony looking over Kyrenia and a vast stretch of bay. We settled down to feta cheese, olives and toast. The manager looked at us with the fond eyes of one who had seen many holiday romances but was not yet disillusioned by them. He pretended to fiddle about re-arranging the olives while his ears were flapping for a romantic story he could take home to his wife.

We took a hire car to a little beach to the east of Kyrenia and spent the morning swimming, followed by a leisurely lunch at a little restaurant. We had no idea what to order and the waiter suggested fish metzes. It seemed a good idea for someone else to make my decision and after five minutes a bottle of cold white wine was produced. We sat and drank it and when the food arrived it seemed a good idea to have another bottle. The owner had lived in London for three years and seemed delighted to have English customers and produced a running commentary on the food as we ate. There was a delicious chick pea humus and sharp salty cod roe taramasalata with about eight other dishes of spicy fish and vegetables. We just about managed to finish this and leaned back groaning when a large plate of mullet and some other fish and chips appeared. Under the beady eye of the proprietor it seemed churlish not to get stuck in. With feigned enthusiasm and by spreading the chips about the plate we managed to convey an impression of doing justice to the meal. We managed to gracefully decline a sweet course and settled for coffee, which was accompanied by large complimentary brandies.

At this stage the Cypriot approach to life had begun to appeal to me but my blood alcohol level must have been at heights unreached since drinking eight pints of Guinness after scoring a goal at a football match. The bill was a little blurred and to my horror, I finally deciphered that it was for five million lire. I envisioned us washing up for the next ten years to repay it, but Kate, who had drunk much less that me, translated this into twenty five pounds which seemed very reasonable. After this we went for a five minutes sleep on the beach and I woke up three hours later with a dry mouth and sunburnt nose. Another swim restored me and when we got back to the hotel I managed a reasonable dinner on the terrace, but declined the wine.

The next morning I woke up feeling better than I deserved. We had an early breakfast and left the car in the middle of Kyrenia without the usual parking problems, and the town only had a single set of traffic lights. We walked past the Bristol Hotel and made a mental note that there were three café/restaurants which had a view of the front entrance to the Bristol. We settled for the nearest one and I sat with my back to the hotel wearing a straw Panama hat pulled well down at the front while Kate faced the hotel with her long hair in plaits and wearing dark glasses against the strong morning sun. We ordered toast and coffee and sat for an hour while nothing happened. After this time we paid the bill and moved to the second café/restaurant and ordered exactly the same.

After half an hour of inactivity I felt waterlogged and went off to the toilet at the rear of the premises. When I came back, Kate said that a blonde man and another wearing a hat tilted to the right had emerged from the entrance to the Bristol a minute before. I sent Kate off down the street while I quickly paid the bill and followed her. She told me that they had headed left parallel to the harbour and she went ahead to follow them while I trailed fifty metres behind. She hurried back after a few minutes and said they had gone into a car park. We went back to our car knowing that they had to leave the town through the one way system. Kate sat in the driver's seat while I kept my head down. She looked backwards through the rear view mirror and spotted them approaching us. "A red car with a small T on the grill," she said. I deliberately stared ahead and recognised the profiles of the two men as their car pulled in front of us. We let them go and then drew out with a taxi between our cars because of their permanent suspicions about being followed. They headed east along the coast road and we soon lost the protective cover of the taxi and were forced to fall back to about half a kilometre behind. Our car was a non-descript white Fiat but it had the red tourist number plate.

After twenty kilometres we entered a long straight stretch of road not containing the red car. As we drove down it there was a signpost to a village on the left in the direction of the sea. The road was basically a rough track and I felt uncertain whether it might be wise to turn around in case we had a reception committee around the next corner. After five kilometres we passed a small bay and saw the red car with the two men walking away from it carrying towels and beach mats. The man with the hat had taken it off and was instantly recognisable as Reilly. When they heard a car approaching they both looked long and hard at us, but I felt fairly secure in my disguise and the Panama hat and we drove past.

"We've got them," I said triumphantly and saw that they had continued their walk to the beach. When we got back to the hotel I telephoned the number McDonald had given me. A woman's voice answered this time. "It's the man from the Halfpenny Bridge," I said, using the code that he had stipulated.

"Hello Eamon," said a different voice, which I

recognised as that of McDonald. "Have you met any friends on holiday?"

"Yes, two lovely people."

"You might be able to introduce them to some friends of mine from London who will be coming out to Cyprus in a day or two. Could you phone back in an hour and I can speak to the friends and check that the provisional arrangements still stand?"

I telephoned again later hoping that James Miles would still be prepared to stick to the agreement we had made in Ireland. McDonald told me that he would and someone would be in touch with me at our hotel the next evening. Meanwhile we should stay out of Kyrenia so that there was no possibility of the hunted finding the hunters.

The next day the temperature at 9 a.m. was already 25° with more to come and I suggested to Kate that we drive to Saint Hilarion Castle where it would be cooler. The road from Kyrenia to the castle passed in front of the hotel so it seemed a safe place to go.

The castle was perched on a crag, three hundred metres above Kyrenia with a view for miles in every direction. The road up to the castle passed through one of the military reservations which are everywhere on the island. A warning notice banned stopping the car or photography on the approach road and half way up it was the entrance to an army camp guarded by two bored looking conscripts toting rifles. As they did elsewhere on the Island they peered hard in an intimidating fashion at passing cars and presumably this was part of their instructions. Our tour guide had told us that officially there were 35,000 Turkish soldiers on the island, but the true number probably exceeded this. They were mostly poorly paid conscripts who had nothing to do and whose meagre pay was spent on cigarettes and telephone calls to their families in mainland Turkey.

We parked in the car park outside the gate of the castle. There was an outer retaining wall with a fortified gate leading into a field which sloped steeply up to a second wall and gate containing the living quarters, a cistern and a chapel which were all perched on the edge of a cliff. The whole site must have been impregnable as a fortress. Leading up from the second part of the castle was a steep rock stair one hundred metres high. This led to a keep perched on a pair of rocky outcrops. We were breathless and sat on the wall of the top keep admiring the view in the hot sun and drinking from a bottle of water. The keep was empty and the steep climb discouraged all except the fairly fit. I felt drowsy and sat with my legs stretched out and heard the steps of some tourists approaching the top of the keep from our right side. I opened my eyes and to my horror saw that it was Reilly and Blondie. They looked relaxed and just like any other pair of tourists. Reilly looked straight through me, but as his gaze passed over Kate, I saw his attention concentrate. She was a striking girl and looked distinctive in her plaits. Reilly had survived pursuit by the police over the last ten years and I could see him mentally registering that this girl had passed him in a car the day before. His eyes swung back to me and looked at me hard. He reached into his haversack and pulled out a pistol with a long barrel.

"Well, well Eamon, you look very pretty as a blonde. Now don't tell me, it is coincidence that we are both here. What the bloody hell are you and your girlfriend spying on me for? I am not the sort of man that you mess with, so start talking or your girlfriend gets a bullet in the belly."

Rationally it seemed unlikely that he would use the gun. A gunshot would be audible to the few, visitors to the castle, but if reported by the man who collected money for the entrance tickets or by the souvenir shop or café, then a telephone call to the army camp down the single access road would result in five hundred bored Turkish Army conscripts blocking the road and fanning out over the approaches in the best sport since fox hunting. This was the rational argument but these two were mad dogs and might not have reached the same logical conclusion as myself. Unfortunately I was not only gambling on his decision with my own life but that of Kate as well.

"All right," I said, "let's talk about it rationally." What I was going to say next I had no idea but it seemed important to placate them. As I spoke there were again footsteps to our right and a crowd of ten tourists begun to emerge onto the keep roof. The ladies were vast and the men large with money pouches round the front of their large bellies. Thank God for the Germans, I said to myself. Reilly could not be seen waving a gun at me but continued to point it covered with his haversack with the clear intention of resuming our interesting conversation once the tourists had passed. Under the cover of their babble of conversation I murmured to Kate, "Exit left when I say."

On the way up to the keep I had noticed that the approach path forked in two directions and we had taken the right turn and I prayed that the door to our left led down to the other path. Reilly and Blondie had their backs against the precipitous drop from the keep while Kate and I sat with our backs to the opposite wall. The only route for the tourists was between us and I let the first two pass as they headed for the door on our left. "Go!" I said to Kate and she streaked off left followed by myself. We elbowed the German man and woman aside and they protested indignantly. Reilly and Blondie took off after us but by the time they reached the door, there were now four Germans either in the doorway or in the tunnel beyond it and they were very annoyed about the young couple who had so rudely pushed past them. I took a quick look behind as we ran down the stairs and saw the delightful sight of our pursuers waving their arms and attempting the impossible task of squeezing past some large uncooperative Germans in a narrow passage. We shot down the steep steps from the keep to the second level. As we got to the bottom, I saw a red faced Reilly emerging at the top of the stairs. This part was particular steep and

Blondie was ahead of him. He had obviously misjudged things and taken the section too fast as he stumbled and fell about ten steps with a shout of pain and some language which made the Germans shrink back into the exit tunnel. Reilly hesitated and stopped to help him. We continued to run down to the outer curtain wall. I told Kate to stay there and run like hell when they came out of the inner gate and into the intervening field. I knew this would give us a start of three hundred metres and I had a task to do while they were delayed.

I ran down a hundred metres to the car park and saw their red car. I took my own car key from my pocket and used it to depress the valve on the inside front tyre which deflated with a satisfying hiss. After a minute the tyre was flat and from the corner of my eye I saw Kate emerging from the gatehouse. As we accelerated away in the car, I could see Reilly accompanied by Blondie whose fair hair was matted with blood. I could not hear their voices but got the general impression that they were arguing. They leapt into their car and set off with screaming rear tyres and a very ominous flapping noise from the front. Reilly braked hard and got out and I saw him gaze at the front tyre with a look of disbelief and frustration. I tooted the horn and was unable to resist the temptation to blow him a kiss as we set off down the road from the castle at a sober pace. "Right my girl," I told Kate, "we do not leave the hotel until that pair are safely sorted and someone else can take the risks."

That evening towards the end of dinner, the head waiter discreetly told me that a Mr Miles was waiting for me in the bar when we had finished dinner. We walked down to the bar and James Miles stood there looking like a transplant of a British civil servant. I introduced Kate and he suggested that we had a drink in the quiet poolside bar where we could speak in confidence.

I explained to James Miles that the situation had changed since my conversation with McDonald the day before and that we were now hunted rather than hunters. They would assume we were working with the IRA or British Intelligence and their first reaction would be to kill us and the second to escape from Cyprus.

"Escape is not quite so easy," said James. "They can either get out through Ircan Airport or by the two ferries or the hydrofoil service from Kyrenia which all go to Turkey. We have permanent assets in North Cyprus of ten people. When I say we, I mean MI6 not MI5, but the Prime Minister has given firm instructions to MI6 that total co-operation is given or else. If they turn up at any exit my lads will say hello and tell them that they will be met when they arrive in Turkey. The Turks will co-operate with a request to extradite a pair of known terrorists because they certainly will not want them in Turkey. If they help us we will owe them a favour which they can call in at some future date. That is the way Intelligence Services work with another - they have a sort of central favour bank. There was another interesting suggestion from MI6 that we tell the Turks that we are after them for terrorism in Britain but that the reason for their visit to North Cyprus was to meet the illegal Kurdish Resistance who are fighting a guerrilla war in mainland Turkey. Their intelligence outfit practices a rigorous form of interrogation accompanied by a high mortality rate. If they die in Turkish custody, then we announce that those who did the Severn bomb job died in a Turkish jail and this will save us the expense and trouble of a trial. British juries are cynical about the evidence in 'terrorist' cases because of the miscarriages of justice, which are persistently exposed. I would burst into tears if that pair were found not guilty."

Kate looked horrified at this tortuous and rather unscrupulous approach. My own disbelief was based on a difficulty in the concept of any British agent saying hello to Reilly. It seemed much more likely that once spotted, they would be killed in North Cyprus and James' story of giving him a trial was to spare our feelings.

"Spare us the details, we would prefer not to know them, but why do you need Kate and myself?" All we want to do is get out of here and lead a normal life like the rest of the world."

"Put frankly, you pair are bait. We know that Reilly never forgives an informer and we know of five that he has certainly killed and there were probably others. He may have some escape route we don't know about and there is a large frontier with South Cyprus. We want him to come after you before he runs. Anyway, you have little choice. If they get away you will both be looking over your shoulders for the rest of your lives. Now having decided that," he said imperiously, "I need to think it through. They will certainly have checked out of the Hotel Bristol and could be staying anywhere on the island. We cannot ask the local police to check the hotels because they would tell us to get stuffed before deporting us as undesirable agents of a Foreign Intelligence Organisation. The British Government would be put in an embarrassing position and my plans for a nice quiet retirement would be torpedoed".

I groaned at the thought of being ground between a pair of psychopathic killers on one side and a set of gung ho official British killers on the other. "We have no choice," said Kate firmly, making up my mind in what I saw was going to be a life long trend.

"Excellent!" beamed Miles. "Now they will think that you are probably freelance and will go back home and try to strike a deal with the British police probably through a solicitor. I doubt if they will consider that you might have done the deal first because they will be unaware that it was brokered through the IRA. They must be baffled how you tracked them here and are probably blaming each other for some lapse in security. We need to get you to a safe house and hide the hire car because they will have taken the registration number and will be working their way around hotel car parks looking for it. We have a farmhouse on the road to Bellapais Abbey about five kilometres from

Kyrenia. Tell the hotel reception here that you bumped into some old Turkish Cypriot friends from London who have a family home near Famagusta and they were very pressing with an invitation to stay there. The manager will be delighted because the tour company have prepaid your accommodation and he will not need to provide meals or service the room and may be able to let it."

James gave instructions how to get to the farmhouse and we went to our rooms and packed quietly. I assured the lady at reception that we were not leaving because of dissatisfaction with the hotel, but because it seemed rude to decline the invitation of our Cypriot friends. She understood this and I told her that we would return in a few months for our honeymoon. The head waiter was hovering in the background and I thought should he have been playing a romantic melody on a violin. He shook hands emotionally as we went out and his wife would have got a full report that night.

The farmhouse was at the end of a lane and built on a low hill. As we entered the gate a man stepped from a ruined outbuilding. He had a bulge in his trousers which did not result from the normal male cause of this phenomenon. He had a fit, aggressive appearance and relaxed as he identified us. "Just go up to the house and they are expecting you. There are two of us in the grounds so no need for alarm if you spot us." As we drove up, James emerged from the house and directed the car into the barn. When we went into the house, he closed the barn doors to hide the car from any prying eyes. In addition to the guards in the grounds, there were two other fit young men in the house who had the characteristic stamp of soldiers.

We sat down at the table. James sat at the window seat. "We have little to go on," he said gloomily. "The two men outside will rotate every six hours with another six who are flying in tonight and who are based at Hereford. The only positive things we have are their descriptions, the fact that Kate and Eamon recognise them and the model and registration number of their car. We have staked out the Onar Village Hotel but it seems unlikely they will find out you were there because the car is no longer parked in the hotel. The exits are plugged apart from the border and that is packed with Greek and Turkish soldiers glaring at each other and filled with the conviction that the other is about to invade. Even if they got to the South, there is a large British garrison who would welcome the entertainment of a manhunt. It would keep the rough soldiery occupied and stop their usual method of entertainment of getting objectionably drunk and beating up the locals. Relations are quite good with the Greeks and they would be on a RAF jet to Northolt a few hours after any Greek police or troops picked them up. Their problem is that there is nowhere they can safely run and if I put myself in Reilly's mind I would lie low, wait for the uproar to settle and meanwhile kill you pair. So here is the plan. All our sources will keep a lookout for the car. Eamon and Kate will separately drive with two armed men sweeping the island. They will travel in the back of a four wheel drive jeep with the roof up, so it is difficult to identify anyone in the back."

"I would feel safer for Kate if we were together," I said.

"That would halve our number of agents and I doubt if a muscular Mick would be much use against a gun," said James sarcastically. "We can assume they are both armed and not just Reilly. With all the fighting on the island in 1974, every family has at least one hidden firearm in case the Greeks come back to claim their property. Oh, and another thing Kate, cut off those bloody plaits. They immediately identify you and I know that some of our lads have fantasies about schoolgirls and you wouldn't want to encourage that."

I was sometimes tempted to punch James. He was very intelligent but had an abrasive tongue and an irritating air of superiority and competence. He sensed my irritation. "Sorry Eamon," he said, "I am used to dealing with soldiers and policemen and you will forgive me if I am more direct than civilians expect. The main thing is to get the job done."

Over the next three days we spent twelve hours out of the twenty-four, being bounced about in the rear of four wheel drive vehicles with cartspring suspension. Every two hours, each vehicle telephoned the farmhouse for any positive sightings. James felt that portable telephones or radios were potentially insecure in such a militarised country. On the third day, our driver stopped at a small bar in a country village to make his standard report of no progress while I sat and sweated in the back of the jeep. The soldier came running back to tell me that one of the other units had spotted the car going east on the road from Kyrenia to Kantara. This was a secondary road leading to a long finger of the island pointing east into the Mediterranean in the direction of Syria. All the cars were concentrated on that end of the island for the rest of the day but nothing turned up. That evening we all felt depressed and we sat down to our usual meal of Turkish bread tasting of cardboard, some salty feta cheese and the inevitable tomatoes and cucumber, all washed down with a few bottles of passable Turkish Dikman wine. The British Army approach to food was less enthusiastic than that to its weapons and the team which now included six SAS men spent the evening cleaning their weapons before going to bed in bunks in one of the bedrooms.

It was a hot sticky night and we sat on the veranda of the farmhouse sipping some fiery local brandy. We all became more despondent as the evening passed by and I knew that Kate and I had to return in a week or she would lose her job. James had a telephone call just after dinner to which he responded with cryptic monosyllabic answers giving the impression that his superiors were asking him why he was not meeting with any success. We were all sitting thinking our own thoughts when a voice from the left side said, "Nice to see you boys and girls."

We swivelled around and saw Reilly covering us with a rifle. "Don't even think of it," said a voice on the other side, where Blondie stood holding a heavy handgun. "Now, nice and gently, just put your hands on your dicks where I can see them and you, madam, put them where you would if you were lucky enough to have one. All I need is an excuse to kill the lot of you. We can get you to do the talking Eamon because you have certainly had practice talking to someone. If you get hesitant, the young lady gets a belt across the head from the butt of my rifle and if you do it twice, I can easily think of some other method of persuasion that would make Blondie happy. First, tell me who your friends are?"

"British Intelligence," I said without hesitation, because there was no choice.

"How the hell did you find where we were?"

"You wrote the telephone number of the hotel next to the telephone in the farmhouse and I memorised it."

"Aren't we the clever boy then and was I not a bit silly. Never mind, I always wanted to do a spectacular which cleaned out a British Intelligence outfit. The other nice thing is that the British Government will be very embarrassed when nine of her finest are shot in a country which it does not recognise. I could help with an anonymous telephone call to the local military saying that they had been meeting some Greek friends to discuss the future plans for North Cyprus and they had a quarrel. Given the suspicious nature of the Turkish mind, this could raise a few more problems for HMG. Now let's all go inside and we can continue our nice little chat. Now Blondie, open that bedroom door, switch the light on and tell the fairy princesses that it's time to wake up because the prince has arrived. If anyone moves, kill them."

"How did you find us?" I asked Reilly.

"Your friends flatter themselves by calling themselves Intelligence. Me, I'm just cunning. So I thought, Eamon is not going to come looking for me just with himself and the girlfriend because he knows well that I am a dangerous man, so he must have done a swap with the Brits - me for him. The British are unlikely to have much help on the ground in North Cyprus so the first thing they would do would be to move in some heavies from the UK. Because of the diplomatic problem they would have to come in on a scheduled flight. They would probably have staked out the departure area of Ircan Airport looking for Blondie and myself and the last place they would look for me is in the Arrival section. Blondie did a reverse Eamon and dyed his hair black - I'm sure you agree it makes him look more attractive. So he waited until six fit young men arrived on one flight. You did very well to give them T shirts labelled 'Birmingham Sub-Aqua Club' and I'm sure this would have convinced any immigration officer who wondered why six fit looking young clones would arrive on the same flight. Where the plan fell down was that you can see the passport control office from the arrival hall and they all stood to attention whilst they presented themselves to immigration. By a strange coincidence, they all got into two four wheel drive vehicles awaiting them and all Blondie had to do was to follow them. That friend of yours at the gate - or more properly, your ex friend at the gate, had a nice chat to them so we had a nice chat to him a few minutes later."

The farm kitchen was a large room and they herded us into the far corner making us sit with our hands on our heads. "Now, first a little information," said Reilly, "before we start to enjoy ourselves. Eamon, you can tell me how a nice lad like you with an interest in blowing up bridges, could get involved with British Intelligence for I doubt that you answered an advert. Would it perhaps be through a sell out by some ex friends of mine?"

My guilty silence confirmed his suspicions.

"I'm not talking to myself and I meant it about your girlfriend," Reilly said.

"Yes," I told him, "the IRA tracked me down and offered a deal with the British. You left me hanging in the wind and I owed you nothing."

"Fair enough, but you underestimated me. Now you trash," he said to Miles and slammed the barrel of his gun into his belly so that he collapsed groaning to the floor. "What I'm going to do is to have a nice little massacre so that a group of armed men with UK passports will be found dead in mysterious circumstances and after my telephone call, the excitement will be fantastic. Remember that Turkey is a member of NATO and supposed to be on the same side as you lot. They will not be speaking to you for a few years and Blondie and myself can rest up on the island and nobody will bother us."

James Miles lay on the floor holding his gut. "Fair enough, Reilly," he said, "you and I are soldiers and know the risks but how about letting Kate and Eamon run. They are not professionals and won't be able to hurt you."

"That bastard Eamon grassed on me once and no-one who does that lives. Now Eamon, I am going to make you an offer; either the girlfriend gets a shot in the belly or a shot in the head and you have the same choice. If you give me some useful information then you die easy and if not, you both die hard." I could think of no useful information that he would want except the details of my contacts with the IRA.

"As long as you go easy on Kate, then I will tell you what you want to know."

"That's the boy," said Blondie. "I knew you were always a nice helpful lad, so tell us everything we want to know." I sensed, rather than saw, a movement at the open window behind Blondie.

"Just stop it there," said a crisp voice. "I have a gun pointed at your ear so just drop your gun on the floor." I saw it was the soldier who had originally let us in at the farmhouse gate.

"Very interesting," said Reilly in a relaxed cool manner. "It's the Mexican stand off. You have a gun on Blondie and I have one on James Bond here," and he gave

James Miles a kick in the ribs. "So let's put it all together. You shoot Blondie and I shoot your man. If I do you will be responsible for the death of a very senior man in MI5 and it will all be your fault, so that should mess up any more co-operation between SAS and MI5 for the next ten years - what a tragedy. I can probably kill a few other people as well. It seems to me that mathematically speaking, you are on a loser so why don't we relax and negotiate. What we both want is to get out without casualties. You also need to avoid political embarrassment and we can help you. Here is what I propose. Everyone walks away. You take Blondie as a hostage and I take 'mastermind," and he gave Miles another kick. "I telephone you when I feel safe. You then let Blondie go and I release your man. We are both professionals and see the realities of the position. Eamon is decoration on the cake. I would love to shoot him but I can close him down at leisure and give him no guarantees."

"Fair enough," said James from his position on the floor. "No doubt we will meet again somewhere in the world and we can resume our discussion."

Reilly and Miles set off in the jeep and as the engine noise faded, I felt relief that at least Kate was safe but I felt anxious about James Miles. Thirty minutes later there was a message that we could pick up James Miles at a bar in Kyrenia in exchange for Blondie who had sat quietly on the floor.

The money was kept in a battered suitcase. Blondie was uncertain how much was left. Before each visit to Britain he would go with Reilly to an old farm in a deserted village near the east of the Island. It was an eerie, lonely place and it was easy to imagine the Greeks running for the safety of the South side of the island carrying their children and a few portable objects. In a stable at the back of the farmhouse, the floor was of brick. They would lever the bricks apart with a crowbar and the suitcase was buried beneath, secured with a rope and a lock. Reilly always made Blondie go outside when he opened the case but from the weight when he last lifted it from the hole he could tell that it still contained a substantial sum, especially as Reilly always paid for their activities in England with twenty-pound notes. Blondie realised that there was only one way of getting at the money and then escaping safely to a new life.

Blondie and Reilly sat by the side of the hotel swimming pool and watched the stars emerging as they sat and drank brandy after dinner. Over the last month Reilly's drinking had become uncontrolled and Blondie usually had to help him to bed. The hotel did not seem to mind because Reilly got quietly drunk and promptly settled his enormous bar bills. On this evening he had a bottle of wine with his dinner, and the half bottle of brandy he had brought to the poolside had almost gone. "I have another bottle in my room and I'll go and get it," offered Blondie and the only reply was a morose grunt. He went back to the room and took out a full bottle emptying three quarters of it down the lavatory. From his pocket he took three wax covered capsules of Temazepam. A single capsule of ten milligrams gives a good night's sleep. The tablets are popular on the drug scene as they confer a floating sense of drowsiness and peace and were easy to obtain from dealers in British pubs. Crushing the tablets he tipped them into the remaining brandy in the bottle and shook it vigorously so that the drug dissolved.

Blondie went back to the poolside where Reilly asked where the hell he had been because he needed another brandy.

"Thought I had a full bottle, but there's enough here," said Blondie cheerfully and poured a full wineglass of brandy.

"That's a bloody good drink and only a little bit left for you."

"I feel pissed already," Blondie replied and poured a

small measure for himself which he put to his lips but did not sip. Over the next five minutes, Reilly drank the wineglass to emptiness. Blondie had previously experimented with the mixture and knew it to be tasteless.

After fifteen minutes Reilly started to snore. Blondie gave him a shake but the mixture of wine, brandy and Temazepam was a powerful one and he was unrouseable. Blondie piled three sponge poolside mattresses between the recliner and the pool and very gently lifted the edge of the recliner so that Reilly tipped onto the mattresses. Save for a sigh and a cough he showed no appreciation of his change of position and the pool was now dark and invisible from the lights of the hotel fifty metres away. Lifting the edge of the mattresses, he rolled Reilly gently into the pool with a soft splash. He sank to the bottom and then started to rise so that as he came near to the surface, his arms and legs could be seen waving frantically. His hair reached the surface first and clinging to the rail, Blondie grabbed the hair in his hand and thrust down holding the body and head beneath the surface. Reilly's arms and legs thrashed silently. There was a bubbling and a noxious smell as Reilly lost control of his sphincter, stopped jerking and sank to the bottom of the pool where he was invisible in the darkness.

Blondie knew that the body would be seen as soon as anyone passed the pool after first light. He returned to his room and packed a minimum of personal effects as he had acquired few and had the soldier's capacity to travel with little baggage. The car was in the hotel car park and quietly unlocking the door, he let it run down the drive to the road outside and started the engine there. His intention was to get the money from the farmhouse and to catch the morning ferry to Turkey leaving the car behind. Once in Turkey he could use a new name and passport and return to Britain by an indirect route. If anyone were looking for him they would not be looking too hard at passengers arriving at Harwich from Sweden.

He parked the car a kilometre from the farmhouse and carefully locked it. In his usual cautious manner he circled the building which seemed as empty as it usually was. He had brought the crowbar and a torch and rapidly unpicked the bricks in the stable floor. After each visit the hiding place was concealed by sweeping dust over the bricks and he checked that they had not been disturbed. The suitcase was intact and again needed a good heave to lift it from its resting place.

Before opening the case, Blondie again checked that there was nobody observing the farmhouse. For a few minutes he sat and thought about a cottage in a village in Scotland with a pub and a crowd of lovely young women who had never previously met an attractive experienced man. He had a great sense of contentment knowing that Reilly would never come and kill him and he smiled to himself at how easy it had been to dispose of such a formidable man.

To open the suitcase he used a key which he had found in the lavatory cistern of Reilly's bedroom. He had visited the lavatory during one of their drinking sessions when Reilly had started to snore. On two occasions in the past, they had been armed with revolvers for a job involving planting bombs at railway stations. On each occasion before finally leaving their hotel, Reilly had retrieved the revolvers from the lavatory cistern in the bedroom where they had been stored in watertight plastic bags.

Blondie turned the key and opened the lid. There was a two-second pause. Just enough for him to see an enormous heap of twenty pound notes secured in thousand pound bundles; each contained by a rubber band. On top of the notes was a detonator wired to a kilo of semtex. He started to scrabble around looking for the switch to disconnect the semtex which Reilly must have fitted and alarmed on each occasion he opened the case.

His last thought before it blew was that it all seemed so bloody unfair after all his careful planning.

They landed at Heathrow on a scheduled flight from North Cyprus and felt tired and defeated.

"Eamon, I think it's better if I am frank with you," said James. "As far as Kate is concerned we can talk her out of trouble. Strictly speaking she is legally an accessory after the fact because she helped you hide from the law knowing that you were involved in the Severn bombings. Frankly, she is small fry and I doubt if the police will be very interested in charging her. The problem with you is different. There were three people who planted the bombs and two got away leaving you. The public and the police are still baying for blood and yours would do nicely. On the credit side, you gave us enormous help in Cyprus but it never led us to catch the others. Your story about your part in the Parliament bombs sounds like a fantasy and your Counsel will feel embarrassed at having to present it in Court and it should raise a good laugh. I suspect that the best I can do is to say that you co-operated and that you were stupid and misled but it would be difficult to see you getting less than twelve years. If you are a really good boy inside you might get out in eight but that always assumes that there is no forthcoming Election or Party Conference when the Home Secretary has to demonstrate how tough on crime he is."

Eamon gloomily contemplated the prospect, and Kate cried.

"You can run if you want to Eamon, but it would be easier to plead in mitigation that you gave yourself up voluntarily because you knew yourself to be innocent."

"You're right," said Eamon. "It's hopeless and if I come back to your office we can telephone the police from there." Eamon looked out from the taxi knowing that traffic and people in the streets were sights that he would need to remember for the next eight or ten years. "I will wait, no matter how long," said Kate and Eamon kissed her as James tactfully looked out of the opposite window.

The gloomy procession tramped into James' room at Millbank and Hilary smiled at them. "Welcome back Mr Miles," she said. "Who are your friends?" James introduced them and tersely told Hilary that they had been helping him in a project in North Cyprus. "You look worn out dear," said Hilary to Kate. "I'll get you a nice cup of tea and don't let that Mr Miles bully you. By the way, Sir, I have an urgent message that you telephone the Cabinet office at Number 10 as soon as you got back."

James felt depressed. He had failed his Director, the Service and the Prime Minister. The Prime Minister had a reputation for making short work of anyone who failed him. He went next door to Hilary's office where he could make the confidential call, while Hilary clucked over the young people who brought out all her frustrated mothering instincts.

"What kept you?" said the smooth voice of one of the Prime Minister's male private secretaries. "One moment."

"Ah! James," came the characteristic rather booming voice of the PM. "Bloody marvellous! Look, I don't want to know how you did it in case I ever have to lie to Parliament, but you got them both and the locals think they killed each other in a quarrel about drug money. Case closed - headlines in the local paper about British criminals deserve their fate sort of thing."

"Er, thanks Prime Minister," said James quite taken aback and not having a clue about what had happened.

"Yes," babbled the PM. "The blonde one drowned the other and the local police found the blonde with no hands or head and surrounded by twenty pound notes."

James was not a man to miss an opportunity. "There are a few little loose ends, sir. There was a third bomber who agreed to lead us to the other two if we gave him an amnesty."

"An amnesty, be buggered. Give him a medal but tell him if he ever breathes a word, we'll crucify him and send him down forever." After a little more delighted babbling the PM rang off.

James telephoned the Director. "We chased those two all over North Cyprus. They gave us the slip but they must have quarrelled and killed each other. The PM has just been on and thinks we did it and I didn't have the heart to disabuse him."

"James," said the Director. "All the Service usually gives the Prime Minister is bad news so let's leave him with his delusions and take the credit. Now go and have a nice holiday and can I give you a piece of personal advice. Could I suggest that you marry that nice secretary of yours, she's mad about you."

James put the telephone down thunderstruck. He had always been attracted to Hilary since the death of his wife but felt that nobody would want to marry a cynical fat old widower with rapidly failing career prospects and was frightened that she might laugh at him.

He went back to his room. "Eamon, things have happened which you do not need to know about but Reilly and his friend are dead. I have spoken to the Prime Minister and you are both off the hook. Now get out of here and if either of you talk about what happened, even in your sleep, I shall find out and put the handcuffs on personally." Kate kissed James who blushed deep red. Hilary had evidently been let into the secret that they wanted to get married, but that Eamon faced a long jail sentence and she dabbed at her eyes with a handkerchief. "Now go with God," he said and ushered them out of the door.

"Now Hilary, a little personal matter I wish to discuss with you..."